Back to
Blue

by

Dillon Watson

Bella
BOOKS

2013

Bella Books, Inc.
P.O. Box 10543
Tallahassee, FL 32302

Printed in the United States of America on acid-free paper.

First Bella Books Edition 2013

Editor: Medora MacDougall
Cover Designed by: Judith Fellows

ISBN: 978-1-59493-347-9

Some of the locations in this book are actual places, but the characters and story are fiction.

Other Bella Books by Dillon Watson

Keile's Chance

I think I know
I hope it shows
That I am whole
Because of you
You brought me back
When things were black
You brought me back to blue

CHAPTER ONE

"You can do it this time," Summer Baxby muttered, coming to a stop in front of the bike racks. The mini-pep talk did nothing to still the shaking of her hands as she threaded the bike lock through the spokes. The thought of entering the twenty-story office building in downtown Seneca, Georgia, had her pressing a hand against the major skirmish occurring inside her stomach. She tried not to give into the uneasy thought she wasn't ready to function in an office environment. Tried to slough off the guilt that she didn't deserve the job she'd only gotten as a favor to her dad. But most of all, she struggled against giving in to the siren's song coming from the safe haven that was her parents' home.

Thinking of what her parents, especially her mother, had gone through to get her to this point, she stiffened her resolve. She'd made it this far, and this time she'd damn well make it upstairs and report for the first day on the job. But the throng of workers crowding the area in front of the bank of elevators shot her nerves through the roof and put a big dent in her resolve. Reciting the multiplication table to herself, Summer detoured past the bank of elevators and into the lobby bathroom.

Once inside, she made it to fifteen times fifteen before remembering the deep breathing technique she'd practiced with her shrink. It took a while, but gradually it worked. When her nerves and her stomach settled enough for her to think she could get on one of those elevators and go to work, she mentally added another item to the growing list of things she owed to Dr. Veraat.

After sluicing her face with cold water, she looked at the reflection of the woman who was slowly becoming less of a stranger. Aside from helmet hair, she looked like any normal person nervous about returning to the workforce after three years. "This is for you, Mom." With a quick fluffing of her short, dark brown hair with the contrasting white streak on the left side, she made her way to the elevators.

Summer arrived seconds behind a sharply dressed guy who she placed in his late twenties. He was muttering under his breath about the parentage of people who couldn't be bothered to hold a damn elevator. When he stabbed the Up button repeatedly, she decided a smartass remark was not called for.

"Four elevators. You'd think one would come." He turned and gave a start as if he'd just realized he wasn't alone. "Hey," he said with an obviously practiced smile. "I don't think I've seen you around here before. You must be new."

"First day," she admitted with the barest hint of a smile, then quickly looked away from unwanted scrutiny. She was sure he'd see a woman too pale and skinny to be attractive and lose interest. She was wrong.

"Thought so." He sidled closer and threw back his shoulders. "You I would have noticed."

She gave a mental sigh. First day and she'd run into Mr. "Thinks-He's-a-God."

"Are the elevators always this slow?" She stepped around him and drilled the Up button.

"They are this time of day. But for some reason I don't mind today. Care to guess why?"

The doors to elevator number three slid open, saving Summer from having to respond. As she entered the elevator, her only regret was that no one had dashed up at the last minute to save her from being beleaguered by God's Gift. When he pushed the button for the eighth floor, she wondered if the gods were laughing their fat asses off.

"What floor for you?"

"Eight's good."

"What a sweet coincidence. Looks like we'll be seeing each other regularly." He leaned back against the wall in a pose Summer was sure he practiced regularly along with the smile that accompanied it.

"How great is that?" If he worked at Tathum, Inc., she was going to have to find another job.

"I'm Rich—" He broke off and yelped as the elevator jerked to a stop.

Summer splayed herself against the wall behind her and began to recite the multiplication tables again. She hadn't gotten to five times five when the lights flickered and the elevator dropped. After everything she'd lived through it came to this? The faulty elevator was going to do what not wearing a seat belt three years ago hadn't? In a small way, it was a relief to close her eyes and wait for impact while listening to Rich's unmanly scream. No more trying so hard to get back to the woman she once had been. No more being out of step with the world around her.

Her knees turned to jelly as the elevator came to a grinding stop. She swallowed hard against the bile threatening to break free, slid down, dropped her head between her knees and prayed. Maybe she wasn't as ready to leave this life as she thought. Rocking back and forth, she went back to the security of reciting the multiplication table.

"You still with me?"

To Summer his voice sounded as rough as tree bark with an undercurrent of fear. "Uh, yeah." She rubbed her arms, trying to still the shakes. "Please don't tell me this is a regular thing."

"No. No," he repeated more firmly. "It's gonna start up any minute." The emergency light came on as if to back up his claim. "The building is only three years old. It's gonna start. It *has* to start." Now there was desperation added to the roughness, the fear. He sounded like a frightened child.

Summer darted a glance at him and he looked the way he sounded. "You're right," she said quickly. "Still, maybe one of us should push the Emergency button as backup." She made it onto her knees before the elevator gave another gut-dropping jerk and the lights blinked out, leaving them in total darkness. Giving a quick prayer this wasn't an omen of what her new job was going to be like, she pushed to her feet.

"What are you doing?" Rich whispered.

"Looking for the Emergency button. You have a better idea?"

"There's supposed to be a light. There's always supposed to be a light."

"Obviously there isn't," she snapped back, frustrated as much with the childish whine in his voice as her inability to find the right button. God's Gift obviously had a marshmallow center.

"I don't like the dark," he said softly, breathing hard. "Make it go away or he'll come back."

She opened her mouth to tell him to get a good, hard grip—
and suddenly she wasn't in the elevator. She was in a darkened closet, her mouth covered by her mother's hand, clutching a bedraggled teddy bear. Summer could hear what sounded like a rabid animal screaming for the whore to show herself. She flinched at the sound of fist meeting wall and the ensuing howl. Could feel her heart stop when the door to the closet was yanked open. Feel it start up and beat rapidly as madness spread across the face of her father smiling down at them. When a fist slammed into her mother's face, she could smell the urine permeating the stuffy air, the warm dampness spreading in the crotch of her worn jeans...

As suddenly as it began, the vision ended. She was back in the elevator, the darkness punctuated by the loudness of Rich's breathing. Putting her hands to the throbbing beat at her temples, she squeezed. What the hell had just happened? She leaned her forehead against the coolness of the wall, afraid her grip on sanity was more tenuous than she'd thought. Why else would she be hallucinating? And about some kid she didn't know of all things?

She zipped through to twenty times twenty before her panic subsided. So what if she'd had an out-of-body experience? She'd come out of it whole and without the ritual probing the people in the movies always talked about. That counted for something. Something had to count for something or else what was the point of counting?

It was the sound of ragged weeping that made the connection for her, that drove her to renew her efforts to find the alarm. The kid was Rich. It had to have been Rich, stuck in the dark and waiting for a monster to strike. Once she found the panel, she settled on the button that stuck out more and pushed, then pulled until the alarm sounded. She almost cried herself when a distorted voice echoed over the sound of the alarm.

"We're stuck," she yelled. "With no lights." She thought the garbled response said something about working on the problem. Not that it mattered what had been said. She was going to choose to believe a solution was being found.

With the memory of Rich's possible—*no, probable*—trauma fresh in her mind, she felt her way to him, slid down and, without a word, threw an arm around his shoulders. She almost laughed at the thought that she, with all of her issues, was capable of providing comfort to someone else.

Summer wasn't sure how much time had passed when the lights flickered two times and then came on full force. She was sure her ass had fallen asleep on the unforgiving floor. Rich stiffened, his embarrassment filling the elevator. Without looking at him, she dropped her arm, scooted to the opposite side of the elevator and stood to massage her sore behind.

Taking stock, she gave herself credit not for being alive, but for not falling apart. Best of all, she'd known what to do. Dr. Veraat would be proud. Especially if she left out the part about…Well, the part that she wasn't sure had happened.

"Thanks," Rich said softly. "I…Just thanks."

"We all need help sometimes. Usually it's me." She finally thought to look at the watch she was getting used to wearing. They'd been stuck for over two hours. "I'm really late. Wonder if I can get the elevator person to write me an excuse?"

"I'd do it, but not sure it would count for much. Low man on the pyramid and all. I'm Rich Slator."

The practiced smile was back, but now she glimpsed the frightened child underneath as well. It made him easier to take. "Summer Baxby. I think I have a job at Tathum, Inc."

"I work on the other end of the floor at Abstracts. We're in project management."

They looked at each other in concern as the elevator jerked, then made a grinding noise before beginning a slow descent.

"Maybe you should, you know, sit down," Rich suggested.

"Good idea." Summer wrapped her arms around her legs and worked to keep her breathing even. When the elevator finally came to a stop at the lobby level, she exhaled. Scrambling to her feet, she waited, not so patiently, for the doors to open. To her dismay, they stayed closed. Hearing Rich's heightened breathing, she repeatedly hit the Open Door button.

"There's no basement, so we can't fall," Rich offered, his voice thin and reedy.

"Some comfort," she muttered. Before she could pull the Emergency button again, the doors were forced apart.

"Everyone okay?" the older of the two technicians asked.

"I'll let you know," Summer said, hurrying away from Rich as much as the faulty elevator and heading up the stairs to the eighth floor.

Ten minutes later she could only wish to be back in the elevator. Even going through the multiplication table wasn't enough to block the tsunami-strength waves of disapproval pouring off of her supervisor, Marcia Meachem.

Sure, she should have used her cell phone to call and explain she was held up. And maybe she would have if the damn thing wasn't so new to her. She'd only had it for a couple of weeks and using it wasn't something that came natural to her. Not that much felt natural to her.

"You're right," she said when Marcia paused to take a breath. "I should have called when I realized we would be stuck for a while. I apologize again."

"Fine. Next time show a little more courtesy." Marcia pursed her thin, blood red-lips and drew herself up to her full height.

She looked to be about five feet six inches, thanks to four-inch heels, but she was still two inches shorter than Summer. "Have a seat. I'll see if Mr. Knowelton can fit you into his busy schedule."

Summer didn't exhale until Marcia was out of sight. Being stuck on an elevator was not a good way to start a job. Having her supervisor hate her guts for no apparent reason trumped that. But she'd fix that. Tomorrow she would come early and take the stairs again. Problem solved.

Feeling better, she wondered if the caked-on makeup the other woman wore hid a skin condition. If so, Marcia was wasting her money and time. Her generously sized breasts, encased as they were in a tight, low-cut sweater probably did a better job of distracting from any facial blemishes than buckets of makeup. At least with men. And some women.

"He'll see you now."

Summer decided she detected a good bit of disappointment in Marcia's voice. She allowed herself a smile as she followed the other woman. They walked down a long hall past occupied offices. Summer imagined she'd have to do an introductory round later, and her smile faltered as she considered that her other co-workers might have Marcia's unwelcoming attitude. The smile on Garland Knowelton's face said otherwise.

"Welcome, Summer," he said, holding out a hand that was large like the rest of him. "I hope you won't let faulty elevators run you off."

"No. It's not your fault. I'm grateful for the opportunity to work here."

"Good deal. I'll handle it from here, Marcia."

Marcia looked as if she wanted to protest, then gave him a blinding smile and retreated.

"Have a seat." He motioned toward the chairs facing a desk laden with sports memorabilia. "As I'm sure you know, Kevin's out of town. But even if he weren't, as your boss, I'd still be having this conversation with you. I'd like to start off with your special situation and our expectations."

She swallowed hard. Expectations did not sound good to her. Not before she'd had a chance to screw things up. "Of course." She focused her gaze on some point over his left shoulder. It wasn't that he was hard to look at. The opposite was true. With his handsome square face, sky-blue eyes and dazzling smile, lots of women must look at him all the time. Not her, though. Even if she'd been straight she wouldn't dare. There was no room in her life, in her recovery, really, for a relationship. She forced herself to pay attention; her heartbeat slowed eventually as Gar detailed her job duties. She was going to be a "gofer" and that was something she thought she could handle. She stood when he did, gave him an appreciative smile and returned to Marcia's glassed-in office, located behind the reception area. Given the situation between them, she knocked on the open door and waited for Marcia to acknowledge her presence before speaking. "Gar said I should report back to you."

"Yes. By all means let's find something you can do." Marcia pushed back her chair, acting as if she was about to make a sacrifice of Biblical proportions. "You do read, right? I mean, I heard you suffer from brain damage." Marcia made it sound like a lobotomy.

"Yes."

"Yes what?"

"I do read," Summer said. She added very slowly, "As long as the words aren't too big. I can recite the multiplication table too." She wanted to laugh at the look on Marcia's face. A look that said she wasn't sure if Summer were joking or not. Marcia probably had her categorized as somewhere between moron and smartass. She could live with that.

"Good for you. Filing then, I think." Marcia led the way once again, not bothering to stop at any of the eight offices they passed.

The filing room seemed amazingly large to Summer. She could easily imagine getting lost in the maze of legal-sized cabinets. The walls were sterile beige and there weren't any windows. Fluorescent lights kept the room bright.

"I must remind you that you signed a nondisclosure agreement, so any information you see is to be kept strictly confidential." Marcia stopped in front of a file-laden desk. More files were stacked on the floor. "Do you understand?"

From the tone, Summer figured she'd been placed in the moron column. She furrowed her brow. "You mean like I have to say it's good?"

"Not 'complimentary.'" Marcia pursed her lips and looked at Summer through narrowed eyes. "Confidential. That means you can't tell anyone what you see in these files. Not that you should be reading them anyway."

The words "you moron" seemed to fly through the air and slap Summer in the face. She nodded. "It's a secret. Sorry. Big words still confuse me sometimes. What do I do?" She almost felt sorry for the look of doubt on Marcia's face—almost.

"Obviously, you need to put these folders that are on the desk and on the floor into the filing cabinets. All of the folders are marked with a name and number. You match the number with the number on the file drawer and then place the folder in alphabetical order within it. I hope that wasn't too hard to understand. I tried not to use big words."

"Like a match game. Got it." Summer hoped her smile was idiot-savantish.

Marcia glanced at the slim watch on her left wrist. "I'll be back to check on you in thirty minutes. If it's too challenging, that is, too hard, you come find me before then. I can probably come up with something to match your intellect."

Summer pulled a face once Marcia left trailing perfume behind her like a crop duster trailing pesticide. Playing the idiot was surprisingly fun. Very different from the times she'd felt like an idiot. Thankfully those times were becoming more of a memory than a frustration. Dr. Veraat said she had to move past that time and that the only way to do that was to stay in the present.

Of course that was easy for Dr. Veraat to say. She hadn't woken up three years ago dumb as a rock. Summer grabbed a stack of folders, pleased to find they were mostly sorted. She spent the next thirty minutes reducing the stacks, finding the repetitive motions soothing. The numbers helped keep her in the present. Keep her thoughts focused.

"How's it going?"

Summer gave a start and dropped the stack of folders she was holding. Putting a hand to her galloping heart, she studied the attractive brunette who'd managed to catch her unawares. Nothing like Marcia, she had an athletic build that was tastefully covered in a gray suit, and though there was a look of concern on her face, it wasn't overlaying a sneer.

"Sorry I startled you. I'm Liz Fears."

"Summer Baxby." She shook the proffered hand. "Not your fault. I was caught up in the world of numbers." She stooped to pick up the files. "I'll never get this stuff back in the right place."

"Let me give you a hand. Some of those are bound to belong to me." Liz looked at the top folder. "Yup, this one is mine." Within minutes, she had all the pieces of correspondence back in their respective folders.

"Thanks. You saved my life."

"If you're not part of the solution, you're part of the problem, right? Oh, wait, I *was* part of the problem." Liz gave an infectious laugh.

"I still appreciate it." Her smile disappeared as she heard the rapidly approaching footsteps.

Marcia burst into the room. "What is going…Oh. I didn't realize you were in here, Liz. I hope Summer's not keeping you from your work."

"Not at all. I just dropped by to welcome a new employee. I'm surprised you didn't take the time to introduce her around."

"Well… It's just…" Marcia raised her chin. "I know everyone is busy this time of month. I didn't see the need to disturb you." She folded her hands over her chest and glared at Summer. "I have work to do myself. I thought it was enough that I have to take time to check up on her."

Summer chewed on her lip and recited the multiplication table while wishing herself away from the sharp animosity filling the room. What had she stepped into?

"Fine." Liz's smile was anything but friendly. "I'll take care of introducing her around. I can spare the few minutes it'll take to do it."

"I don't need you doing my job," Marcia said heatedly.

"So you do realize it's part of your job? Imagine that." Liz turned her attention to Summer. "Since Marcia has graciously agreed to introduce you around, I'd like to be the first to invite you to lunch. Is twelve thirty okay?"

Summer shot a quick glance to Marcia before nodding.

"Good. My office is the second on the left. See you then." Liz brushed past Marcia.

"I hope going to lunch is okay?" Summer said.

"What do I care?" Marcia flipped her platinum blonde hair over her shoulder. "What have you done so far?"

Summer thought she caught a flicker of surprise on Marcia's face when she saw how much work had been accomplished. A closer inspection showed she'd been wrong. Marcia had the "I'm so much better than you" sneer firmly in place.

"You seem to have caught on. Which is good. I have more important work to do than babysit you. Keep at it and report to me at the end of the day." Marcia was gone in a click of heels and another cloud of perfume.

Any more compliments like that, Summer thought, opening a file cabinet, *and I'll get a big head*.

CHAPTER TWO

"I feel I should tell you straight out that Kevin informed us about your coma and memory loss," Liz said, reaching for the large glass of iced tea. She was seated in a booth opposite Summer at a bustling Mexican restaurant a block from their office. "My dad was in a coma for only three weeks and it took him months to get close to what he used to be." She tucked her curly hair behind her ears and leaned forward. "And why am I telling you this, you wonder? I want you to know you don't have to worry about doing something strange around me. I'll shut up now and look at the menu."

"It's okay." Summer looked around the noisy restaurant filled with office workers. The décor was Americanized Mexican with an abundance of cactus plants and the smell of sizzling fajitas. "I take that back. It's more than okay to have someone who understands a little of what I'm going through." She flipped open the paper menu. "It's nice, so thanks."

Liz nodded. "As far as the menu goes, everything here is great. And fattening. I try not to eat here more than twice a month. No self-control." She plucked a warm tortilla chip from the basket and dipped it in salsa.

"You don't look it." Liz wasn't thin by any standards, but she was toned and shapely.

"Only because I exercise like a demon and watch my intake for the most part. Hey, any chance you play sports?"

"Me? I do okay on a treadmill, but that's hardly a sport. My little brother tells me I've always been more the artistic type."

"Too bad. My soccer team needs a couple of players who actually show up for most of the games." Liz closed her menu as their waitress breezed up to their table.

"Hey, y'all ready to order now?" She whipped a pad out of her apron.

They both ordered. Chicken quesadillas for Summer and a taco combo for Liz.

"How long have you worked at Tathum?" Summer asked once the waitress had scurried off to place their order.

"Going on eight years. Started right after college. It was my first real job, but I did internships, so I can say it's a great place to work. For the most part, anyway. I probably should keep my big mouth shut, but what the hell. Don't let Marcia get to you. She's had it rough, so we cut her some slack. Only some, though."

"Can't say I blame her for being upset about having to deal with me. I come with my own set of problems."

"Doesn't everybody? All I'm saying is sometimes you have to plant your foot. And yes, sometimes it's up her butt. Remember you're doing work that she doesn't want to do. Hence the big piles. She should be more grateful."

"I can handle her. It's kind of fun to play up to her image of me." She toyed with a chip. "Can I…ask about your dad?"

"Sure."

"How long ago did it happen?"

"Five years in May. He was reporting in the Middle East when a bomb exploded, hitting his head with shrapnel. At first they thought his brain might be scrambled. It's a good thing his skull is hard." She blinked rapidly and exhaled. "He had some relearning to do. Things he'd been able to do since he was a kid. But he's adjusted better than me and my mom."

"Must have been tough on you two. I mean, seeing him struggle to do the simple things." Summer had only seen her mom's guard slip once, but that was enough to make her realize the strain her mother had been under. Enough to make her save her own frustrations for when she was alone.

"It was. For a while it was like I was the parent and he was the child. He was always second-guessing himself."

"I can totally relate to that. I was out for eleven and a half months, in case you're wondering. It was something of a miracle that I woke up. Then two years in rehab and therapy to relearn everything I needed to know to live on my own." She leaned back to let the waitress place a plate in front of her. Her eyes widened at the amount of food. "This looks great," she told the waitress and declined a refill of her Coke. "Smells good too."

"Tastes even better. I know they have all those fancy tacos these days, but give me an old-fashioned one every time." The taco shell crunched as Liz took a bite. "If you can't eat all that, there's a fridge in the break room."

"There's a break room?"

Liz rolled her eyes. "I'll give you a real tour when we get back."

Summer hastily swallowed. "You don't have to."

"I know. Coma sympathy thing."

She grinned. Maybe she *could* function on the outside. "I don't mind taking advantage of that."

* * *

By five o'clock, Summer was more than ready to be gone. The dent she'd made in piles had her riding on a huge sense of accomplishment and the majority of her co-workers were friendly, but she needed a break from Marcia's sharp tongue and disapproving manner. She stopped by Marcia's desk on her way out and was pleased to find it empty.

"Problem?"

Startled she turned to see Gar, lightweight jacket settled over his arm and a messenger bag in his hand. "I...I wanted to, uh, let Marcia know I'm leaving for the day. But she's, uh, gone already."

"Contrary to what you may have heard, you're not required to check out. Nobody's watching the clock for when you get in or leave. Especially me."

"Okay. Good to know. Uh, see you tomorrow then."

"I'll walk out with you. You can tell me about your first day since I was unable to check in earlier."

"My stuff is in the file room."

"I can wait."

Taking him at his word, she hurried back to grab her bag. She was on twelve times twelve when she returned. To her relief, Liz was waiting with Gar. She wouldn't have to wrack her brains for how to make spending the day filing sound like something more.

"What a colorful bag," Liz commented. "The daisies scream spring."

"It's for my bike." She turned it around so Liz could see the hooks on the other side.

"You biked here?" Gar asked.

She could tell she'd gone up in his estimation. She wondered if she'd go back down if he knew she couldn't drive or, rather, couldn't bear to be behind the steering wheel. She shrugged. "Only takes ten minutes to get here. And that's from start to finish."

"Then you must live downtown," Liz said, opening the door to the suite.

"Fifth near Langford."

"Nice location," Gar remarked. "Plenty of bars in walking distance."

"I like it so far. Like you said, it's close to everything I need."

"Not enough green space for me." Liz handed her briefcase to Gar and slipped on her coat.

"Central Park is only thirty minutes. That's green."

"We should go riding one weekend. I'll show you plenty of green. Couple of weeks and the weather will be perfect. Not too cold, not too warm."

"Count me in," Gar said.

"Fine. But you don't get to lead." Liz turned to Summer as they waited for an elevator to arrive. "Last time he had us peddling all over the place looking for some restaurant that used to be a barn. I was ready to eat just about anything by the time we found it."

"Hey, now. Don't listen to her, Summer. That was one time out of what? Fifteen, twenty?"

Summer hoped the surprise didn't show on her face. Liz and Gar were obviously more than co-workers and didn't seem to care who knew it.

"That one time wiped out all the others," Liz claimed and jostled her way onto a full elevator. "Come on, there's room," she told Summer.

"I...I'll get the next one," she replied, remembering the morning's ordeal. The mere possibility of getting stuck on a crowded elevator to be bombarded by memories was too much. When the next two elevators proved to be equally crowded, she headed for the door to the stairs. *Going down is not so bad*, she told herself, then almost changed her mind when the door opened with a loud squeak. "Needs oil, that's all." But before closing the door, she checked the inside handle to make sure it wasn't going to lock behind her. Getting stuck twice in one day was not on her schedule. And given the vast number of people leaving, she could be stranded until the morning.

The lobby was bustling as workers poured out of the elevators, seemingly in a rush to leave. Tomorrow she'd hang around upstairs, wait for the rush to die down.

"Summer? Summer Rain Baxby, is that you?"

She faltered. Nobody here should know her full name. She turned—and a memory surfaced with the force of a whale breaking water. *Freshman year. Fierce crush. Waiting in the dorm lobby hoping for a glimpse, a chance to make conversation. Kylie? No, that wasn't quite right.*

"It *is* you. Remember me? Keile Griffen from Bradford House."

"Of course. Key, not kai. I would have recognized you anywhere. You look the same." *Better, even*, she admitted to herself. Keile was wearing a red sweater that contrasted nicely with her light brown skin. Her dark brown hair, cut short, framed an attractive face set off by expressive brown eyes and full lips. "It's good to see you again." *Great to be able to recognize someone from before, actually!*

Keile smiled. "You, too. You work here? I know I haven't seen you around before."

"Started today. Tathum, Inc., eighth floor."

"Cool. I gotta get home to kid duty, but I'd love to have lunch someday. Catch up." She set down her backpack and pulled out her wallet. "Here's my card. Give me a call if you're up for it."

"Tomorrow? Are you…Would tomorrow be okay?" Summer knew she sounded desperate and didn't care. Before her was a piece of her past. A piece her mother couldn't give her.

Keile checked her phone. "Sure. Lobby at one?"

"I'll be here." Early. She'd be here early. "Tomorrow," she said softly and hugged herself as she watched Keile stride confidently away—much as she had during freshman year.

* * *

Summer's phone beeped as she unlocked the door to her condo. For a second she was transmitted back to the hospital when a beep meant her heart was still beating. Out of habit more than worry she put her hand to her chest. By the time she realized the beep was from her phone, it had stopped—as was usually the case.

Despite her argument to the contrary, her mother had insisted on giving her a cell phone. And had insisted she carry it everywhere she went. Recognizing the fear behind her mother's request, Summer had eventually given in and promised to keep it charged and turned on. Now she just had to learn to associate the beep with the phone. Then maybe she could answer it before her mother's imagination had her fifth daughter lying in a ditch.

She wheeled her bike inside, and when the phone rang again, she answered by the third beep.

"Are you okay?"

"I'm fine, Mom. I told you—it takes me two calls to figure out it's ringing and remember how to answer."

"You've had it for fifteen days, Summer. I'm beginning to think this is your way of rebelling. And when I think about that some more, I'm sure that's a good thing."

"You're making too much of tech incompetence." She locked the door and crossed through the foyer to drop onto the plush living room sofa.

"When was the last time you ate?"

"Lunch," she shot back, knowing her mother expected her to be unable to answer quickly. "Chicken quesadillas from Matador."

"Maybe working is good for you. Just maybe."

Her mother had been against her seeking employment. Against her leaving the childhood home that had sheltered her for almost two years while she went through rehab. "I had a memory today. An actual memory."

"Oh, baby…" Her mother's sympathetic words were followed by a loud sigh. "I hope it was a pleasant one."

"It was. At this point though I'd take any kind. Mom, I have a memory that's older than two years. I'm not two years old anymore."

"Oh, baby," she said again and broke off, her voice tremulous. "Tell me."

"Freshman year after we moved me into the dorm. You and Dad had left and I didn't feel like sitting in my room alone. I was in the lounge and she walked in, all shy, unsure. Keile Griffen was her name. Thanks to her I now remember part of the first semester. How she made my heart beat faster without trying. We're having lunch tomorrow. Hopefully more will come. Memory, that is."

"That name sounds familiar. Was she the serious one who was all about studying? The one you talked about all the time?"

"That's her. I let her think she was the reason I passed algebra. Oh my God. Another memory. Dr. Veraat was right. It just takes one to get started. Keile and I would meet at that little grill place in the student union. I bought her food in exchange for tutoring. And as hard as I tried I could never talk her into doing anything that wasn't school related." Summer rubbed a hand over her mouth. She wasn't a blank slate anymore. "Oh my God."

"What a nice memory, honey. But I wonder if you shouldn't see Dr. Veraat. Memories, even good ones, can upset your sense of order. I'll come by tomorrow and we'll see if she can squeeze you in."

"No. This is good. I need this. You know I do. And I can't continue to run to Dr. Veraat for every little thing. The whole point of me moving out and getting a job was to help me learn to function on my own. To be semi-independent. Let me try to deal with this on my own first. I promise to call if it gets to be too much."

"Okay," her mother said after a prolonged silence. "I'm not trying to run your life, honey. I want…I worry about you."

"I know. I really do. But remember Dr. Veraat thinks I'm ready to take some lumps and I can only do that by expanding my comfort zone. I get that you've had to let me go once and that this time it's probably harder."

"Last time I had eighteen years of lead-up time."

"Oh, Mom, I love you." Summer couldn't begin to understand the magnitude of the agony her mother had lived through the past three years, but if she was going to get better, she had to start making her own decisions. Had to start doing things for herself—hence the condo, the job, the not running to her parents for every little thing. They needed this as much as she did. Probably more.

"I love you too, baby. I'll try not to call until Friday. Your dad's been talking about taking a trip to Callaway Gardens. With spring around the corner it'll be nice to see the plants getting ready to bloom."

"You could go to that spa you told me about. Get the full treatment."

"That does sound like a wonderful idea. Maybe we'll stay a few days. Order room service, stay in bed and pretend we're still young."

"TMI," Summer warned playfully. She'd picked up that expression from her brother. "You should call right now. You deserve it."

"Maybe I will. It's not that far away. We could be back in less than two hours if…"

"I did the job today. And I recognized an old friend. I'll be okay, Mom. You need to hang up and make reservations now. Promise, okay? I need you to do that for me."

"Then you'd better be prepared for me to check in on you. Twice a day."

"I'll be here."

CHAPTER THREE

Feelings of hunger eventually got through to the right side of Renny Jamison's brain. She absently rubbed her belly and stretched her back, pleased with the day's work so far. Chapter Ten was practically writing itself, the words flowing from her brain about as fast as she could type them. Maybe that had something to do with the subject matter, she thought with a sly smile.

Pushing back from her desk, she was surprised to discover it was after five. No wonder she was hungry. The stale oatmeal packet she'd scrounged for breakfast had long since been digested. She took a step toward the kitchen and groaned. The only reason oatmeal had been on the menu was due to the lack of other edible foodstuffs in her kitchen. And hadn't she meant to make a grocery run during the early afternoon when everyone else was at work? she mused, frowning. Well, she'd have to suck it up and fight the traffic in and out of the store. Takeout was not an option considering it had been on the menu three nights in a row and she was now afraid to get anywhere near the scale.

But looking at the detailed schedule for completion of her novel plastered on the wall of her office, she couldn't help thinking that dodging traffic was a small price to pay for today's accomplishments. At the rate she was going, she would finish the first draft by mid-March, two months earlier than projected. Being the superstitious sort, she rapped her knuckles against the wooden desk on her way out of the room. She was almost to the front door when she realized she needed to change before going out in public. She didn't consider herself too vain, but the holey sweats she was wearing with her favorite writing shirt, now off-white because it hadn't seen bleach in years, were not fit for public consumption.

Her cell rang before she made it to the bedroom. She glanced at the caller ID—Eve Jamison—and sighed. She was tempted to let it go to voice mail. In her upbeat mood, she wouldn't mind putting off talking to her mother until hell froze over. But that would be cowardly and she wasn't a coward—much. Reminding herself she could handle anything her mother had to dish out, she answered the call. "Hello, Mother."

"When are you coming back? You've been in that forsaken place for six months now. Surely that's enough time to mourn my mother."

"I'm doing fine, Mother. How are you these days?"

"Renee, tell me you're *not* staying there," her mother demanded.

"Do we really have to go through this every time?" Renny sighed. She could count on her mother to demand her return once a month. And now twice in February. "I'm not coming back to California. This is my home now. And for your information, I will mourn Gran for the rest of my life."

"And you could mourn her here as well as there. Is it the drugs? You can tell me if you're afraid—"

"No! I was clean for two years before I left, remember?" Her mother had a way of remembering only the worst parts of her history. "I like it here. I can write here."

"Oh, well, then you must stay. We wouldn't want being a star to get in the way of your little hobby." Her mother exhaled.

"I thought you might be interested in this script I managed to get my hands on early. It's a made-for-TV movie that's perfect for you. One word from me and you'd have an audition. This is your chance to get back in the game. To get back on top."

"Eve, when will you get it through your head that no one wants to see me act. Hell, *I* don't want to see me act. I appreciate the offer, but as I explained the last seven times, I am not interested in being in the business anymore." She'd been in her first movie at six months and by the time she was old enough to realize not everyone lived in the land of make-believe, acting had been her life, a sure way to keep her mother's approval. "If that's all you needed, I have some errands to run." Her answer was a dial tone.

Renny breathed a sigh of relief as she placed the phone on the counter. The requests from her mother were getting easier to deflect. She no longer had that tightness in her chest after a conversation with Eve Jamison—the movie star and demanding mother. She no longer had even the tiniest longing to be back under the lights, either on the set or out on the town. What she told her mother was true. She liked living in Seneca, the growing town an hour south of Atlanta. She loved living in the house her grandmother had left her. Loved the location with its friendly neighbors and a park in walking distance where she could sit and write or people watch. Most of all she loved being in a city where she wasn't always regarded as the child actress who had turned into a teenage fuck-up.

There were so many reasons for her to stay and no reasons for her to go back. No use telling her mother that. Eve had never understood her, never known her well enough to know where she was coming from. When Renny had finally accepted that fact, she was able to turn her life around for good. No matter what her mother thought, moving back to Southern California wouldn't change who she'd become. *And I'm finally stable enough to know I don't have to prove that to anyone*, she thought, absently answering her phone, which was ringing again. "Hello?"

"Keile here. You interested in dinner with strings attached?"

Her stomach rumbled. "No food, hungry, so yes. When?"

Keile laughed. "When you get here. Be warned, there are three kids over here and only one adult. Even my fur baby deserted me to go help train Marcus's puppy."

"Three? Sweet! Be there in five." She rushed to her bedroom and did a quick change. Over the past six months, she'd gotten to know Keile and her partner, Haydn, very well and volunteered her babysitting services regularly for four-year-old Kyle, eighteen-month-old Chelsea and Can, their four-legged child.

Keile somehow managed to open the door while carrying two babies, one of which looked very much like her. She was also sporting a big welcoming smile. "Yeah. Which one do you want? This one then," she said as Chelsea lunged toward Renny.

"Love you too." Renny kissed Chelsea's soft brown curls, then smiled at the blonde tot hiding half her face against Keile's chest. "Hey, sweet thing."

"Hey, back," Keile said, grinning when Renny swatted her arm. "Oh, you were talking to Zelda? According to Edan, who is having a night out with my better half, she's going through a shy phase. That means she won't be climbing all over you for another five minutes. Give or take five minutes," she added as Zelda held out her arms to Renny.

"Where's my little man?" Renny asked, balancing the girls on her hips.

"Probably choking on mac and cheese by now. You're just not important enough for him to stop stuffing it down."

"As hungry as I am, I can't blame him."

"Then let's join him." Keile led the way down the hall to the kitchen. "It's not haute cuisine, but it should fill you up. Chelsea and Zelda have already been fed, so they can go in the playpen while we eat."

"Don't have to tell me twice." She placed the girls in the playpen and ruffled Kyle's hair before taking a seat. He wasn't choking, but he was shoveling down mac and cheese at an alarming rate. "Hey, Kyle." She laughed when he grinned at her, mouth full of food.

"No eat and show," Keile admonished and set a plate in front of Renny.

Renny filled her plate with rotisserie chicken, mac and cheese, green beans and coleslaw, then grabbed a couple of rolls. "This looks fantastic. More so because I don't have to do a thing but eat it."

"I picked it up on the way home from work since Zelda's other mom called to say she couldn't make it. Haydn suggested I tag you as Edan pulled her out of the door."

"I'll thank your lovely wife later." She moaned at the first bite of a moist chicken breast. "Sorry. Haven't eaten since breakfast. Oh, this is good." She took another bite and wiggled with satisfaction.

Keile transferred some chicken to her plate. "Hope that means the book's still going."

"Oh, yeah. Great. It's going great. Something about this town brings the muse to full force. I'm ahead of schedule. Not that I would ever tell my agent that."

"Is this one about the child musician with the demanding mother who turns into an addict or the one about the psycho cop killer?"

Renny finished chewing, then swallowed. "The former. They say you should write what you know and I know all about demanding mothers and addictions. If I thought Eve was going to read the thing, I might be worried she'd recognize pieces of herself. I say pieces, but it's more like chunks. Big juicy chunks. In case you haven't guessed, I have mommy issues."

"Never crossed my mind," Keile said with a straight face. "Seems like writing about her is the best kind of revenge. She can't accuse you of slander without giving herself away."

"Priceless," Renny all but sang.

"Mama Kee, can I have some more mac and cheese?"

"Finish your green beans first."

"Aw." Kyle stuck out his bottom lip, looking pitiful.

"Green beans are good." Renny forked a few and made a show of eating them. She pretended not to notice when Kyle followed suit.

Keile mouthed a thank you as she placed more mac and cheese on Kyle's plate. "Are you sure you weren't around kids before you got here? You're too good with them to be a newbie."

"Really I wasn't. But if I'd known how much fun they are to be around, I would have found some to play with sooner."

"What about having one of your own?"

"Have to find the right girl first. And even then I'm not sure it's for me. I like being able to give them back. Can't do that when they're yours." Renny grimaced. Keile didn't look offended, but Renny knew that due to having an unstable mother, Keile had spent most of her life in the foster care system. "Anyway, I'm only thirty. I'd say that gives me plenty of time to make a decision."

"Speaking of plenty, there'll be plenty of single women here Saturday night to tempt you. Between Haydn and my good friend, Jo, I believe every lesbian in Seneca got the invite."

"And who wouldn't go for a February-Is-History party. I can't be the only one looking forward to February being gone. Not to mention a party. Please tell me there'll be dancing."

Keile nodded. "That's Edan's job. Maybe you could give her a hand."

"Maybe I could." Renny pushed her empty plate away. Considering the size of her first helping and her impending diet, seconds were not on the menu. "I dated this DJ once. I have vague memories of being shown how to scratch."

"Uh, don't think we'll have that kind of crowd."

"Didn't think so. I'll burn a couple of CDs. Now it's time to play with the kiddies."

CHAPTER FOUR

Summer jerked awake, a scream caught in her throat. Fighting against the covers, she struggled to breathe. Once free, she turned on the bedside lamp, letting the light bathe her and her fevered imagination. "I am *not* in the closet." She had to say it out loud. Saying it out loud made it true. "I'm not." Hugging her knees, she rocked back and forth, willing her mind to let go of the vivid dream featuring a young Rich. He had been sitting in the closet, watching as his crazed father pounded on his mother. She could still smell the mixture of blood, booze and the emptying of bowels as the poor woman died. Could feel the terror as Rich whispered prayers and waited for his father to start on him.

"No!" She shook her head and took a deep breath, held it a moment, then let it out slowly. "It didn't happen." After a couple more breaths, the trembling slowed and her mind cleared. A look at the clock and she groaned. Five thirty. Too early to get up and too late to get any decent sleep. Not that she wanted to sleep. Not if it meant going back to the closet or back into Rich's mind.

She wondered how the hell she had gotten there as she swung her legs over the side of the bed. Maybe if she had thought through her earlier experience, written it down before going to sleep, she wouldn't be awake now. Taking another glance at the clock, she dismissed thoughts of calling Dr. Veraat. What could she tell her anyway? That she'd had an episode on the elevator and fallen into a stranger's memories? On her first day on the job too. Dr. Veraat would write it off as stress, the anxiety she had said would come with each step forward. She told Summer to remember that the little wayward backslides didn't take away from the forward motion.

See, she told herself, *you don't need a shrink. You need exercise. Looking like a scarecrow is no reason not to be an in-shape one.*

Thanks to her mother, the treadmill in the third bedroom was top of the line. But then again, everything in the condo was new and top of the line. Sandra Baxby had spared no expense when setting up her daughter's new home. Summer made her way to the exercise room, hooked up her MP3 player and set the speed for a brisk run. As her feet slapped against the treadmill pad, finding her rhythm, her mind wandered. There were plenty of areas in her life that needed work, but the physical was working for her. She was eons away from the days of having to use a walker because she lacked the strength to stand on her own. Now she could walk, run, bike—that was her miracle. Her freedom. For now her bike or her legs got her where she wanted to go. Maybe one day she would be able to get behind the wheel of a car.

Summer grimaced. The last time her mother convinced her to try that, she had coated the dash with vomit, unable to fight off the panic that had gripped her. Now she could almost smile about that day, remembering the quickly disguised look of horror that flashed over her mother's face—as if she were wondering if her daughter were the Antichrist.

Summer didn't need a shrink to tell her the answer to her problem was buried with the rest of her memories. It was strange that she equated being behind the wheel with danger because she hadn't been driving when the accident occurred.

So she'd received with skepticism Dr. Veraat's assurance the fear would pass, much like her fear of being inside the car had. She'd experienced the cramping in her stomach, the sweating, the feeling faint the first few times she'd sat in a car, but only being behind the wheel had induced vomiting. She didn't see that little side effect going away soon.

And how would she know if it did? Even her mother got a tick in her eye when she talked about Summer getting into the driver's seat of her car. Her father flat-out refused to let her near his beloved Mustang, and her sisters were quick to find errands that had to be done elsewhere if the subject came up. Her brother, the only one who wouldn't care if his beat-up pickup got spewed on, lived three hours away. In crazier moments or when she needed a good laugh, she fantasized about asking some poor car salesman if she could take a luxury car out for a test drive. Her conscience had prevailed so far.

Hitting the four-mile mark on the treadmill's counter, she switched to cool-down mode. Fifteen minutes with the dumbbells and she'd be finished. Then she'd shower, grab some chow and wait until it was time to leave for work. Not a bad way to start her day when she added in a book to keep her company. She had become addicted to reading during her recovery. In a lot of ways, books had been her salvation, reintroducing her to the world and explaining how she should act in certain situations.

It was eight twenty-five when she hurried into the lobby of her office building. The book had been excellent company, keeping her turning pages as she tried to figure out the identity of the killer before he or she was unmasked. She took a quick look at the elevators and veered to the stairwell. Her thighs protesting as she crested the eighth floor, she prayed she wasn't developing an elevator phobia to go along with her other issues. Running her fingers through her hair, she entered the reception area and smiled at the unfamiliar woman sitting behind the front desk.

"Hello. Can I help you?"

"I'm Summer Baxby. I, uh, work here." She fumbled through her bag for her wallet and pulled out her employee ID.

"Oh, right." The petite brunette with the spiky hairdo held out her hand. "I'm Fiona. I was out sick yesterday."

Something about the way she said it made Summer think Fiona hadn't been sick. She knew that for certain when she shook Fiona's hand and—

she was on a bed, a man behind her, and they were looking into the mirror as they had sex...

Mild pain flashed through her skull and her heart hammered. A fleeting trip this time. Still, she felt her cheeks burning as she pulled her hand back quickly, looking anywhere but at the woman she'd just seen naked. "Gotta, um, go," she blurted out. "You know, Marcia, late, that kind of stuff." She hurried away, not caring that judging by the look on Fiona's face she had just been branded a kook. Because considering what just happened, she *must* be one. She might be able to rationalize away the thing in the elevator as stress-induced. Maybe. Both she and Rich would have scored high on the stress scale during that. No way could she say the same about the deal with Fiona just now.

In the file room, she rested her forehead against the coolness of a file cabinet, unsure of what she should do. She didn't want to jump into other people's heads, absorbing the gritty details of their life, their secrets. Her own was scary enough. Had she pushed too fast for independence? Maybe she needed to move back to her childhood room, return to being cocooned in her parents' house.

"You okay?"

She plastered on a smile before lifting her face. "Trying to figure something out."

"So it's not problems with M&M?" Liz asked.

"M&M?"

"I know it's difficult to think of Marcia and chocolate at the same time. And it probably gives the candy a bad name."

"M&M. Marcia Meacham. I get it." Summer tapped her forehead. "That reminds me I forgot to stop by and check in."

"You shouldn't have to."

"It's better that I do."

"If she gives you any grief, tell her I held you up."

"Thanks." Summer went to Marcia's office and once again knocked on the open door. She wanted to laugh when Marcia made a show of checking her watch. "Liz stopped me."

Marcia frowned. "For what?"

"A question," she said vaguely. "Should I continue filing?"

Marcia pursed her lips, making them look even thinner. "I suppose. You didn't seem to mess things up yesterday as I expected."

My head's going to explode from the praise, Summer thought as she returned to what she considered her office. The image of her brain matter splattered all over Marcia's low-cut white sweater and her pristine office pushed the incident with Fiona to the back of her mind. As she filed, she entertained herself by coming up with different ways to slime Marcia. The morning passed quickly.

At ten to one she left a note on Marcia's desk as to her whereabouts, then took the stairs to the lobby. She spotted Keile standing by the elevator and was filled with anticipation. Here was somebody she remembered. Keile looked competent and very professional in a charcoal suit with a crisp red shirt. Summer was glad her mother had helped her pick out the dark blue pants and tapered light blue shirt she was wearing. Left to herself she favored baggy jeans and oversized T-shirts. "Hey. Thanks, you know, for doing this right away."

"No prob. There aren't too many people I remember from back then. It'll be fun to talk over old times."

"Funny you should mention that." Summer gave her a strained smile. "Unfortunately I only remember a few things from my past. And what I do remember only happened since I ran into you." If Keile was surprised, she was too polite to show it. "Why don't I fill you in on the way?"

As they walked to restaurant row, Summer explained her situation. "So you see why I was so eager to have lunch."

Keile nodded. "I can't imagine how terrifying that would be. Memories, good and bad, are at the base of who we are."

"Right now my base is a little over two years old. My family has filled in some of the blanks, but as I've discovered since running into you it's not the same as having the actual memory. So thanks again for that."

"Glad I could help. Is there any particular place you'd like to go? What with you being two and all?"

Summer laughed and to her surprise discovered she was hungry. "I could go for a burger."

"Mac's then," Keile said and backtracked half a block.

Mac's was more pub than restaurant and claimed to have the best selection of beer in Seneca. The inside was a casual collection of wooden tables and chairs, in addition to a bar that ran halfway down a side wall and round the back of the establishment. It was crowded, but Keile spotted an unoccupied table in the back.

Summer took a deep breath as she opened the menu. "Smells good."

"Best burgers in town," Keile assured her. "The problem for most people is deciding which one of the ten specialty burgers to order."

"But not for you?"

"I'm still more the 'stick with what I know' kind. But I forgot you don't remember that. You were always trying to get me to try new things, not study so much."

"I don't know about the trying new things, but I do remember me trying to talk you into doing something non school-related with me. You never would."

Keile shrugged. "It was nice you tried. You were so the free spirit extraordinaire to me."

"Hi." A perky African American waitress with intricate braids hanging down to her waist breezed up to the table. "I'm Katrina. Have you decided what to order or should I come back?"

"I'm ready," Summer said. "I'll have the avocado burger with Swiss cheese and a Coke."

"Good choice." Katrina gave her a beaming smile. "How would you like that cooked?"

For a second Summer drew a blank. "Uh…medium?"

"Okay." Katrina turned her attention to Keile. "Philly rare with a Dr. Pepper for you?" At Keile's nod, she said, "I'll be right back with your drinks."

"Is it bad when the waitress knows what you want?" Keile asked.

"Only if you wanted something different. I'm all about consistency. It's a check in the success column if I can follow my day-to-day routine *without* consulting a list. Obviously not the free spirit you remember."

"To be expected. Do you still paint?"

"I've tried," she said, shaking off the twinge of pain the reminder brought. "I've seen some of my work and it's impossible to imagine I had that kind of creativity inside me. I've been told it may come back. To give it some time. I figure after two years it's gone. That's one of the hardest things to take. Being told what I used to be able to do, who I used to be and not seeing a way to get back there." She sighed. "It's tough."

"I still have that drawing you did of me," Keile admitted. "The one time I gave into you and instead of tutoring you, I sat for a picture. You always said you didn't need math to fill a canvas. Since I'd seen some of your work, I agreed but never let on. You even paid me extra."

"It sounds…" She broke off as the waitress plunked down their drinks.

"Sorry it's taking so long. You need anything else right now?" When they shook their heads, she hurried off.

"You were saying," Keile prompted.

Summer frowned, rubbing her forehead. "I don't remember now. That happens more than I like."

"You'll remember later."

"That should be my motto," she said, dunking the straw into her drink with more force than necessary. "'You just wait. It'll come back to you.'" She exhaled. "Like I believe that."

"You remembered me. That means there's a chance other things will come to you. If you'd seen me three years ago, you'd believe in chance."

"Don't tell me. You turned into a party animal and flunked out of school?"

"Okay, maybe the changes don't seem so drastic on the outside, but they were huge on the inside. Three years ago I was more like the person you knew in college. My main goal was to have money."

"Who doesn't want to have money? Everyone—"

"Are you going to let me finish?"

Smiling, Summer pantomimed zipping her lips.

"I guess a better way to say it is that I was focused on having money to the expense of everything else. I was working like crazy, getting bonuses and watching my savings grow. Didn't matter about not having a life outside of work. Then one day I'm taking my dog to the park and this little kid finds me. I don't know how it happened, but while he and I waited for his parents, we connected. I met his mom, fell in love and realized what I'd been missing." Keile pulled out her cell phone. "This is Kyle now. He was eighteen months old when I met him."

Summer looked at the photo, then quickly back at Keile. "But he looks like you."

"Wait for it." Keile scrolled through more photos. "This is his biological father, Marcus, who is also Kyle's mom's brother and, as it turned out, my long-lost brother."

"Whoa. Just whoa." Trying to make sense of what she'd just been told, Summer gave the waitress a distracted smile as she placed her burger in front of her.

"Confusing, right?" Keile grinned. "I love to freak people out with our supposed incestuous relationships. In reality, Marcus is my partner Haydn's adopted brother. When she decided she wanted to be a mom, he was her first choice for a donor. He's also the biological father of our daughter, Chelsea." She thumbed through more photos. "This is old, but here's Haydn with Chelsea. It's all very surreal how it worked out."

"I don't know, Keile. Sounds more like fate." Summer studied the smiling redhead and bundled up baby. "And incredibly romantic. Like Beauty and the Beast romantic."

"Are you calling me a beast?"

"If the shoe fits. But my point is that it was an incredibly romantic movie and one of things the old me has in common with the new me is a love of reading. Especially romances. Which makes no sense when I think about it. I can't see myself ever falling in love. Can't see myself ever being ready for a relationship. Not like I am now."

"Thought the same thing." Keile doused her fries with ketchup. "It was going to be just me depending on me. You don't get hurt or disappointed that way. You don't do much living either. Love changes you for the better."

"It seems to have changed you. Looks good on you, but my situation is different. I'm a wreck. Anyone who'd take me on is suspect. No, crazy. They'd have to be crazy. It's better I be crazy by myself." She took a bite of her burger and agreed with Keile's assessment. It was great.

"We won't talk about love. But friends. You gotta have friends, right? And to get friends you have to meet people."

"Why do I feel like I'm about to be sold something?"

Keile smiled. "Have I got the perfect opportunity for you! We're having a party Saturday. Nothing fancy, just food, drink, conversation and maybe a little dancing. No pressure. You can talk or not talk. Meet women or not meet women. You don't have to stay long."

"I don't know. I'm not good at that kind of thing." Nerves danced up and down her spine. The thought of having to deal with strangers was a little frightening. No, she corrected herself, it was terrifying. As her breath quickened, she raced through the multiplication table. But even that wasn't enough to douse the fear of being exposed, of being surrounded by women who expected her to know how to act, what to say, how to be normal. "I can't. I'm sorry, but I can't."

"That's okay. You don't have to come. Maybe you could come over another day. I'd love for you to meet Haydn and the kids."

"I could do that." Suddenly her chest wasn't so tight. "I'd like to do that. Like to meet the woman who accomplished what I couldn't."

CHAPTER FIVE

Saturday morning found Summer on the treadmill assessing her first week of work. Her Wednesday night session with Dr. Veraat had been a success. So maybe she hadn't mentioned the head hopping deal. She was allowed. She had gotten some good strategies to deal with Marcia and her continued displeasure with anything that was Summer, and that was a good thing. It was hit or miss at times, but more hit than miss, so she felt overall work was going well.

On the other hand, she'd let herself be convinced that going to Keile's party would be a giant step toward independence. A step that would do Summer and her mother a lot of good. And later, hearing the excitement in her mother's voice when she learned of her daughter's plans, Summer had been forced to admit once again that Dr. Veraat knew her stuff.

Flying on hope, she was letting herself believe her memory would return one day. That every step she took forward was a step toward the old Summer. The one with the free spirit who didn't sweat the small stuff. The one who didn't look at a pad and pencil with trepidation.

"I'll get there," she said, breathing heavily. How could she not when yesterday she'd managed to take the elevator down without a hitch? An elevator packed with boisterous workers, eager to begin their weekend.

At the three-mile mark, she gradually slowed to a walk and toweled off sweat. It wasn't yet eight, which gave her more than seven hours to obsess over everything about the party. From what she was going to wear to how stupid she was going to sound trying to make small talk. Maybe she could stay long enough to meet Haydn, then sneak out the bathroom window when Keile wasn't watching. *Officially reaching pathetic*, she thought as she removed her workout clothes.

Studying her naked body in the full-length bathroom mirror, she looked for signs of her improved appetite and found none. She was still thin. Painfully so when compared with old photos of herself. While she hadn't been fat, there had been enough bulk to constitute a medium build. Of course her hair hadn't sported a white, lightning bolt streak then either. No, that was one of the side benefits she'd discovered when she woke up from the coma. A benny that drew unwanted attention.

"But you did wake up," she reminded her reflection, fingering the streak. It was a small price to pay for coming back to life, for having her family's prayers answered. She was grateful for that.

Of course during those first few months of consciousness, gratitude had not been at the top of her list of emotions. If she was a wreck now, she'd been a catastrophe back then. Fighting the nurses, doctors and her mother with what little strength she had. She'd been confused, and, though she wouldn't admit it at first, frightened about everything.

She turned on the water in the shower and stepped inside as scenes of those first months played in her mind. She'd been like a lump of clay that needed to be shaped into a person. Everything had to be learned and with varying degrees of success. Walking had been the easiest. Her mother claimed that was because it enabled her to get away.

So many little things she even now took for granted had frustrated her, angered her, shamed her because somewhere in the deep recesses of her brain she seemed to know how she had been, how she should have been. When Dr. Veraat had tried to explain what was going on, Summer had silently dismissed it as psychobabble. From everything she'd read, and she had read plenty, the functioning of the human brain was still a major mystery. Her brain, she'd been told by many of the doctors-in-training at Emory Hospital, was even more so. One of the neurologists had written a paper on her recovery. She'd declined his offer to study her further—like some kind of lab rat. If he hadn't learned what he needed in a year of study, he wasn't ever going to learn it in her opinion—in this case, the only one that counted.

Her stomach grumbled as she was getting dressed, an unusual but not unwelcome occurrence. To celebrate, Summer decided to try something different for breakfast. She'd go out, a kind of dress rehearsal for tonight. The deli two blocks away would do. It was small and not overly crowded when she passed it in the mornings on the way to work, unlike the Starbucks a street over. She wouldn't be overwhelmed by people desperate for coffee. And if she were, it was only a quick jog back to the safety of the condo.

The number of people milling about on the sidewalk outside her building surprised her. While it was nothing like the almost frantic pace of a weekday morning when everyone was on a deadline, everywhere she looked there were families with kids. A lot of kids. Nothing like the mostly single, mostly younger people she was used to seeing.

After a moment's hesitation, she moved forward into the throng, ducking her head down to avoid making eye contact. Anxiety didn't pull at her confidence until she was a block away—halfway to the deli, halfway to safety. Her footsteps slowed as she debated the decision she'd made earlier when she hadn't been surrounded by people talking, laughing, enjoying the cool morning air and each other.

Her plans shifted when she saw the line stretching out of the deli's door. She could go back, grab some cereal, but that seemed like a cop-out. Getting jostled from behind, she moved forward, scanning side streets and discovering restaurants never noticed before. There had to be some place she could go.

It took almost six blocks before she spotted the sign for a bakery. She maneuvered through the crowd, backtracked and made a right. Inside the shop, which looked bigger than it had on the outside, the smells of yeast, cinnamon and sugar melded into something heavenly. Her midsection reacted as she spotted the display cases filled with various kinds of breads and pastries. The difficulty would be in picking just one. But maybe she didn't have to. Maybe today she could have two.

The place was busy, but the line was moving fairly quickly and there were places for her to sit. When she finally made it up to order, she picked the breakfast sandwich on a croissant and a chocolate-filled doughnut, along with a hot chocolate, since she had as not yet regained her love of coffee. With her hot chocolate and an order number plaque in hand, she found a small table near the front window. While waiting for her food, she amused herself by making up stories about the other people in the restaurant. There was the overweight couple with plates piled high who had been together long enough to eat off of each other's plate. There was the harried mother who was struggling to keep her baby happy and at the same time stop her two older boys from smearing food on each other. The abundance of freckles and mischievous eyes of one of the boys made her fingers itch for pencil and paper. A few strokes and she could have his likeness down on paper. Then she could attempt to capture the frenzied look on the mother's face. Maybe add the grumpy baby and the older boy with spikes in his dark hair for a family shot?

Realizing where her thoughts were taking her, Summer caught her breath. Could she do it? Was she finally ready to put pen to paper and create? Her gaze returned to the redheaded boy. What was it about him that made her want to capture his image? That stirred her imagination? If she could figure that out, maybe, just maybe she could find her muse, paint again. The thought was as terrifying as it was thrilling.

Her order number was called before she could figure it out. When she returned with her food, the family was packing up to leave. She felt regret, as if an important opportunity had passed her by. Suddenly the food on her plate wasn't as appetizing. She picked at the buttery croissant for something to do rather than out of hunger and watched as the kid with the freckles beat his brother in a race to the door. Her fingers itched again, seeing the triumphant smile that split his face.

A bump against her table had her turning her head in time to get hit in the face with food and drink. *I'm lucky the tray didn't hit me*, she thought, grabbing a napkin and wiping ineffectively at the scrambled eggs with cheese mixed with orange juice now spattered on her face and chest. When she blinked her eyes clear, she saw Rich standing in front of her looking like a fish trying to get oxygen, his face and throat a mottled red. She could only sigh.

A petite blonde rushed from behind the counter, towel in hand. "Are you hurt?" she asked, her voice surprisingly deep.

"I'm okay." As she accepted the towel, embarrassment had her wishing the earth would open up and swallow her. She had no doubt her face was as red as Rich's.

"I'm so sorry," Rich finally said. "I'll get you...let me... I'll uh...Damn, I'm sorry. I'll get you more food."

"No," she said more forcefully than she intended and stood, dumping food from her lap. "I mean, I was done." Summer made the mistake of looking around only to see they had the attention of everyone in the bakery. "I...I gotta go." She backed away from Rich, then fled, reciting the multiplication table until she could lock her apartment door behind her, away from the all-seeing eyes.

* * *

Renny blotted her lips with a tissue, took one last look in the mirror and declared herself satisfied with the color of her lipstick. The coral was pinker than she usually wore, but it worked against the brown tones of her skin. Not that it mattered considering where she was going. Still it was nice to make an effort now and again.

In the kitchen, she covered the large square casserole dish filled with warm banana pudding and hurried two doors down to Keile's house. As she shivered on the porch, waiting for the doorbell to be answered, she was glad she'd grabbed her coat. February was hanging on tight to winter, making sure March would come in like a lion. The midafternoon temperature was in the low forties and windy.

Haydn Davenport opened the door, tendrils of auburn hair escaping the band she'd used to pull it back. "Hey. Don't you look nice." She pulled Renny into a hug. "Thanks for helping out the other day. Sorry I missed seeing you, but Keile tells me the book is going well."

"I feel like I should knock on wood before I agree with that. As for helping out, I should be thanking you for suggesting Keile invite me. Dinner was right on time. So I guess this is my show of thanks." She held out the dish with pudding.

"It's warm." Haydn's green eyes lit up as she hugged the offering. "Come on. I have to find a hiding space for this in the kitchen before the hordes of hungry lesbians descend."

Renny laughed, but she got a kick out of Haydn's reaction to one of the few dishes she prided herself on. One of the few dishes her grandmother had taught her how to make. "Where are my kids?"

"Chelsea's finally taking her nap, no doubt fueling up for the party, and Kyle and Can went shopping with Keile. She decided at the last minute she didn't have enough charcoal or chicken."

"Isn't it a lot cold for that?" Her southern California roots were alive and well.

"Preaching to the choir." Haydn shrugged. "When she gets these ideas in her head there's no talking her out of them. She would tell you she's determined. I say hardheaded."

It was said with such affection that Renny smiled. "If she's willing to freeze for us to have barbecue, who am I to object? What can I do to help?"

"Don't tell anyone else about the banana pudding for starters."

"You would only regret it if you ate it all."

"I know. And since I've finally shed the extra weight from having Chelsea, technically I shouldn't have any." Haydn placed the bowl on the counter.

Taking in Haydn's woebegone expression, Renny said, "On the other hand, not having some would be downright rude. As the hostess it's your duty to sample it and shower me with praise."

"You got me there. Dear Abby would say it's my sworn duty. Or is that Miss Manners?" She grinned. "How do you feel about stuffing eggs?"

"No problem." Renny washed her hands while Haydn removed the halved eggs and stuffing from the fridge. She picked up the decorator tool and filled it with stuffing.

"Tell me about your book," Haydn said as they worked side by side.

"It's about an addict. Darker, grittier, more real life than I usually write. My agent's scared it'll drive away my regular readers."

"What do *you* think?"

"It could, but at some point I have to write what's inside me. Writing's a business, don't get me wrong. At the same time, I feel I have to take chances, expand my horizons in order to grow as a writer."

"What happens if it doesn't turn out like you want?"

"I think my readers are forgiving enough to give me another read if this one isn't to their taste."

"As one of your fans I'd go there with you," Haydn said, deftly chopping green onions. "You have a unique way of telling a story. I don't see how that could change because of the subject matter."

"Can I have my agent call you? She and I have been over and under this issue for a month now. I almost regret telling her about it. Should have just dropped the completed manuscript on her. The way things are progressing, I feel like this is the best piece I've ever written. But I tend to think that about everything I write."

"Then you have to go with it." Haydn scraped the onions into a bowl of spinach and grabbed an orange pepper. "How autobiographical is this?"

"There are pieces of me in the main character. Pieces of people I knew when I was using. Cleverly disguised, of course, so they can't sue me."

"So if you have a beautiful, intelligent woman with red hair and freckles I shouldn't assume it's me?"

Renny laughed and gave Haydn a quick hug. "Exactly. Now if she's an accountant you'd better watch out."

"When are you going to write a story about an actress? I have to confess the whole Hollywood scene sucks me in."

"When I feel I can do it justice. Be more objective." She shrugged. "Trust me. If I wrote it now, it would be a lousy novel. Maybe one day after I've made peace with that time in my life." *With my mother*, she added, to be strictly honest with herself. "And I'm sure that's more angst than you wanted to hear."

"No. The process fascinates me. I'm a numbers person who can remember struggling to write a short story in my high school English class. Having an idea is easy. Putting all the words together to make it interesting is the hard part. Read 'impossible' for me. How do you do it?"

"One of my secrets is having a great editor. The other is putting ass to chair and pushing through. That's especially important on the days when I think every word I've written is crap. Are you thoroughly disillusioned yet?"

"No more than when I see how special effects are created. I still enjoy the movie. And I can still get lost in a book despite knowing what an author has to go through to write it."

"Good to know. Being able to help someone get away even for a little while is rewarding. We all need that kind of outlet."

Renny placed the decorator tool on the counter and admired her work. "Not bad. Should I wrap this up and put it in the fridge?"

Haydn peered at the clock on the microwave. "Wrap, yes. I need to make some room before you can put it in, though."

"I'll finish chopping the veggies while you take care of that."

"That works." She paused at sound of Can's bark followed by Kyle's excited chatter. "Our quiet time is over."

CHAPTER SIX

Summer stopped a block from Keile's house and maneuvered her bike onto the sidewalk. Her heart was racing so fast she wondered if she was having a heart attack. Her throat wasn't closed so it couldn't be a full-blown anxiety attack. Maybe she was having an "I shouldn't have listened to my mother" attack. Lord knows that was the only reason she had left her condo. The only reason for fighting the frigid temperature that she was sure had frozen her nose and cheeks.

How does she talk me into this stuff? she wondered, pressing a gloved hand against her frozen nose. Most mothers would have advised their daughters, especially the ones who couldn't drive, to stay in and out of the cold. Not *her* mother, who had insisted her daughter was healthy enough to withstand the cold and who had brushed aside Summer's comment that she would be out in the elements for an hour with the return trip. When she had pointed out that she'd run all over town finding the all-weather gear to ensure Summer could bike or walk in every kind of weather, Summer had thought it prudent to promise to attend the party.

"Hey, you got bike trouble?"

Heat rushed to Summer's cheeks, defrosting them as she glanced at the full-sized pickup truck that had pulled up alongside her. The two female occupants looked at her in concern.

"Uh, no, thanks. Just making sure I'm going the right way." Summer was glad the cap under her helmet obscured her face somewhat.

"Happy to give you directions," the butch-looking driver said. "Know this area well."

"It's, uh, right down the block," she replied, pointing. "I'm, uh, good now."

"Are you going to Keile and Haydn's house?" the attractive African American passenger asked. "If so, Terri can throw your bike in the back and you could ride with us. We're good friends of theirs."

"It's okay. Really."

"If you're sure. I'm Lynn Thompson and this is my partner, Terri Ocalla."

"Summer Baxby."

"Great. We'll see you there."

"Yeah," Summer muttered as they drove away. "Great." She didn't have to make an entrance to make a fool of herself. Hands against her cheeks, she gave serious thought to heading back to the condo, her figurative tail between her legs. But what possible excuse would she have for Keile, who would soon be hearing from her friends that she was a block away? Kidnapped by aliens?

Her phone buzzed before she could contemplate a more original excuse. She groaned, seeing her mother's name, but answered anyway. "I'm on my way there. I swear."

"You're not biking and talking, are you?"

"No. I had to stop for a minute. Uh, check the directions."

"Call me when you get there."

"Mom, I'm not a baby."

"You're *my* baby and I don't trust you to go. I think you got halfway there and chickened out. I bet when I called you were thinking about turning around and going home."

"More than halfway there, okay? I was more than halfway there. And it was more of a panic attack than chickening out."

"Oh, baby, I know this is all so hard for you. Do you want me to come get you and drop you off? Maybe even go in with…"

"Or you could just paint a big L for loser on my forehead and be done with it." Summer's cheeks burned at the thought of showing up with her mom in tow. Far better to go to the party and take credit for her own embarrassment. "I'm leaving now, Mother. Expect my call in five minutes."

Sandra laughed. "I thought that would motivate you. Try to have fun. You can wait, call me tomorrow and tell me all about it."

Muttering under her breath about sneaky mothers, she eased into the street. Keile's house was three-quarters of the way down the block. A string of blue lights were draped around the front door. Summer swung off the bike and walked it up the driveway. She was looking for something to lock it to when Keile stepped out of the house.

"Hey."

"You made it," Keile said, returning Summer's smile. "We can take your bike around back. It'll be safe there. How was the trip over? Not too cold, I hope?"

"It was okay." Summer followed Keile around the side of the house to a fenced-in backyard where the smell of barbecue emanated from a large grill being tended by two women. "You make your friends cook outside in this weather?" She returned the wave of the truck driver who'd stopped to check on her, then flipped down the bike's kickstand. Terri was her name, she remembered. Terri, who was with Lynn.

"If you can ride your bike in it, they can grill in it. And I didn't have to make Jo or Terri do anything. Grills have a gravitational pull for them."

"My dad's like that. Here's hoping they don't need to have the food rescued from burning like he does."

"Please don't let them hear you casting aspersions on their grilling abilities," Keile said, her voice lowered. "I've heard people have been maimed for less."

"I'll keep that in mind." Summer removed a box of Godiva chocolates from one of her bike bags. "It's not much, but it travels well."

"You didn't have to bring anything, but thanks. Come inside. I'll introduce you around."

"Uh, yeah. Inside." Summer slowly attached her helmet to her bike, then took a deep breath. "Okay." Looking at the back door, she tried not to think about all the unfamiliar women she'd encounter there. With shaky hands, she pulled off her skull cap and ran her fingers through her hair. "Okay," she repeated.

"Relax." Keile placed a hand on her shoulder and gave a gentle squeeze. "Everybody's friendly and if it gets to be too much you can always hide in Kyle's or Chelsea's room for a bit."

When Keile kept a hand on her shoulder, Summer wondered if it was for support or to keep her from escaping. *Maybe both*, she decided as they stepped into the brightly lit kitchen. She recognized the redhead with a smattering of freckles who was standing by the sink as Keile's partner, Haydn, from the photos Keile had shown her at lunch.

"You must be Summer," Haydn said, wiping her hands on her apron.

"Summer Baxby, my partner Haydn Davenport."

"Nice to meet you." Summer shook Haydn's hand. The sound of banging drew her attention to the kitchen's other occupant, almost hidden by the mesh of the playpen.

"And that's my Chelsea." Keile crossed the kitchen, scooped up her daughter and flew her overhead a couple of times. "Watch out for her," she warned as Chelsea dissolved into giggles. "She's an attention hog."

"She's beautiful," Summer marveled. "Looks just like you, Keile."

"The red highlights and freckles come from her mama," Keile said, obviously proud.

"You were right, Haydn. The hummus…" Renny came to an abrupt stop just inside the door. "Hi. I didn't realize anyone else was in here."

"Don't stop now," Haydn said. "Not when you were praising my rightness for all to hear."

"Don't listen to her." Keile poked Haydn's shoulder. "Renny, come meet my newly re-found friend, Summer."

Renny set the empty dish on the counter. "Renny—"

"Jamison," Summer finished. Before she could stop herself, she blurted out, "I've read all your books." Realizing she sounded like fangirl-ish, she put her hands against her heated cheeks. At least she hadn't mentioned that Renny looked better in person than she did in her publicity photo.

"I hope you enjoyed them," Renny said, seemingly unperturbed by Summer's outburst. "Have we met? You look familiar."

Summer shook her head. "I would have remembered that. Summer Baxby," she added belatedly and held out her hand.

"Summer, as a Renny Jamison fan, would you read a book about an addict that was…" Haydn pointed at Renny. "How did you describe it?"

"Darker, grittier, more like real life."

"That's right. So, Summer, would you buy it?"

"Oh yeah. If Renny Jamison's name is on the cover I know it'll be a good read."

"Too much of this and my ego will get out of control. Maybe both of you should tag-team my agent. Assure her I'm not committing writing suicide."

"Has she read it?" Summer asked. "I can't imagine how she could say that if she's read it."

"Not finished." Renny slid her hands into the pockets of her slacks. "This is based on the detailed synopsis."

"What happens if she says no?" The heat in the kitchen had Summer unzipping her coat, revealing a long-sleeved purple sweater, which barely met the top of hip-hugger corduroys in the same color. "While I can't really see her saying no to Renny Jamison, does that mean you toss your book?"

Renny smiled. "I'm exaggerating. Janine might grumble, but she hasn't said no so far."

"And why would she?" Keile said as she played peekaboo with Chelsea. "You're a bestselling author."

"I'm only as good as my next book sells. And before I forget why I came in here..." She grabbed the empty bowl. "We need more hummus."

"Can't have that." Haydn opened the fridge. "Summer, what can I get you to drink?"

"Coke, if you have it." She accepted the can as the back door opened.

"The last of the chicken's done," Terri announced, coming in the back door and holding up a filled platter. "Anything else need to go on?"

"More veggie kabobs." Haydn returned to the refrigerator.

"Glad to see you got here okay," Terri said to Summer. "Summer, meet my ugly sister, Jo."

Summer looked from one to the other. Their faces were identical. "Hi. Summer Baxby."

"Jo Ocalla, the better looking sister. Nice to meet you. Any chance you're in the market for a dog?"

"Geez, Jo, give it a rest." Terri rolled her eyes.

Jo glared at her sister. "As I was saying, I work with rescue dogs and we're always looking for responsible parents. You decide you're ready, Keile knows how to find me."

"Oh...Okay." Summer wondered in what universe she could be classified as responsible. She could barely take care of herself.

"She's really not as crazed as she comes across," Terri said to Summer in a loud whisper. "Just humor her."

"You two." Keile shook her head. "Now that the humor portion of our program has been dealt with, I'll take care of the kabobs." She handed Chelsea off to Renny. "I didn't invite you guys to make you watch the grill."

"Nope." Jo stepped around her and plucked the plastic-wrapped platter from Haydn. "You just want to hog all the fun," she accused Keile before slipping back out the door, followed by Terri.

"Told you about the lure of the grill," Keile said and shrugged. "You'll have a chance to talk to them later. Despite evidence to the contrary, they're definitely in the category of good friends to have around."

"Keile, you can go ahead and take the chicken into the dining room," Haydn ordered. "And show Summer around before she thinks we only have a kitchen. And check on Kyle. He's being entirely too quiet."

"Yes, boss," Keile said with a snappy salute. She laughed when Haydn shot her the bird. "Later. Come on, Summer, you heard her."

Summer took one last look at Renny and the comfort of a relatively empty kitchen. Telling herself that mingling wasn't the end of the world didn't slow her heartbeat. Nor did it soothe her nerves. She focused on reciting the multiplication table, but couldn't miss the buzz of conversation and laughter that grew louder as they approached the dining room.

"Chicken and Summer," Keile announced loudly as they stepped into the packed room.

"Summer and swimming pools," someone yelled back.

"Swimming pools and bikinis!"

"Bikinis and dieting."

Someone near the table groaned. "No talk of diets with all this good food around."

"Oops. Did I say 'diet'? Really, I meant 'chicken.'" A thin brunette with spiked hair transferred a piece of chicken to her empty plate.

Summer relaxed and joined in the easy laughter.

"Don't pay any attention to them, Summer," Lynn said, walking up to her, a toddler attached to her hip. "So, no trouble making it the rest of the way?"

"Yeah. I mean, no. Uh, thanks, you know, for stopping earlier. Is this your child?"

Lynn laughed. "No. You've already met my child, Terri. This little darling belongs to Edan." She placed a hand on the brunette with the spiked hair. "Edan, this is Summer, the warrior who rode her bike in this weather."

Edan nodded. "You're Keile's friend from college." She shot out a hand. "She's really psyched you could join us."

"Seems safe as long as you don't mention dieting," Summer replied.

"I said 'chicken,' remember?" Edan whispered and winked.

After that, Summer had no trouble hanging around the periphery, occasionally getting drawn into conversations going on around her while nibbling her way through varied dishes. When Terri entered with the veggie kabobs, Summer discovered she was actually enjoying herself.

It wasn't until an hour later that she saw an opportunity to speak with Renny again. She drifted back into the dining room and hung around on the outskirts of the group Renny was in. When most of them left to grab more beer, she found her backbone. "Hey."

"Hey back at ya," Renny said with a smile. "A live fan. Now I can be a bore and quiz you on my novels."

Summer liked the gentle teasing. "Be careful what you wish for. Which book do you want to start with?"

Renny laughed. "You're serious?"

Summer's heartbeat quickened, and she quickly tore through the multiplication table up to five. What had made her think she could fit in? "I'll, uh, just go," she said quietly.

"Hey, wait." Renny grabbed her arm. "I'd love to hear what you have to say. Sounds like you're an avid reader. Nothing this author likes more."

Summer looked into Renny's light brown eyes before she, haltingly at first, talked about the things she liked. From there they moved on to other best sellers, discovering they had some likes in common, but also areas of strongly held differences of opinion.

"So what's your favorite genre?" Renny asked, plucking a cherry tomato from Summer's plate. "And be honest," she warned with a shake of her little finger.

Summer hastily swallowed a hummus-laden cracker. "I guess I have to say romance because it can be all genres."

"Lesbian or straight?"

"Lesbian, but I read both. A good story is a good story."

"I don't see you as an Oprah watcher, so how did you stumble onto my books?"

"My mom's library. I've spent a good part of the past two years reading my way through it. And she's not really an Oprah fan. Not that I know what that has to do with anything." She met Renny's dubious glance head-on. "I was, uh, out of it for a while. Not up on current happenings."

"Were you on Mars?" Renny quirked an eyebrow. "You're going to stand there and tell me to my face you don't know about my mother hyping my book on Oprah? And FYI, that wouldn't be considered a current event."

Summer's nod seemed to harden Renny's expression.

"Next you'll tell me you don't know who the hell my mother is."

The note of accusation in Renny's tone startled Summer. She swallowed past the lump in her throat and took a step back. What had just happened? What had she missed? "I, uh, I'd better go." Summer fled, making a stop in the bedroom to pick up her coat and scarf. She managed to get to the back door without anyone stopping her—and then her manners kicked in. Backtracking, she found Keile, Haydn and a sleepy-looking Kyle on the sofa in the living room with a mellower crowd.

"Leaving so soon?" Keile quizzed.

Summer tried for a smile. "I made it past the 'not staying very long' stage, right?"

"You need a ride?" Haydn asked. "It's dark, as well as cold. I bet your bike would fit in the back of Keile's Jeep."

"Oh, no. I'm good. I have a light and a beacon. Thanks for having me over. It was nice getting to see you and the kids."

"You'll have to come back when the house isn't so full," Haydn said. "We didn't really get a chance to embarrass Renny by fawning over her books some more."

"Sure" was the polite response. No sense telling Haydn that having Renny attack her for no discernible reason had ensured she wouldn't read another one of her books. She put a hand on Keile's shoulder as she made to get up. "I'll see myself out."

As she walked her bike from the backyard to the street, she wondered if bad endings to outings like the two she'd had today were going to be her future.

* * *

"You didn't have to stay and help with final cleanup." Haydn plopped down on the sofa with a sigh. "But I'm glad you did."

Renny stretched out her legs, feeling pleasantly tired from dancing. "All I did was convince Kyle to go to sleep."

"That's always the hardest part of cleanup." Keile settled next to Haydn and pulled her close. "I had a great time. How 'bout you two?"

"I obsessed over the food too much as usual," Haydn admitted, turning sideways to rest her legs across Keile's lap. "Don't let me do that next time."

"As if there's a way to stop you," Keile and Renny said simultaneously.

Haydn glared at Keile, then Renny. "Come on, I am not that bad."

"So, Renny, how's the book going again?" Keile asked.

"Real good. Making progress every day."

"See if I try to drum up sales for it," Haydn said. "I'll even wait to buy until it's on the discount table. Better yet, I'll borrow it from a friend."

Renny put a hand to her heart, affecting pain. "Now you're getting vicious. How will you feel if I have to bankrupt my pride and ask my mother to go back on Oprah?"

"Vindicated." Haydn jerked when Keile pinched her thigh. "Hey!"

Keile shook her head. "Beautiful, but heartless."

"That's me." Haydn preened. "Renny doesn't need me anymore. I noticed she and a certain someone seemed to talk for hours. She could be the publicity tour."

"Yeah, right." Renny caught herself before she rolled her eyes. That was one of her mother's trademark moves and she tried hard not to be like her mother. She didn't want to talk about Summer. She was mad at herself for being taken in by her enthusiasm and, she was forced to admit, her flattery. *Probably figured she'd suck up to me and get an introduction to Eve Jamison, the movie star*, she thought with disgust. "Where do you know her from again?"

"College. We lived in the same dorm when she was a freshman," Keile replied. "What's the problem? I thought you were getting along."

"Problem? No problem. I've dealt with her type too many times to count. Got taken in by a few before I wised up. For some stupid reason I didn't expect to run across one in Seneca. Live and learn, right?"

"Type? What are *you* talking about? Or should that be 'who'?"

Keile asked the question, but Renny caught a matching look of doubt on Haydn's face. "That Summer's one of those who plays head games. Come on. She tried to convince me she didn't know about the whole Oprah thing. But she topped that by playing dumb about knowing who my mother is. I mean, really? I'm supposed to buy that crap in these days of instant media frenzy? That would be a big no."

"She's telling the truth." Keile rubbed her forehead. "Listen, there are legitimate reasons for her not knowing."

"Let me guess. She's from Mars?" Renny rolled her eyes before she could help it.

"It's hard to believe, but there are extenuating circumstances, Renny. You're reading her all wrong."

"If you say so." Not wanting to end the evening on a bad note, Renny stood. They would have to agree to disagree about Summer Baxby. "Time for me to head out."

"I'll walk you," Keile said instantly.

"I only live two houses over and it's cold. I'll be fine."

"I owe Can a quick walk for being confined most of the evening."

At the mention of his name, the black lab stood, stretched, then left the warmth of the fireplace to nudge Keile's thigh.

"How can I refuse such an escort?" Renny watched Can's tail go into overdrive as Keile bundled into her coat. As soon as they stepped outside, a cold wind seemed to wrap around her. "Jeeze, February's going out with a bang," she said, wrapping her arms around her upper body.

"Since it's after midnight, this is the lion of March."

"March? That can't be," Renny said, shaking her head. "If it's the first of March I should already have the gift I'm giving my father when I have dinner with him and Lisa...Shit, that's tonight." She exhaled, her breath a puff of white. "Damn, Sunday does come after Saturday, doesn't it? This is what happens when the muse and I are clicking. I disassociate days and events."

"You have most of today to pick something up," Keile said as they stopped at the end of Renny's driveway. "And if you don't, he'll probably still be glad you're making an effort to meet him halfway. When you and I talked earlier this week it didn't sound like you were going."

She shrugged. "I decided it was time to grow up and stop judging him by what Eve has to say about him. He hasn't done anything to deserve that from me. The opposite, in fact. I don't know if it's the town, but I see more clearly these days. I like it." With a wave, she hurried inside.

After completing her nighttime rituals, Renny slid under the thick down comforter and sighed in contentment. She would get a full eight, then worry about what to get her father. Turning on her side, she closed her eyes and waited for sleep.

Ten minutes later she was still waiting. Her body was pleasantly tired. Her brain was another matter. She shouldn't have thought about the gift for the father she didn't know. The right gift was important. More so to show his wife she was making an effort than to please her father. And that was the wrong attitude to take, she told herself, bunching up a pillow. She didn't want to fall into the same old rut. Lisa Gulatt was nothing like her mother or any of the mothers of friends she'd known growing up. For one thing, she came across as genuinely nice, never saying one thing with her mouth and something entirely different with her facial expressions. Not once had she made snide remarks about Renny's weight, her past wrongdoings or the attention Renny was taking away from her or her daughter. Best of all, Lisa seemed to love her husband. Renny had to admire that, given the marriages she'd witnessed—her mother's many, among them.

Wine, she thought. She could get her father a nice bottle of wine. She remembered him saying he and Lisa liked to sit in the sunroom and talk over their day with a nice glass of wine. This way she would be getting something they both could enjoy.

As she drifted off to sleep, Summer's stricken face replaced thoughts of whether to buy white or red. A niggling feeling of guilt quickly followed. Maybe she had overreacted, but really! Anyone who knew as much about her books as Summer did should know how she had hit the big time. Eve was a huge part of that.

Her first book had flown off the shelves after Eve hyped the book on Oprah's show. A book tour had followed to keep the momentum going, and Renny hadn't looked back, polishing stories that she'd woven as part of rehab into one bestseller after the other.

So maybe she could be forgiven for being skeptical of Summer's claim. The woman would have had to spend the last four years in a cave or on a desert island not to know about Eve and Oprah. Every time Renny released a book or did an interview Eve's appearance on the show popped up as a question or a clip. It would be annoying if she didn't know that at the same time Eve was getting peppered with questions about her daughter's books.

That had nothing to do with Summer, though, and the way she'd looked at her before she fled. Keile said there were extenuating circumstances, so maybe she'd have to think about apologizing next time she ran into her. Ask for a do-over. Because they had been having a damn good time up until then, and she couldn't say that about a lot of the women she'd met.

CHAPTER SEVEN

Summer dusted off her hands with a great deal of satisfaction. Her weekend had been a nightmare, but Monday was turning out okay. *Better than okay*, she corrected, looking at the empty shelves that this morning had been filled with dusty files. Marcia was going to have no choice but to admit it was a job well done, she thought as a sneeze blew from her mouth.

"Whoa. Summer, is that you behind that cloud of dust?" Liz jokingly waved a hand in front of her face.

"Hey, following orders to clear off these bookcases, then the rest of the room."

Liz peered around the small dusty room that mainly served as a dumping ground for old files, outdated computer equipment and discarded furniture. "She must be running out of things for you to do. No one cares about this stuff in here."

"Oh no, there's more filing. She said Gar told her to give me something different to do."

"I don't think this is what he had in mind," Liz said, frowning.

"I don't mind," Summer said quickly. Marcia was already in a bad mood. The last thing she wanted was for Liz to go to Gar with complaints and feed the fire of Marcia's dislike.

"I'm sorry, but the cleaning service could have done this. It's a total waste of your talent."

"If I had any talent, you mean. This type of work suits me."

"No talent? Who was it that divided the lunch tab into five, with and without tip, in her head on Friday?"

"Lots of people can do that." Summer shrugged and glanced away from Liz's pointed look. "I just, you know, did it faster."

"Because the rest of us had to use our phones. And you're the one who recited the multiplication table at the drop of a hat. Nobody outside of grade school can remember that stuff."

"Exactly. I'm functioning on a grade-school level. Cleaning and dusting *is* my level.

"Is there a problem?" Marcia's lips glistened as if she'd recently reapplied lipstick. The color matched her top, which had a neckline that almost plunged to her navel. Her black skirt was a conservative length for her, but that effect was somewhat offset by the patterned fishnet stockings she wore.

"I almost finished one of the bookcases. Do we have any furniture polish?"

"I certainly do not expect you to polish the furniture," Marcia said, her gaze fixed on Liz. "And I certainly did not tell you to clean off the bookcases. You were supposed to be filing."

"No," Summer disagreed, shaking her head vigorously. She might get some things confused, but the orders from Marcia had been very clear. She held up the dustrag. "Remember? You gave me this to wipe down the shelves once I found a place for the other stuff."

"Liz, would you excuse us? Summer might appreciate some privacy for the rest of our conversation."

"Summer or you?" Liz asked with a hint of a sneer. "I'm going," she added before Marcia could respond.

It wasn't until Marcia closed the door that Summer realized how small and dimly lit the room was. She wiped the already clean shelf, waiting for Marcia's rant.

"You had to run and tattle to Liz, didn't you? You think this is beneath you because you're from a wealthy family? Think *I'm* beneath you because you're from a wealthy family? I'm here to tell you you're wrong on both counts."

Her heart pounding, Summer shrank from the vindictive tone and the hate in Marcia's eyes. She didn't do confrontations. Didn't want to do confrontations. Instead she recited the multiplication table, faltering when she reached seven times seven. *What the hell is seven times seven?* she wondered as the air in the room seemed to thin and breathing became harder. Something bad was going to happen. Something she couldn't stop.

"Oh, now you have nothing to say," Marcia charged, jabbing a finger in Summer's direction.

On one level Summer heard her. On another she was reasoning if six times seven was forty-two, then seven times seven had to be forty-nine. Eight times eight was sixty-four and nine…

"Well!"

"Nine times nine is eighty-one. I'm sure of it."

"You think that's funny? You think you can stand there and make fun of me?"

"I…" Summer broke off, looked at the floor. Looked at anything but the anger and accusation in Marcia's eyes. "All I did was what you told me to do," she finally said quietly. "That's all. That's all."

"Then why was Ms. Know-It-All in here?"

"I don't know. I don't know," she said, thinking feverishly that twelve times twelve was one hundred and forty-four and how badly she wanted to be away from here.

"I doubt that. What I think is that the two of you are working to get me fired. She never liked me. Never liked the way Gar and the rest of the guys around here look at me."

"What?" Summer's head jerked up. Fifteen times fifteen got lost as her brain rejected what Marcia was implying.

Marcia's eyes narrowed to slits. "I've been here longer than either of you. I'll be here after you're gone. Best you remember that the next time you try to make trouble for me with Gar or Kevin."

"But I didn't. I haven't."

Marcia held out her hand, palm first. "Stop already. Don't try that lost child look on me. That 'I'm so pitiful, feel sorry for me' crap. Seems I'm the only one around here who can see through your act. You be careful because you don't fool me one bit. I have my eye on you."

"For what? I come to work, I do my job. Liz came looking for me. I didn't call her."

"Don't lie. Don't you stand there in front of me and lie. Oh, I forgot. You got bags of money on both sides of the family. Bet your parents raised you to lie."

A memory tried to surface and Summer strained to bring it into focus. Someone else had berated her this way—full of hate and disdain. But who? It wasn't Renny. Renny hadn't been this bad. She swallowed hard, pressing a hand against her stomach. How had a simple conversation with Liz turned the day to black?

"Talking to you…" Marcia poked her arm, turning the memory to smoke, but igniting an anger intense enough to break through Summer's fear.

"You have no cause to talk to me like that. I spent the whole day following *your* orders, Marcia. That's all I did. That's all I was supposed to do. You want to pretend I took it upon myself to clean this filthy room, then that's on you." She pushed past Marcia, determined to get away before the tears started. She stopped in the filing room, grabbed her things and hurried down the stairs, her eyes glistening with tears.

The tears didn't fall until she was on her bike and on the road. She let the brisk, cold wind dry them as she peddled furiously, trying to outrun the hate and the deep-seated fear it brought. Hate that had been there from the beginning. Hate she couldn't understand, let alone know how to deal with.

Without conscious thought, she took a right instead of a left and made the thirty-minute ride to what Seneca called Central Park. By the time she arrived, the sky had darkened and filled with dirty gray clouds. Clouds which might herald rain. *Just perfect*, she thought, hooking her helmet onto the end of a handlebar. The cold, stormy day was in keeping with her mood. In keeping with her view of Marcia Meachem.

Summer eyed the empty playground equipment and kicked at the ground. This was where she belonged. She was a freak, a two-year-old in a thirty-three-year-old body. A freak who was a failure at everything from going out to breakfast to talking with authors to cleaning up a storage room. A freak who obviously belonged in her mother's house, away from situations where she could upset other people. No. Upset was too mild a word. Her superpower seemed to be making people hate and despise her. All she needed was a catchy name.

The tears returned and she wiped at them, annoyed at their presence, annoyed at the world. If she were a two-year-old, she decided, she should do what they did. She settled into a swing, and pushed off. Somehow her body knew what to do as she pumped her legs, swinging higher and higher until a feeling of euphoria balanced the darkness and her spirits lifted.

"I won't let her get to me," she screamed and pumped her legs harder, going so high she felt giddy. "I'm a survivor!" Without warning—

she wasn't swinging anymore. She was just sitting on the swing, kicking the ground and mad at the whole world. It's the stupid baby's fault, she thought, wiping away tears. Everything was all about him now. Couldn't do this, couldn't do that and all because of him. She hadn't wanted some snot-nosed brother anyway. He was supposed to be a girl. A girl she could play with and share her dolls with. All he did was drool on everything and try to put her dolls in his icky mouth. That wasn't her fault, but she sure got the blame.

She lifted her head as she heard the excited barks of a puppy. He was so cute. Brown and cuddly-looking as he nipped at her feet. She forgot her mother's warning about touching strange dogs and slid down onto the ground beside him. She laughed in delight when he licked her face as his tail wagged hard.

"What's your name?" She dodged his kisses while trying to read his tag. "'Brownie.' That's a good name for a brown dog." She pulled him close and squeezed until he squirmed. "I wish I could take you home with me. You're ten times better than a stinky baby brother."

"There you are, Brownie. Didn't I tell you to stay put?"

She let go of the puppy and scrambled to her feet. She hadn't heard the red-faced man come up. He looked funny with his long beard and short hair. "Is he yours?"

"Sure is." He bent over to stroke Brownie's head. "He has a sister who needs a good home. You know anyone looking for a dog?"

She felt a spurt of joy. "I am," she blurted out, then frowned. "But my mom won't let me have one because of the baby." She sighed, watching Brownie chase his tail.

"That's too bad since I can only keep one. You sure you don't know any other kid who might like a puppy? She's very sweet."

"Can I...Can I see her?" If she was as sweet and as cute as Brownie maybe her mom might say yes.

"Where are your parents?"

"Home. They let me come here by myself because I'm seven," she lied, playing with her ash-blonde ponytail. "I'm a big girl."

"Okay, big girl. But you just get to look unless your parents say you can keep her." He clipped the leash onto Brownie's collar. "You want to walk him?"

"Can I? I've never walked a dog before." She giggled as Brownie pulled her across the playground to the man's white van. "Heating and Air," she said, reading the sign on the side of the van.

"You're a good reader for a seven-year-old. What's your name?" he asked as he opened the back doors of the van.

She ignored the question and scrambled around him, wanting desperately to see the puppy she just knew she could talk her mother into letting her have. The inside of the van was empty. "Hey. Where's the puppy?"

"Good question, kid," the man said.

Suddenly his voice didn't sound so friendly. The warning her mother had given her about talking to strangers came back loud and clear. "I have to go." She fought him when he grabbed her arm and squeezed tight. She managed one scream before a rag was shoved into her face. Then she felt nothing...

As abruptly as the vision had begun, it ended. Summer was surprised to find herself still soaring through the air, her legs pumping rhythmically. She dragged her feet until she slowed to a stop. What was she supposed to do now? Go to the police and tell them some white guy with a long beard and a buzz cut had kidnapped a little girl? Pressing her palms against her eyes, she became aware of the pounding behind her eyes and the soreness in her throat. She must have cried out, tried to stop the girl from going with the man. Tried to tell the girl to run.

Whatever had happened, she was here and the girl was not. That meant something had to be done. But what? She couldn't go to the police. They weren't going to believe some story about a, for lack of a better word, out-of-body experience. She wasn't sure she believed it herself. What she'd experienced could have been a flashback from a movie or any one of the numerous books she'd read.

But what if it was real? Summer took a deep breath and let it out slowly, then repeated the process until her heartbeat slowed and the throbbing in her head was bearable. Now she could think. The first thing was verifying the kidnapping. If there was any validity to her mystery novels, some sort of alert would have been released by now. To find that, she needed to get home and watch the local news or, better yet, search the Internet. Once she'd determined that a kidnapping had occurred she could somehow let the police know about the man and the white van without mentioning how she came by the information.

Her legs were shaky, but she made good time getting across town to her condo. She wasn't sure how she felt when her search of the Internet came up empty. There were no alerts or reports about a missing seven-year-old girl. No reports of a missing white girl with long, ash-blonde hair and a stinky baby brother. There hadn't been an alert issued in Seneca for the past ten months. And the one that had been issued was for a teenager who turned out not to be missing.

She stared at her laptop and wondered if she'd made it up, if it was a product of her anger and lingering damage from the brain scramble. But what if the parents had been too enthralled with the new baby to notice their daughter was missing? What if they didn't care?

"No." She quickly dismissed that thought. If the girl lied about being able to be in the park by herself, it was because her parents had set rules. Parents who didn't care wouldn't bother to set rules. "They also don't warn their kids about not talking to strangers." She breathed a sigh of relief. If the girl was missing, it would be in the news. What she'd experienced in the park wasn't real. Couldn't have been real.

Then why didn't she believe that?

Summer closed her eyes and replayed the scene, keying in on the man's appearance and his van. His hands had seemed large to the girl when he petted the puppy. And maybe his pants had been brown and his shoes black and scruffy looking. And hadn't she seen the girl's jeans and red sneakers when she looked down at the puppy? There'd been no rings or bracelets on either the girl or the man.

Summer opened her eyes, set her laptop aside and grabbed a pad. She wrote down the descriptions of the man, his dog and the girl. There wasn't much to say about the van beyond its color and the Heating and Air sign. The girl had never looked at the license plate, being too eager to see the nonexistent puppy. But the inside of the van had looked too clean for something used to haul around tools or equipment. It was probably part of the disguise, like the beard.

Satisfied that she had done all she could, she painstakingly typed her notes and saved the file. Keile had kids. Maybe she should talk to her, see if she knew anything about a missing girl. And maybe she should expand the time frame to a year and the location to anywhere in north Georgia. She quickly scratched that thought. If it happened, it was in Central Park. How else would she have established the connection? There was no other way, because anything else would be too scary.

"No coats," she all but sang triumphantly. Neither of them had been wearing a coat. The girl's arms had been bare and the man had worn a long-sleeved dark blue work shirt to go with his brown pants.

Summer keyed in the information, then jumped up when she heard a key strike the lock on the front door. Fear that the kidnapper had somehow found her had her looking around the living room for a weapon, a hiding space. She darted to the coat closet in the short hallway leading to the kitchen. Once inside it, she ran through the multiplication table, her method of prayer.

"Summer? Summer? Are you here?"

The sound of her mother's frantic voice had her bolting from the closet as quickly as she'd entered it. "Mom? What are you doing here?"

Sandra Baxby put a hand to her heart and exhaled loudly. "Where have you been? I've been trying to call you for hours. Do you know what time it is?"

Summer took a furtive glance at the antique mantel clock. "Almost nine?"

"Exactly." Sandra smoothed back wavy brown hair, which hung halfway down her back. She was an unashamedly throwback hippie with pots and pots of family money. Today she was wearing an ankle-length full skirt and Birkenstocks with thick black socks. "What have you been doing?" She unzipped her thick coat as she crossed the room to lay a hand on Summer's forehead. "Have you been sick? I should have gotten you a landline. I'll take care of that tomorrow."

Seeing the worry on her mother's still youthful-looking face brought on the guilt. "Oh, Mom, I'm sorry I worried you yet again." She leaned into her mother's touch. "I got caught up on the Internet. My phone must be set on buzz from work."

"You're okay and that's all that matters."

"No. I was selfish. I should remember by now you'll call to check on me. You always do."

Sandra kissed Summer's forehead and then unknowingly letting Summer know how worried she was, ran her fingers along the white stripe in her hair. "Maybe I should stop. Give you some space, the freedom to check in when you want to."

"I don't mind. Really, I don't. It's just I switch my phone to buzz at work and I forgot to switch it back when I left." Another strike against Marcia, she thought darkly. This one was by far the worst. "I'll pay better attention from now on. I promise."

"Then you're forgiven, despite the fact I'll never get back those years you cost me tonight." She grabbed Summer's chin and looked at her closely. "Did something happen at work today? Have you had a setback you're afraid to tell me about?"

Summer battled the desire to look away and won. "Work stuff. A personality thing. I can handle it."

"You're sure?"

"Positive."

"Good. Now tell me again all about meeting Renny Jamison." Sandra shrugged off her coat and threw it over a chair. Grabbing Summer's hand, she led her to the sofa.

Thankful for the change of subject, Summer gladly gave her a carefully doctored version of meeting the famous author.

CHAPTER EIGHT

Summer jerked herself out of a nightmare the next morning only to discover she'd slept through her alarm. She had just twenty minutes to get to work on time. Of course this was the morning she was missing a matching sock, out of Toaster Strudel and in an incredible grumpy mood.

With a minute to spare, she squeezed onto a crowded elevator at work and dared it to malfunction. Secure in the power of her unspoken threat, she tried to relax and concentrate on blocking out the other occupants. In her frazzled state it would be easy to hop into someone else's head, see their darkest hour. She didn't need that this morning. Not when the nightmare was fresh in her mind.

The elevator stopped on every floor, of course, so it was three minutes past eight thirty when she walked into the suite.

"The big man is here," Fiona whispered.

Summer assumed the big man was Kevin Tathum, the owner and a college pal of her dad. "Thanks." After a moment's hesitation, she stopped by Marcia's office.

"You're three minutes late," Marcia said, looking at her watch. "Since you left fifteen minutes early yesterday, I expect you to make up those eighteen minutes this afternoon. You're on file duty today. Is that clear enough for you, *Princess*?"

"If I'm the princess, does that make you the evil stepmother or one of the ugly sisters?" She kept her tone sickly sweet. "Just saying." She left the office without offering Marcia the one-finger salute. Considering her mood, she thought that should have earned her sainthood status or at the very least a boatload of points—the positive karma kind.

In her office, she had a chuckle over her clever comeback, then fell into her filing rhythm. By the time she heard the telltale sound of heels slapping against the floor, her mood had improved so much she couldn't even work up a decent frown.

"Mr. Tathum would like to see you in his office now." Marcia snapped her fingers like she was trying to hail a cab.

Summer hoped one day she could look back on this time and have a good laugh. She was smart enough to know that would be a day far in the future.

Kevin Tathum stood when they entered his office. He was tall, befitting the power forward he'd been in college. He and Summer's dad had a regular date to down a few beers and brag about glory days. These days he was carrying a little more weight. His hair still hung to his shoulders but now was liberally sprinkled with gray. "Summer, great to see you again. Have a seat. That's all for now, Marcia." He perched on the edge of his desk once they were alone. "You're looking much better."

"I feel like it. I guess I should call you Mr. Tathum in the office."

"You should know by now we go by first names around here. Even for me. Kevin or the Big Guy work fine," he added with a wink.

"Now that I've been working, I want to thank you again for giving me this job. It's what I needed. I, well, I hope it doesn't cause you any problems with the staff."

"Don't worry about that," he said with a wave of his hand. "I brought you in at the bottom. Everybody here knows no one got stepped on or shoved aside to make room for you."

She was certain that "everybody" did not include Marcia. "Good to know."

"How have things been going for you around here?"

"Okay." She gave him a pained smile. "Is this about yesterday?"

He patted her shoulder. "You have the same look you used to get as a kid when you thought you were going to be punished."

"I just…I don't want to sound ungrateful, but I don't want any special favors. Other than that you created this job for me, that is."

"I don't consider it a favor to intervene in work-related matters when it's needed." Kevin held up his hand when Summer opened her mouth. "Let me explain. I pay good money for a cleaning service. If they aren't doing their job I want to hear about it. What I don't want to hear is that one of my employees is doing that job because it means I'm paying for it twice. That doesn't make good business sense. Now Gar and I talked this out, and I expect you to go to him if you're given another dustrag. And since Marcia seems to be having trouble finding something for you to do, he and I decided to rotate your services among the teams. See what they can come up with."

"What if I can't, you know, do what they need? God, Kevin. I'm okay with dusting in addition to the filing. They're both something I'm actually good at. That's saying a lot right now."

"Calm down. The work thrown your way will be on par with filing. No one's going to ask you to write a report. If it makes you feel better, I'll have Gar outline the types of assignments you should be getting and we'll go from there."

"Okay." She ran her fingers through her hair. "Change is so hard for me. But you know that already."

"Change helps you grow." He patted her shoulder again. "You've grown so much in the past two years. I'd hate to see that slow down because you fear failure. Everyone here knows your situation and with one possible exception, no one's going to expect miracles. And if they do, tell them to call a saint."

She exhaled loudly. "I can live with that. Do I still report to Marcia?"

"Unless you tell me no. I could easily switch you to Liz. Something she seems to be angling for."

Summer shook her head. That would be too easy, and at a deeper level, she knew she didn't want or need easy. "I'll deal with her."

"That's my girl." He gave her a thumbs-up. "Now clear out. I've been away for a week. I have real work to take care of."

She took the long route to her office. The one that skirted Marcia's office. She wasn't ready to talk to her yet, and she had the idea Marcia was dying to talk to her. She needn't have bothered as her supervisor was lying in wait and with what looked to Summer's eyes like a giant stick up her butt.

"Satisfied?" Marcia managed to put enough venom in that one word to kill a snake.

She must have gotten acclimated yesterday. The confrontational manner didn't bring flashes of fear. Didn't fill her stomach with acid and make her want to run. She took a moment to celebrate that tiny victory and then asked casually, "About what?"

"You know exactly what."

Summer took in the shake in Marcia's voice, the anger stamped on her body, and thought the only thing to do was to woman up. But she could do that just as easily from a step or so further away. Marcia looked like a volcano about to spew molten lava in an effort to level all in its wake.

"You'd better watch yourself." Marcia punctuated each word with a stab of her finger.

Stepping back had saved her from getting jabbed by one of Marcia's talons. The force of the jab could have been painful. Summer rubbed her chest against a phantom pain and stared in shock when her hand came away bloody. She looked in fear at the woman responsible and—

suddenly she wasn't in the file room. Suddenly she wasn't looking at Marcia. She was looking at a woman who, though taller and heavier, resembled Marcia. She was looking into eyes filled with anger and trying hard not to cry because of the slap, the bloody lip.

"I'm sorry, Mama. I didn't mean it." Again she wasn't quick enough to dodge the backhand that knocked her to one side.

"Slut! You get in the bathroom and wash your face. Wash your whole body. No telling what you let that boy do to you." Her mother bristled with rage.

"He didn't touch me, Mama. He didn't touch me," she swore, her cheek on fire from the hit.

Thin lips stretched into what might have passed as a smile. "We'll see what your daddy has to say about that."

Fear clenched in her chest and moved down to parts below. Her daddy would be mad if he thought someone had touched what he considered his. He'd come to her room for sure once her mother was asleep. She couldn't stop him. She was never able to stop him...

"Are you listening to me?"

Summer came back into herself with a pounding headache and bile at the back of her throat. She swallowed hard and waited for the fog clouding her brain to dissipate. She was getting used to the feeling. What she wasn't getting used to, would never get used to, was the horror of the situations she had found herself in. Was this what the rest of her life going to be about—reliving the tragedies of abused children? She pressed her hands against her temple and felt panic take hold.

"I said, 'Are you listening to me?'" Marcia repeated slowly. "What's wrong with you now? Coma relapse?" Her lips stretched into a smile reminiscent of her mother's.

"I wish I knew," Summer said, battling the tears that wanted to fall, the hysteria that wanted to take her over. "I need..." She dropped to the floor and rested her head on her knees. How she wished she was anyplace else. Someplace she wouldn't be bombarded with suffering. If these experiences were to be her future, anyplace else needed to be a padded room with limited outside contact.

Oh God, maybe she did die in the accident and this was her version of hell. What started as a laugh turned into sobs that wracked her body. Filled with sadness and hurt for those who couldn't protect themselves, Summer didn't notice when Marcia slipped away, shutting the door behind her.

Eventually the tears dried up. With her head beating like the drum section of a marching band, she used the desk to pull herself up, then grabbed a tissue. The tissue was no match for the ravages of tears. She bit her lip as they threatened to return and headed for the bathroom, hoping—praying really—that it would be empty. Her luck held and she splashed water on her face until the redness around her eyes didn't scream "crying jag." There wasn't anything she could do to soothe her soul. The residue left from what she'd experienced was probably permanent. She could only trust that it would eventually fade to something so dim she'd only feel it under duress.

Staring at her reflection, she could see the horror and sorrow lingering in her eyes. But only Kevin would be able to tell and she didn't expect to run into him again today. What she had to do now was return to her desk and get through the rest of the day. Preferably without another word from Marcia.

Later, when she was thinking more clearly, she called her shrink. There was no need for her to go through this angst alone.

"I'm sorry, Ms. Baxby, she's out of town with a family emergency. I'd be happy to schedule an appointment for you with Dr. Suit, who's agreed to see Dr. Veraat's patients in her absence."

But I don't trust anyone else, she wanted to say. It had taken her a long time to get comfortable with Dr. Veraat. She couldn't share her craziness with a stranger. "Do you know how long she'll be gone?"

"I'm sorry, I don't. Dr. Veraat is still assessing the situation, but she does not think there'll be a quick resolution to the problem. Are you sure you won't see Dr. Suit, Ms. Baxby? His credentials are impeccable and he's been practicing for twenty years. Dr. Veraat holds him in the highest regard."

Summer could only think the hard sell meant she must have sounded desperate. "I'm sure, but…I'll check back in a few weeks. If she hasn't returned, I'll consider it." Who was she trying to fool? They'd have to admit her before she voluntarily spilled her guts to this Dr. Suit. She hung up the phone wondering if it would come to that.

* * *

"Hey." Renny looked down at the puppy chewing on her ankle. "Trying to work here." As was usual when she talked to him, Chazz jumped up and tried to lick the skin off her face. "Work," she reminded him, trying to dodge his huge tongue. "No work, no food, buddy. As much as you like to eat that would hurt."

She shoved the pup aside, trying to figure out how the hell she let Jo talk her into taking him. Sure, her heart had softened when she learned he'd been abandoned, left to wander along the highway cold and hungry. According to Jo, his rescuers had done a great job of fostering him. All he needed to be a good family member was consistency and continued training. How sympathy at his plight had morphed into her opening her mouth and agreeing to take him home was a mystery even five days later. Gazing at the little giant, though, she thought maybe this was a mystery she didn't need to resolve.

Stretching her back, she checked the clock on her monitor. She closed her eyes and opened them, but it was still five o'clock. No wonder the poor dog had been trying to get her attention. "I've been a bad mommy, haven't I?" Petting his head, she sniffed for signs that she'd been too distracted and found none. "Aren't you a good boy! Yes you are. You deserve a walk in the park." She laughed as he barked and pranced around, then cringed when he bumped her desk hard and tipped over a bottle of water sitting on it.

"Easy, Chazz." She scooped it up before much damage was done. She decided again that she needed to invite Jo over to help her rearrange the house to accommodate him. Although he was no older than six months, he weighed forty pounds. Jo thought he might be part Leonberger. When Renny looked up the breed on the web, her heart almost stopped. Leonbergers were one of the largest dog species. A full-grown male could get up to one hundred and seventy pounds and stand over thirty-one inches tall. Renny was hoping the Leonberger part of Chazz wasn't dominant. Still, if it was, they'd make do. She had a large house and a decent size fenced-in backyard for him to roam around in. Her new baby couldn't be blamed for his genetic makeup.

In addition, he was affectionate, loved kids and played well with other dogs. He'd only been to one training class, but the teacher claimed he was already ahead of the other dogs. And best of all, he forced her to push away from the computer regularly and get out of the house.

Wanting to stretch her legs as much as Chazz seemed to, Renny took the long way to the park. The cold weather from earlier in the week had turned mild and some of the trees were starting to bud. Before she knew it the dogwoods would blossom, showcasing their signature white blooms. She'd been told it was a wonderful sight to see.

They entered the park from the west side, closest to the playground. Unlike earlier in the week, the equipment was getting good use. Renny slowed, then stopped to watch a young mother help her son onto the swings and give him a push. She moved closer to see the boy pump his legs and give a cry of triumph as he flew high. She knew that feeling, had experienced it during the best summer of her childhood. Or to be more accurate, the best two weeks.

Eve had just begun to date future ex-husband number two and, for reasons Renny hadn't been privy to, she had packed her off for a visit with her grandmother. At first Renny had resisted being banished to a place she only knew from Eve's words. A place Eve claimed was backward and boring. Her resistance had proven futile. Within a day, she was on a plane headed to the deep South and a grandmother she barely knew.

Renny smiled, thinking about how quickly she'd changed her tune once she found out the advantages of being at her grandmother's house. She could be herself without worry of bringing down Eve's wrath because something she said or did had been noticed by the wrong person. For two wonderful weeks she'd been allowed to be a kid. And just when she began to settle into the room her grandmother had lovingly decorated for her visit, when she began to feel at home, Eve had called, demanding her daughter's return. More upset than she'd been at being forced to come to Seneca, an angry Renny returned to Hollywood. Her anger intensified when she found Eve busy with wedding preparations. Apparently getting married without your only child present didn't make good copy.

Chazz tugged on his leash, breaking into her musings. He nudged her with his big, black head when she didn't move.

"I got it." She gave the boy on the swing one last look. "Let's go play." She let him set the pace to the entrance of the fenced-in dog park. Once inside it, she undid his leash and moved to the three benches marked for humans. Her step faltered when she spotted a familiar figure on the other side of the fence watching the dogs as if trying to memorize how they looked. Her first instinct was to continue to the benches and act as if she hadn't noticed her. She didn't yield to it. She was sort of the one at fault, after all. "Hey. You lose a dog?"

Summer briefly met Renny's gaze before returning her attention to the dogs. "I, uh, I'm looking for a brown puppy. Lab or lab mix. Goes by the name of Brownie. Any chance you've, uh, you know, ever seen him?"

"I don't remember that name. But I've only been coming here a couple of days. You should talk to Keile. She and Can are regulars."

"Good idea. Uh, thanks." Summer played with her helmet strap. "I should, you know, go."

"Wait." Renny put a hand on the fence between them. "I want to apologize for Saturday. I guess I was channeling my mother and being a real diva." Seeing the confusion on Summer's face, she added, "Sorry. My mother is Eve Jamison. The actress."

"Oh, yeah. She was in *Five Days To Hell*. My dad loves that one."

"So does she. Won her the big one." *And launched her desperate chase for another*, Renny thought but didn't say. "Anyway. I'm sorry I acted like everyone should know all about me. Which was dumb because the reason I like it here is that people act like they don't."

"That's okay." Summer gave her a sliver of a smile. "Your mom must be proud. Of your success, I mean."

"When it suits her. She's more interested in getting me back into acting."

"Back?"

"Way back when I used to do a show called *Family Time*." She had to admit she felt a tug on her ego that Summer didn't know the show. During its heyday, the show, and she with it, had been very successful. She hadn't been able to go anywhere without being besieged by fans, young and old. With lots of therapy, Renny had come to accept that the loss of the show and the adulation had nudged her into a downward spiral.

"Sorry." Grimacing, Summer stuck her hands into the pockets of her slacks. "Doesn't sound familiar. I've mostly watched movies so far."

"That's not a bad thing. Now you won't expect me to be like Ree."

"No. I promise I won't," Summer said, her manner serious. "Uh, I, uh, well…How long have you, you know, lived in Seneca?"

"Around six months. I love it. It's what I seem to need at this time in my life."

"Good. That's good. Uh, have you, uh, heard of any little kids gone missing from here in that time?"

She smiled. "The last one I heard about was about three years ago. Keile told you how she met Haydn, right? She was sitting around here when Kyle walked right up to her, put his head in her lap and called her mama."

"Yeah, she told me about that. But this one would have been a girl child," Summer persisted. "Around seven years old. White. Blonde hair."

Renny's smile vanished. "Are you telling me a girl's been reported missing?"

"I…no. No. It's just a, you know, a thing. Probably nothing." Summer again looked toward the dogs. "Uh-oh. Looks like your dog's trying to make you a grandmother."

Renny turned to see Chazz picking up a smaller dog by the scruff of his neck. She took off running. "Chazz!"

By the time she straightened out the situation with the other dog's owners, Summer was gone, along with her babble about a missing child. It was probably nothing, she thought, even as she chose the path that led by the playground. When she'd passed before there had been no posters, no obvious unease. Then it hit her. If a girl had gone missing from the park, the playground would have been empty or filled with cops. She almost laughed at her own gullibility. Maybe Summer had picked up a weird sense of humor during her stay on Mars.

At home, she fed Chazz, then fixed herself a salad; she was still doing penance for the amount of food she'd consumed Sunday night when the simple dinner she thought she was going to had morphed into a surprise birthday party for her father. Though Renny had shown up woefully underdressed, she'd been welcomed with open arms. By the time she took her leave, the respect she had for her father's wife had increased several fold.

She ate her salad, trying to imagine it was stuffed shells covered with a creamy lobster sauce. Her imagination was good but not that good. She turned her thoughts to how thin she'd be one day. Model thin, so the clothes in the catalogs would look the same when she tried them on. Daydreams of vamping down the catwalk made the salad more appetizing.

It wasn't until she was lounging on the sofa, Chazz at her feet, and flipping on the TV that she remembered Summer scanning the dog park for a puppy named Brownie and asking about a missing girl with blonde hair. It was probably a hoax or some weird game Summer was playing, Renny reasoned. *Nothing to be concerned about*, she told herself even as curiosity had her leaving the room to retrieve her tablet.

When her search for recent abductions came up empty, she broadened the parameters for date and age. That netted her a fourteen-year-old who thought she could sneak out, spend the night with her nineteen-year-old boyfriend, then sneak back in before her parents noticed she was gone. Definitely not what Summer was talking about.

"Why would she make something like this up?" A snoring Chazz ignored her question, just as she'd expected. She didn't blame him because it made no sense. But if Summer had been making something up, she'd done a good job of playing her part. Could it be because Summer believed it had happened? And if that was true, what should she do?

Renny stewed some more and then decided to sound out Keile for some answers. Perhaps this had something to do with why Summer wasn't up on current events and why she was almost painfully thin.

When she rang the bell, a frazzled-looking Haydn opened the door. In her arms was a grousing baby and at her feet was a roly-poly, brown, part-lab puppy with a shoe in his mouth. Renny was tempted to shove manners off the cliff and run for home. "Not a good time, huh?"

"Do you see that *thing* currently eating my best house shoe?" Haydn demanded. "Isn't it enough I have a miserable teething baby? An overactive four-year-old?"

Renny chewed on her bottom lip and decided silence was the best course for staying alive.

"You're right. Obviously not," Haydn continued as if Renny had answered. "I must need a flea-ridden puppy with no training to consume all my extra time. And the culprit...Where is the culprit you ask? I'll tell you. At a dinner meeting with an important client." She exhaled and thrust the baby at Renny, then clapped her hands. "Not inside!" Grabbing the puppy, she raced to the side of the house.

"Chelsea me girl, it looks like I and my curiosity should have stayed home." Renny patted the fretting baby, working out how long she had to stay.

"Renny!" Kyle burst into the hallway, Can at his heels. "Come see my castle. It's got lights and everything. Even a king."

With a last look at the escape hatch, Renny followed the excited boy to the large family/play room. It was in the new addition to the house, constructed when Keile and Haydn decided to expand their family. Though Kyle had his own corner for his million toys, the plastic gray castle, surrounded by knights and horse, was set up in the middle of the room.

"How cool. When did you get this?"

"Grandpa sent it in the big brown truck. Chelsea only got a stupid doll. Mine's way better."

"Better for you," she agreed, carefully easing down onto the thick carpet, Chelsea in her arms.

"Excuse the rant," Haydn said, entering the room with the puppy in her arms.

Renny watched in amusement as Haydn sat down and cuddled the carrier of fleas who was clearly not fully housebroken. "Did it help?"

"Big time. But I'm sure you didn't come over here to hear me rant or to get stuck playing with the kids."

"The playing's a side benny." She tapped Chelsea on the nose. The baby grabbed her finger and stuck it into her slobbery mouth. After some haggling, she exchanged her finger for the chew toy Haydn threw her way. "I ran into Summer at the park. Before you ask, I did apologize for my behavior. However, I reserve the right to think she's strange. I guess you could say strange. Borderline crazy may be better."

"You're not supposed to call anybody crazy," Kyle said, his eyes wide. "It hurts their feelings."

"That's right," Haydn was quick to agree. "It's amazing the things you learn in pre-K. Renny should say 'strange.' Strange can be good."

Renny shook her head frowning. "Not in this case. First she says she's looking for a puppy. Much like the one you're currently fondling, come to think of it. Then she asked if I've heard about any missing kids since I've lived here. When I questioned her about it, she backed down and poofed. Tell me that doesn't scream 'nut house' to you."

"Keile says her family's filthy rich. She can't be cra—uh, nut house-worthy. She has to be eccentric. It's the rules."

"Then she's full of eccentricity." Following Kyle's instructions, Renny made her knight fight his.

"I've lived here longer than you and I haven't heard of any kids going missing for more than a night except the one you're playing with. And even he wasn't missing for a night. Just long enough to scare me to death."

"She said it was a seven-year-old girl. Blonde hair, puppy aptly named Brownie."

"Maybe you misunderstood her. She might have been giving you ideas for a book. "

Before Renny could nix the idea, Can jumped up barking and raced from the room. The puppy tumbled from Haydn's lap, landed on his butt, righted himself, then scampered after him.

"It's Mama Kee," Kyle announced, tearing after the dogs.

"Three down." Haydn dusted off her hands. "Not too shabby."

"Should I go warn Keile to grab armor?" Renny asked.

"As if that would do her any good."

A minute later Keile entered the room, arms full of puppy and boy, apparently unmindful of the damage they were doing to her white shirt. "Back from a successful evening of hunting and gathering." She let Kyle slid down her body, placed the puppy on the floor and bent to give Haydn a kiss. "Consider yourself off duty."

Haydn pulled her close for another kiss. "So considered."

"Hey, Renny. How's the baby bear working out for you?" Keile crossed the room and picked up Chelsea. She didn't wince when Chelsea sucked on her chin.

"Chazz is doing great. I was telling Haydn I ran into Summer at the dog park."

"She has a dog? Wonder why she didn't tell Jo?"

"I don't, uh…," she paused to consider. "That's not the point. She was there looking for an imaginary puppy named Brownie."

"And a missing girl," Haydn added.

Keile extricated herself from her daughter's strong grip and wiped at her slobbery chin. "I don't think I've seen either. I've certainly haven't heard anything about a missing girl. When did this happen?"

"Good question," Renny said dryly. "*If* it happened. We only have Summer's word to go by."

"Renny thinks Summer is missing some screws. Should we be worried?"

"No. Look, strictly between us she does have some memory issues." Keile rubbed her forehead. "Could be she's remembering events that happened before. Oh God, yes. Freshman year, spring semester, a little girl did go missing. I haven't thought about that in years."

"How old was she?" Renny asked.

"That I don't remember. I do remember she was a cute little blonde with big blue eyes. The media made a huge deal about that. You couldn't walk two feet on campus without seeing a flyer with a headshot. Then school let out and it died away. I don't remember that they ever did find her." Keile tightened her grip on Chelsea, kissed her cheek.

"What about the puppy? Lab or lab mix."

Keile shook her head. "There wasn't any mention of a dog. Like I said it's possible Summer's mixing up two different events. Now I wish I had gotten her number. Sounds like she could use a friend."

Though she was sure Keile hadn't meant it to happen, Renny felt guilty. Whatever happened to Summer was big, and she of all people should be the last one to rush to judgment. There were those in the old crowd she'd hung with who had lingering mental or physical problems from the alcohol, the drugs they'd abused. She'd been lucky, so a little compassion wasn't out of place. "Looks like I owe her another apology."

CHAPTER NINE

Friday morning a nervous Summer applied lip balm to her dry lips as she scanned the lobby for arrivals. She was doing her best to ignore the surreptitious looks being thrown her way, knowing lack of sleep and an excess of worry had her not looking her best. In fact, the walking dead probably looked better. After enduring a couple of nights with little rest, she'd decided to get in early, waylay Keile and ask her to lunch or a drink after work. The waiting was harder than she thought it would be; she was already up to a hundred times a hundred. Any minute she would start to bit her nails.

"Summer. I was hoping to run into you."

She almost jumped a foot when Keile touched her arm and had to consider that home might have been the best place for her today. She was running on nerves and not doing a good job of it. "Hi. I was...I didn't know when you got here."

"It varies." Keile took out her cell phone. "I realized yesterday I don't have your number."

Summer dug through her bike bag for her own phone. "I don't know it yet," she explained as she searched through the menus in vain.

"Let me help you with that." Within seconds Keile found the number and input it into her phone. Then she added her numbers to Summer's phone. "You free for lunch today?" she asked gently.

Summer could have kissed her. "Yes. Yes." For some reason she knew talking things out with Keile would help. Dr. Veraat was still out of the office and she didn't want to burden her mother.

"Twelve thirty okay?"

"I'll meet you down here." Though she felt more centered, she took the stairs. The burst of exercise cemented the calm, and by the time she reached her floor, her stomach was no longer churning and her head felt clearer. She was going to make it through the day. Amazing when she considered the state she'd been in at three a.m.—wide eyed and haunted by a child.

Entering the reception area, she scooted past Fiona's desk. It was empty, which she considered a good sign. Fiona tended to broadcast her emotions, making it difficult for Summer to block them out. An even better omen was Marcia's empty office. For half a second, Summer was tempted to take a seat and wait for Marcia to arrive but dismissed it as too petty.

After storing her gear in the file room, she made her way to Liz's office. She hadn't had a chance to talk to her since her meeting with Kevin. "Hey. You got a minute?" She looked around Liz's organized office. It seemed everything had a place in Liz's world. No stacks of paper on her desk.

"Sure. Grab a seat." Liz turned from her monitor to face Summer. "What's on your mind?"

"Uh, yeah. I, uh, wanted to talk about, you know, doing more stuff around here. That was you, right? I mean, you convinced Gar or Kevin?"

Liz fiddled with a pad on her desk. "I did."

"Why? Filing and a little dusting are okay. For me."

Liz seemed to hesitate. "I sort of met you before the accident."

Summer couldn't have been more surprised. "When? Why didn't you tell me?"

"It was at an opening at this little gallery in New York City. I was visiting a friend and he'd seen some of your work. I thought it would be cool, you know going to a gallery opening in New York. Maybe Paris is cooler. Maybe." Liz smiled. "Anyway, I was immediately drawn in by the images, the faces you put to canvas. And don't worry. With the sheer number of people coming and going, I wouldn't expect you to recall me even if you could remember that time."

"Wow." She flopped back into the chair, hard pressed to believe she'd been a person who inspired admiration in others. "That's…"

"Yeah. What you created was wow. It'd be a shame to let that kind of talent go to waste."

"I don't…" Summer sighed and rubbed her chest. "I don't have that in me anymore. It's gone."

"How do you know if you don't stretch? I thought maybe if you were gradually given more challenging assignments it would, I don't know, help something. And it occurred to me a start would be looking over the graphics for my next report. That's purely selfish on my part."

"What do I know about advertising? You'd have to be crazy to take my word for anything."

Liz leaned forward and clasped her hands. "That's where I think you're wrong. But before you panic, Kevin's made it clear what your role is to be. I promise I won't push. Too much, that is," she added with a smile. "Can you work with that?"

She nodded. "I should probably thank you. Maybe one day I will." She had a lot to think about on her way to Marcia's office. So maybe she could study ads in magazine. Get a feel for what was out there. That didn't mean she had to share how she felt about them. And maybe it wouldn't hurt to keep pencil and paper handy in case she got an itch again. Nothing fancy like the pad with the good paper and the pencil set her father had given her. No, something cheap, befitting her current skill set.

Marcia dispatched her to the file room with only a little snide commentary. The stacks of folders to be filed were dwindling, making Summer realize that her tasks would have changed regardless of Liz's intervention.

The morning passed quickly, interrupted by a request to scan documents from a completed project and create a folder. It wasn't hard to do, but the task was usually handled by Marcia, who was responsible for keeping track of the file numbering system. To Summer's surprise, Marcia logged the file into the database, then handed it back to her without giving her any grief. The day was full of good omens.

Summer was downstairs by twelve twenty-five. She paced while trying to decide how much information to share with Keile. Telling her too much might make her leery. And who could blame her? The whole situation was like something out of the tabloids. Crazed woman sees events that may or may not have happened. Turn to Page Ten to read all about it.

She spotted Keile's confident stride with no trouble. Today she was wearing a lavender knit shirt and form-fitting jeans. She looked competent, the kind of person who could take being leaned on.

"Any place in particular?" Keile asked after they exchanged a quick greeting.

"It doesn't matter." She was too full of worry to be concerned about food.

"Jack's then. The service is quick and it's a little off the beaten track so it won't be as crowded."

Summer followed Keile out the side door that led to the loading dock. She'd never been this way and was surprised when they cut through another building and ended up on Central two blocks away.

"Short cuts," Keile explained. She'd obviously seen the look of surprise on Summer's face. "Gotta love 'em."

Summer nodded and zipped her coat against the cold wind, thinking of the cap and gloves that were keeping her desk drawer warm. "I want to talk, but I don't know how to start. You'll probably think I'm crazy."

"I talked to Renny the other day. She mentioned the missing girl, the dog."

"Oh. Then I'm surprised you accepted the invite. You must think I'm completely nuts."

"No. I think you got confused and remembered something that happened over ten years ago."

Summer gripped Keile's arm, slowed their pace. "What are you talking about?"

"Freshman year a girl went missing. For about a month we were inundated with news about her. Something must have triggered a memory. Were you walking around campus?"

"She's real?" The relief was almost overpowering. She wasn't on the short list for the asylum. "Did they catch the guy who snatched her?"

"It's still an open case. Or I should say a cold case. After Renny mentioned it, I did a little research, read the old news clips. They never had any leads. Never had any idea of where she disappeared from. Like I said it was all over the news. Then it all died away when they couldn't locate the girl or come up with a suspect. The police thought it was done by someone passing through."

Summer chewed on her bottom lip. "When did it happen? I mean what time of year?"

"Early April. Spring break for public schools."

"Could I have known her?"

"You didn't mention it. That I would have remembered. Maybe the story stuck with you because of the search parties."

"I searched for this girl? Me?"

"We did one together. The wooded area beyond the sports arena."

"Yeah. Maybe that's it." But it didn't explain her vision. Central Park was nowhere near the university sports arena.

"This way." Keile made a left into a dead-end alley, then another left and went down a short flight of stairs. "Doesn't look like much I know, but looks can be deceiving. We loyal followers try to keep this place a secret."

Summer was pleasantly surprised at the brightness and, though she wouldn't admit it to Keile, the cleanliness of the small place. The delicious smells spilling from the open kitchen were another plus. A long counter with stools ran along a wall and there were five small tables squeezed together. The restaurant was almost full, but the low hum of conversation was manageable.

Keile grabbed two paper menus from a pocket attached to the wall. "Order first, then sit," she explained. "Everything is good, but I always get the special of the day." She pointed to the chalkboard next to a cash register.

Summer decided that the special—fried chicken, macaroni and cheese and collard greens—would be as good as anything.

After they placed their order Keile led the way to one of the few remaining tables. "It won't be long. So what made you remember the little girl?"

She frowned, unzipped her jacket and hung it on the back of her chair before answering. "It's, uh, complicated." She took a sip from the large plastic cup filled with sweet ice tea. "Do you, you know, believe in psychic stuff?"

"Like seeing dead people?"

"There's more to it. I've been doing some research and there's a lot scientists don't know about how the brain works."

"Summer, are you trying to tell me you're psychic?"

Summer couldn't decide if Keile's tone meant the possibility was good or bad. She looked into Keile's eyes and saw no judgment. "I, uh, I think so. Either that or I'm crazy. Slap-me-in-the-nut-house-type crazy."

Keile smiled. "I don't think one necessarily precludes the other. Tell me why you think you're psychic."

Summer ran her fingers through her hair, zipped through the multiplication table to five, then exhaled. "Okay. Monday I was having a bad day at work, so I went by Central Park. There's something about a park that settles me down. I can't really explain it." She took another sip of tea, then poured out her experience on the swing, going so fast the words almost tripped over each other.

"This is some good information. You have to tell the police. I know they hold back key information sometime, but I bet they have no idea about the puppy being used as bait or the van."

While she was glad Keile seemed to believe her, she didn't believe the same could be said for the police. "I don't…" She broke off, rubbed her dry lips and fought off nerves.

A young African American male with dreads streaming down his back arrived with their food. "Enjoy your meal, ladies."

Though she managed a smile of thanks, Summer was sure she wouldn't. "I can't…I can't do it. They wouldn't buy a word of it. And it happened so long ago."

"We can talk about that later. Now you look like you could use some food."

"You sound like a mother," she said, poking at the mac and cheese.

"And you're acting like a kid. I've found in order to get any nutritional value you have to put the food in your mouth, chew and swallow." Keile demonstrated.

Giving a reluctant laugh, Summer sampled the mac and cheese, found it more than palatable and took another bite, then another.

"Good, huh?" Keile asked with a knowing smile.

She swallowed and wiped her mouth with a paper napkin. "More than good. I love mac and cheese. More than I used to, I'm told."

"You and Kyle could be related. If he had his way, it would be on the menu for every meal. That includes breakfast."

Summer polished off her portion with a little regret. "I don't see a problem if it's this good." Suddenly found hunger had her reaching for a chicken thigh. She managed to finish it and the collard greens before pushing her plate to the side. "I think that's the most I've eaten in forever. And I didn't think I was hungry." She patted her full stomach.

"Jack's will do that to you. Try the peach cobbler. It's very good."

Her eyes widened as the tastes of peaches, cinnamon and sugar mingled together on her tongue. "Better than the mac and cheese." She took a couple more bites before reluctantly pushing the rest away. "Any more and I might explode."

"Not a problem for me." Keile licked her spoon and dropped it into her empty bowl.

"You want the rest of this?"

"Better not or I'll be the one exploding."

"Can't have that. Thanks for bringing me here and listening. I can't begin to understand why you believe me, but I'm grateful."

"Well, a few years ago I admit I would have dismissed your vision as…okay, craziness. But how can I believe fate had a hand in my life and not believe you? It's possible someone on the force would listen, believe you."

"Doubt it. And if one did, there'd be plenty of others making that circle for crazy gesture behind his back. You knew me before, so I'm thinking that you will give me the benefit of the doubt. From their perspective—I can't remember important parts of my life, but I magically have information about a girl I don't know who went missing ten years ago? No. No." She shook her head. "I already feel like a freak. No way I need them piling it on."

"What if I broached the subject with a cop I know? Would you be willing to talk to her if she's receptive? It wouldn't have to be a formal interview."

"I don't know. Maybe." The pressure in her chest didn't lessen until she reached ten times ten. "Would you be there?"

"If that's what you want."

What Summer wanted was for this to never have happened. She pressed her fingers against the first sign of throbbing in her temples. "Yeah. I do."

Keile dropped some ones on the table. "Then I'll be there. You ready to head back?"

"Tell me really—why do you believe me?" Summer asked as they climbed the short flight of stairs back up to the alley.

"You were the first person who tried to be my friend. I wasn't able to accept that back then, but it didn't stop you from trying. You always asked me if I was okay, if I needed anything. Nobody else did. Now it seems like you're the one who needs me to ask if you're okay, if you need anything."

Summer blinked back tears. "You're exactly right. Only I won't be stupid like you and blow off the offer of friendship."

* * *

Despite the threat of rain and the blustering March wind, Summer took the long route home from work, going there by way of the park. It might be Friday night, but she didn't have any plans to rush home for. And with the dread of having to deal with the police firmly lodged in the back of her consciousness, she wanted, no, needed to gather more information. To have something tangible for them, something they could follow up on.

As she expected, the playground was deserted. After propping her bike against a tree, she walked a wide circle around the swing set, searching for a place the abductor might have hidden to wait for a child. She figured he would have watched her for a time before approaching, making sure she was alone. To do that, he would have had to stay out of sight. A man loitering near a playground would have been noticed, remembered.

She wondered if he came to the park often. The girl being alone had been a fluke. He couldn't have predicted she would be there. And yet he'd had the puppy and a story all lined up. Which she thought meant he was a planner and that if he hadn't found her girl he would have waited for a chance with another child. That meant no job or a job where he had pockets of free time. So maybe he did do heating and air type stuff.

She closed her eyes, focused on what she remembered of him. There hadn't been any signs of nervousness, no effort to hurry the move to the van. He'd let the girl set the pace, probably hoping she'd drop her guard. And it had worked. He'd practiced, or, worse, he had experience in ingratiating himself with little girls. If he'd been passing through town, he'd been passing through with the idea of snatching a girl.

As the wind picked up she hugged herself and looked around, suddenly uneasy. Not that there was anything to be nervous about. He wouldn't be here now, over ten years later. Still, the darkness was creeping in, giving the trees and bushes a sinister air. She walked toward her bike, then picked up the pace until she was running. She couldn't help but look back to make sure she wasn't being followed, then she was tumbling toward the ground, tripped up by a mountain of fur. Fighting back a scream, she scrambled to her feet, intent on getting away while she could.

"Chazz! Chazz, come here, boy."

The sound of clapping broke through the haze of fear that had Summer's heart hammering like the pistons of a steam locomotive. Feeling more than a little ridiculous for letting her imagination get the best of her, she identified the mountain as a dog. He nudged her with his big head, then licked her face with his enormous tongue.

"Some serial killer you turned out to be." She stroked his silky strands, waiting for someone to claim him.

Huffing sounds preceded the arrival of Chazz's owner. She was bundled in a thick coat. A scarf covered her hair and most of her face. "Chazz." The word was full of exasperation. "Oh. Summer. Hey. Thanks for stopping him. I hate to think where he would have ended up."

"Renny?" Now she remembered the dog. He'd saved her from Renny's accusatory questions the day before. "Uh, we sort of stopped each other." She watched as Renny clipped a thick leash to his collar, then quickly looked away when Renny's attention returned to her. "I, uh, was just, you know, leaving." This woman had a way of making her feel stupid, something she definitely didn't need help with.

"Are you out here in this weather on your bike?"

"It's not so bad," she said defensively. "I've got on layers." She obliged Chazz with a stroke when he butted against her leg.

"Sorry. I can't believe I said that. I sounded like somebody's mother. Which I guess I am now. Let me officially introduce you to Chazz Jamison, the newest addition to my family."

"He's a sweetie pie. Is he part Saint Bernard?"

"A good part of him appears to Leonberger, which accounts for his size."

"Never heard of them. Is that like a new breed?"

"I hadn't either until Jo, you remember her, right? Well, she convinced me to adopt him. Leonbergers have been around for a long time. The one drawback is he'll be huge when he's full grown. That and the hair. I'll be passing out sweaters for Christmas."

"He's still a sweetie. Has he tried to adopt any more smaller dogs?"

Renny threw back her head and laughed. "Don't remind me. I keep a close eye on him. Not all dog owners have a sense of humor. I was advised to get him a stuffed animal, which we'll do when we go to the pet store tomorrow. Won't we, boy?" She scratched behind his ears, sending him into a spasm of wiggles.

Seeing the woman's obvious affection for her pet, Summer thought maybe Renny wasn't all bad. "How long have you had him?"

"Since Sunday. We've taken to each rather well."

"I can tell. Congrats to both of you. I should go."

"Oh. Okay. Maybe I'll see you around here again." Renny pulled on Chazz's leash as he tried to follow Summer.

"Yeah." She smiled as she slung her leg over the crossbar. That hadn't been so bad. Maybe she *could* be around other people and not totally piss them off.

Summer fought a headwind as she took the side streets back downtown to her condo. The closer she got to the bar and restaurant district, the more crowded the streets and sidewalks became. A pinch of loneliness prickled her skin as she watched the groups, chatting, laughing and having a good time. *Fitting in—that's what they're doing*, she thought wistfully.

Making a left, she rode onto the sidewalk and came to stop in front of her building, a fifteen-story edifice of rose-colored brick. She didn't think of it as home but more like a place to park herself while she figured out the next stage for her life. She was grateful to be here. As a non driver, she loved it for its access to nearby amenities. Had she been a normal single, she no doubt would have loved it for its trendy location too.

"Hey, Summer. Let me get that for you." Stu Kurtz, a buff six-four and two-fifty, opened the door. He was one of the few residents who she spoke with regularly. Or rather, who always spoke to her.

"Thanks. You just getting in from work?" Stu was a personal trainer at a gym catering to women. According to him, they loved him as much as he loved them. Summer thought they couldn't possibly love him as much as he loved himself.

He nodded. "When am I going to have a chance to put some bulk on your bones?"

"I'm still thinking about it" was her pat response to his pat question.

"See that you do," he said and used his key card to access the door leading to the elevator and stairs. "Later." He gave her a nod and went bounding up the stairs.

Summer wheeled her bike to the bank of four elevators. She wasn't up to carrying her bike up fifteen flights of stairs and the garage didn't have a bike rack. As she was getting on the elevator, another resident rushed on behind her. She tensed, then forced herself to relax and return her casual nod of greeting. The elevators were new. Everything would be fine. She quickly squashed the thought that the elevators at work were new as well.

As the past two sleepless nights caught up with her, she halfway listened to the other woman's phone conversation. She was amused and slightly horrified at the information being shared with her. The type of underwear the attractive twenty-something was going to change into for bar hopping was really not something she wanted to know. But now that it was in her head, she'd remember it every time she saw the other woman.

Still, it was better than head hopping, she decided. So much better than reliving some dark terror. Could her elevator jinx be turning? She smiled as the woman got off on ten. The day was going to end on an upswing.

Her mood faltered when she checked her cell for messages. Keile hadn't contacted a cop, but she had gone to a friend who used to be a cop. She wanted Summer to come for dinner tomorrow and tell her story.

"So soon," she muttered as she erased the message. She'd figured on having a couple of weeks to get used to the idea of having to discuss her new abilities with anyone other than

Keile, whom she knew she could trust. She wished again that Dr. Veraat was available for a session. Dr. Veraat knew how to help her when she couldn't help herself. No way that would happen with the replacement shrink.

She thought briefly about calling her mother, then sighed. Her mother had enough worries without adding this. She'd just have to suck it up and trust that Keile's faith in her friend was justified. If it helped solve a case, some parents might get some closure. That would be worth any price of humiliation.

CHAPTER TEN

Surprisingly Summer awoke the next morning feeling refreshed. For the first time in a week there was no leftover unease, no remnants of bad dreams. As she stretched in preparation for her morning workout, hunger reared its ugly head and her stomach reminded her that she'd skipped dinner the night before. Unbidden, the desire for a doughnut popped into her head. She never did get to eat the one she'd ordered last week. If she got it to go, she wouldn't have to worry about someone dumping their own order on it.

Visions of croissants and doughnuts got her through her treadmill workout, ten more minutes of stretching and a relaxing shower, then out the door and down the street through the weekend crowd. The line at the bakery was even longer than it had been the week before. Summer was glad she'd grabbed a book. The lighthearted quirky tale of five lesbians seeking love kept her entertained while she waited her turn. She was giggling over the antics of a miniature German shepherd when someone tapped her shoulder. She looked up to see Renny smiling at her. "Oh. Hey."

"Good choice," Renny said, pointing at the book.

"My mom claims she picked it because of the cover." The cover consisted of a large martini.

"She wants you to drink?"

Summer's loud laughter turned some heads. "I think she picked it because it had the word 'date' on the cover."

"She wants you to date?"

She managed to shrug as her cheeks grew warm. Why hadn't she kept her mouth shut? "It's complicated."

"No. It's cool she cares. Does she pick out the women? I assume it would be women."

"Just books."

"So, was that no to the women or no to dates?"

Summer's insides fluttered at the gentle teasing in Renny's voice. It wasn't an unpleasant sensation. "Books only. That is no women, so far." But now that Renny mentioned it, she wouldn't put arranging dates for her past Sandra Baxby.

"Any chance you'd like to share a table? I don't mind eating alone, but it's more fun with company."

"Uh…yeah, sure," she said slowly. "You, uh, you come here often?"

"More than I like." Renny sighed. "I only get to order food once a month. Other times I come, take a deep sniff, order a skinny latte and run out. And even that adds pounds. What about you?"

"My second try. The first didn't go so well. Someone accidentally dumped their food on me."

"You're brave to come back."

"It's the doughnuts," Summer said before giving her order. "I'll grab us a table, if that's okay." She found one where she could have her back to the wall. No surprise attack for her today.

"I gotta wonder why someone who likes doughnuts and who does not have to worry about her weight doesn't order them," Renny said, pulling out the chair opposite Summer.

"Oh. Uh, yeah." Summer checked her number. "I just thought it would be rude to, you know, eat one in front of you."

"I appreciate the sentiment, but how can I enjoy them vicariously if you don't order any?"

"Next time?"

"At least two. And one has to have chocolate icing. Maybe cream filling."

Summer couldn't help but laugh. "Should I be writing this down?"

"Don't worry, I won't let you forget. Me and doughnuts are like that." She held up two fingers squeezed close together.

"Now I feel guilty."

"Then my mission is accomplished. But seriously, have I made up for being a total diva about my mother and Oprah?"

Summer nodded. "I looked you up on the web so if you want to quiz me, I'm ready. Wait. I should have said 'bring it.'"

"Oh, yeah." Renny rubbed her hands together. "Book three, page twenty, the MC—"

"What?"

"Gotcha." Renny's shoulders shook with laughter. "Okay, easy question. Is your mother the Oprah fan?"

Summer snorted. "My mother? No way. She didn't buy the book when it first came out just *because* of Oprah's endorsement. My mother considers herself one of the last of the holdout hippies. In a seriously rich kind of way," she added with a fond smile. "For her that means that not doing what Oprah says is 'sticking it to the man.' Uh, I hope that didn't offend you?"

Renny shook her head. "I'd love to meet your mother. Do I dare ask why she finally bought it, then?"

"Umm, well…" A spot over Renny's shoulder was easier to look at. "They're slow today."

"I know a stall when I hear one." Renny tapped Summer's hand. "Let me guess. She bought it with the cover torn off?"

"No. No. The sale table," she admitted reluctantly. "She liked the cover. Started flipping through the pages and before she knew it had read the first three chapters. On the better side, she picked up your second one too. For full price. And bought the third and fourth when they came out."

"That makes up for the sales table. Seriously, I'm thrilled she got hooked in by the cover. My publisher and I went back and forth, me advocating for the simple. Rowboat, lake, shoe said it all for me."

"I have to admit covers aren't the draw for me. I'm more into scanning the blurb, then reading the first few pages. If I'm not caught by the author's writing style by then, I won't get caught." Summer lifted her head and listened. "Finally. That's my number. Be right back." Renny's number was called while she was picking up her order, so she grabbed that one as well.

"They apologized for the delay," Summer said, placing a basket in front of Renny. "They offered free doughnuts, but I thought you might kill me if I brought one back for you."

"Probably, but I would regret it after the fact. Killing you that is, not eating the doughnut."

"That's all I can ask for. I did accept a coupon for our next visit." Pleased with her own quick comeback, Summer picked up her fork and speared a potato wedge. She was holding her own. Even Dr. Veraat couldn't ask for more.

As they ate, they talked more about books and Renny's life as a child star. Summer had managed to catch Renny's show on one of the sleepless nights. She understood why Ree had been popular.

"I don't know if I could enjoy having to be on all the time. Must be exhausting." Summer looked at her empty plate in surprise. She didn't remember eating the spinach and egg croissant or the home fries. Good company obviously had a positive effect on her appetite. "What do you miss the most?"

"The family I had on the show. The people. When we were shooting I saw more of them than I did of Eve. I don't miss having to be on constantly, however. As you guessed, it's exhausting. Everywhere I went, everything I did, someone was watching, ready to capture it on film. Being a writer suits me better. I get a lot of solitary time and I get the book tours to meet fans." She crumpled her napkin and dropped it onto the plate. "I told myself I wasn't going to bring this up. I lied. It's obvious something happened to you and maybe if I knew I wouldn't insert foot into mouth all the time."

Summer traced the pattern on the wooden tabletop with her finger. "It's…complicated."

"I don't know how much research you did on me, but I'm betting you stumbled over a story or two about my addictions. I understand complicated. There are some years I don't remember very clearly. They're a blur of parties, booze, drugs and sex." Renny shook her coffee cup as though checking to see if it was empty. "From the way you talk I thought you might have the same kind of issues. Despite my behavior so far, I *can* listen without judging if you need to talk."

At least she doesn't think I'm crazy was the first thing to come to Summer's mind. "Issues, but not the same," she admitted. "I was in a bad car wreck. When I came out of the coma two years ago I didn't remember anything. With the exception of Keile, my memory dates back to then. I know I sometimes come off as stupid. It's more that I don't know what I'm expected to say or how I'm expected to act."

Renny reached for Summer's hand. "Then can I say how impressed I am? I know how hard it is losing track of hours. Okay, maybe a day, but that much? Wow. And scary."

"Very scary. I owe a lot to my mother. She basically put her life on hold to help me. She still does somewhat."

"That makes you very lucky to have a seriously rich hippie mom who steps up when needed."

Summer heard the bitterness beneath Renny's easy words. Not for the first time she wondered about the nature of Renny's relationship with her mother. "I didn't think so at first. She pushed, prodded and begged me to get out of bed, rejoin the world. Then she recruited the rest of my family to do their own brand of pushing, prodding, begging. I had to do something out of self-defense. Getting nagged by your mother *and* four older sisters is torture."

"What about your father? Was he around?"

"Different style. More likely to bring a movie and pizza, tell me to put my feet up because he knows I've been worked to death. I realized later the movies, the conversations were his way of helping me learn."

"The yin to your mother's yang."

"Exactly. That's why you're the writer. I would have never thought to put it that way."

"I have my moments." Renny glanced at her watch. "Sorry to say I need to get back. Have to rescue Chazz and get back to the grind. I had a good time. I hope we could do this again?"

"It would have to be next month, right? You've used up your quota for March."

Renny sighed. "Don't remind me. Okay, lunch or dinner. I can always have salad with low calorie dressing."

"I'd like that." Summer pulled out her cell phone. "I can give you my number."

* * *

"Anything more on the girl? What did she look like?" Dani Knight pressed.

Summer shook her head and exhaled. "I didn't see much of her. Like I already told you, it was like I was looking through her eyes. No mirror in the park, so I can't tell you what she looks like. Since she could see her hands on the puppy and her ponytail, I could too."

Closing her eyes, she resisted reciting the multiplication table. It was beginning to feel like a crutch and Dr. Veraat had warned her against them. But not giving in wasn't an option right now. Not after Keile's friend had been grilling her for what felt like hours.

"I know it's hard, Summer, but the cops will push you harder." Dani patted Summer's thigh. "I want you to take a look at a photo. Tell me what you think."

Summer studied the pretty girl with the shoulder-length blonde hair, the blue eyes and big smile that showed missing front teeth. "It's not her," she finally said, disappointment so sharp she could almost taste it. "Not her."

"What do you mean it's not her?" Keile asked. "I thought you didn't see her face."

"The hair's wrong. The girl had ash-blonde hair and it was longer. When she bent down the ponytail came down to the middle of her chest. The skin on her hands was lighter. More like mine."

"You're sure?" Dani asked. "One hundred percent sure?"

"Positive." Summer bit her lip as anger started to swirl. She wasn't stupid enough to think Dani believed her, so this must be some kind of test. Some way to try and trick the crazy woman. "I gotta go." She pushed off the sofa and shot Keile a glance. "Told you this was a bad idea."

"Wait." Dani strode after Summer, her long-legged stride helping to close the distance. "This photo was taken a couple of months before Ashley Caruthers went missing ten years ago. If you're telling me this isn't the same girl you saw, then we may have a situation." She ran her fingers through her own long blonde hair, sighing. "I hate to think there are two of them."

Summer hugged herself. "There are two. The hair is wrong. You should check, see if Ashley had a baby brother. If she lived within walking distance of Central Park."

"She didn't," Keile said. "They searched for her near campus because she lived in an apartment complex that used to be near there. It would be at least an hour and a half walk for an adult from there to the park."

"Damn," Dani said softly. "No way a kid would do that, and for a swing?" She scanned the information she'd been able to pull together. "Says here she frequented the playground at the elementary school on Royal. Also the woods next to the college. Sorry, Summer, I should have checked that."

"That's okay. What now? How do we find my missing girl?"

Keile slung an arm around Summer's shoulders. "We talk to Carla. Being a cop she has better access to information. I could sound her out first, see what she thinks."

"It'd be better coming from me," Dani said. "I've had to consult with the police about a couple of jobs. I'd like to think she'll give me a chance to lay it out, get her to buy in."

"But will she believe you when *you* don't really believe me?" Summer asked. "Heck, I'm not even sure *I* believe me anymore." She rubbed her eyes, surprised to find them wet. "Maybe it was one big hallucination. Maybe I do need to check into the loony bin."

"Don't," Dani said firmly, her blue eyes fierce. "Don't let my doubts sway you. I'm the suspicious kind until I'm proven wrong. You held up. Your story didn't change. I say we don't know the endgame so we dig. I'm damn good at digging."

"Summer, why don't you stay here tonight?" Keile suggested. "You can take the guest room. It's late. Too late to be out on your bike."

"I don't want to impose."

"It's a good idea," Dani said. "I can see you're tired. I can make a few calls tonight. Might have some info for you tomorrow."

Summer let herself be led to the bedroom with the queen-sized sleigh bed, matching vanity dresser and a welcoming feel. She needed it more than she knew. "What will Haydn say?"

"That she's glad you're not out on your bike this late," Keile responded immediately. "The bathroom's kind of small, but you'll find stuff in there to use. You need pajamas?"

"I'll be okay. Keile, do you still believe me?"

"More than ever." She pulled Summer close for a hug. "Dani's right. You never wavered. We'll find something to make the others believe. Hopefully get some closure for the girl, for her parents."

"Thanks." Summer leaned her head against Keile's shoulder and let herself be soothed for a moment.

Keile closed the door softly on her way out, then rejoined Dani in the family room. "What do you think?"

"I don't know. I was sure it was going to be Ashley and now we have to consider there could be another girl who was snatched. I called Hank. He hasn't heard anything recently about a missing girl fitting Summer's vague description. And that's statewide. I'll wait a couple of hours and try Duvaughn. He keeps a database of missing kids, but he doesn't get moving until after midnight."

"You have such unusual friends."

"I wouldn't call them friends."

"Sources, then. Any chance there are other cold cases?"

"Not of missing girls. Not in Seneca. Keile, I know you feel some sort of loyalty to her, but..." Dani shrugged.

"But nothing. You're the one who said she held up. There's another mother missing her daughter and we need to find out all we can. Summer's having a hard time with this. She's gone through a lot the last few years. I'd like it if we could clear this up for her."

"I'll see what I can do. If I hear anything, you'll be the first to know."

"That's fair."

CHAPTER ELEVEN

Summer was a bundle of nerves when she entered the lobby of her office building on Monday morning. Yesterday had been spent poised on a precipice, waiting for word on the identity of the missing girl with the long, ash-blonde hair. Word that never came. Although sleep had not been her companion the night before, she decided working was better than pacing around her condo like an animal in heat, drinking too many Cokes. And if she succeeded in making Marcia a little crazy today, that would make up for a lot.

"Summer! Wait!"

Recognizing the voice, she turned slowly, prepared for danger. Rich appeared to have come without potential for disaster today, she thought, watching him walk toward her in a nicely fitting pinstriped suit and crisp white shirt. Still, it didn't pay to let down her guard when he was around.

He stopped in front of her looking like a puppy begging for forgiveness. "I've been looking for you."

And I've been dodging you, she thought. *You and your memories.* "And?"

"I wanted to apologize again for dumping my food on you and ruining your breakfast. I swear, I'm usually more adept on my feet."

"Apology accepted." She settled for a nod, ignoring his outstretched hand. Though neither one of them was upset, there was no way she was going to chance touching him. Her defenses were already low to nonexistent.

He stepped in front of her when she tried to skirt by him. "So," he said with a bright smile. "You wanna grab lunch sometime? I'd love to make things up to you, and I do owe you a meal."

For a second she thought she was having another out-of-body experience. How else would Rich get the idea she was interested in him? How else could she *not* have known he was interested in her? She ran through the multiplication table to ten, but he was still there, waiting for an answer, when she finished.

"You gotta eat, right?"

"Can't. Late for work." Despite her aversion to crowded elevators, she bullied her way onto a full one, seconds before the door shut. More dazed than upset, she spent the slow ride up considering the egos of some men. It made a change, at least, from fearing a mind link.

After that surprise, she was grateful that Marcia had written her day's assignment on a sticky note and attached it to her chair. It was a system that worked for Summer. She grimaced. She had yet to exchange more than a head nod with Marcia since Tuesday's blowup. A blowup followed by a breakdown, which for unknown reasons Marcia had chosen not to broadcast. Hoping she didn't owe her anything for the unexpected consideration, she picked up one of the three reports that had been left for her to look over for graphic content.

Summer tried to tap into her creative center—the one which used to allow her to draw, to paint, to know how to arrange graphics for the most impact. It remained largely out of reach, like a carrot dangled in front of a horse. She retained enough to do a decent job with her reviews, she hoped. If she continued to do it long enough, maybe things would come back to her.

When a gnawing emptiness reminded her that she'd skipped breakfast, she glanced at the plain wall clock and discovered it was close to noon. She stretched her stiff back and decided a brisk walk was needed. She'd go to Jack's and this time she'd leave enough room for peach cobbler. No. This time she'd *start* with the peach cobbler.

Her cell phone buzzed before she made it to the door. Her heartbeat sped up when she saw Dani's name. Waiting time was over. "What's the word?" she asked, gripping the phone till her knuckles were white.

"I'm almost a hundred percent sure I found your girl. Her name was Brandy Jones. Her mother identified a shoe found in the parking lot of what is now Central Park. Twenty years ago, Summer."

Bile gurgled in the back of her throat. There was no happiness in being right. At being believed. She sat on the desk, not sure she could feel her legs. Not sure she could feel much of anything besides dread.

"I've spoken with Carla. She'd liked to talk to you. Unofficially for now."

"I can't tell her any more than I told you."

"She'd like to hear it from the source. Cops are like that. The police file on Brandy has gone astray. Anything you give them is more than they have."

"How do they know about the shoe?"

"They don't. I got that from an outside source who followed that case."

"Only that one?"

"It got nasty real quick when they questioned and released a black guy about her disappearance. He almost got beat to death. That guy was my source's cousin, so naturally he took an interest in the case. He swears there was nothing in the file about the van or the puppy. I doubt it was known until you mentioned it."

"All the more reason for them not to believe me." She closed her eyes and took a deep breath.

"I know I was hard on you, but you got through it. Remember that."

"So she's going to believe me because you found the girl?"

"She's willing to listen. Can you meet us in the bar next to the Marriot at seven? It's called Juice. I can't get away any earlier than that."

Can I? She began to shake. It was all so real now and it wasn't going to go away. Not now that some door in her mind had opened and let in the unthinkable.

"You still there?"

The light teasing in Dani's voice did little to help her mood. But ignoring the situation wasn't going to help either. "I'll be there," she said softly. She ended the call without giving Dani a chance to offer more empty platitudes.

Her wallet went back in the bag, thoughts of food buried under an onslaught of queasiness coated with dread. Wishing she'd never gone to the damn park, never touched the damn swings, never let that damn door in her mind open, she sank into her chair and grabbed her head. There would be no going back. Not after she talked to the police, bared her soul for some woman who would have checked her background. Who would know about the coma, the memory loss, and no doubt have pegged her as flaky at best.

She tried to run through the multiplication table, but even that couldn't keep out dark thoughts of being dragged to the station to be interrogated by the police in one of those rooms with the two-way mirrors. Of being forced to tell her story over and over again until she slipped and said something they could pounce on and use to declare her a fraud.

And how could she blame them? Didn't she feel like a fraud deep inside? Like these visions could be hallucinations resulting from the head trauma? Or worse, her first step toward insanity?

Summer blew out a sharp breath. *There*, she thought. She'd acknowledged the thought that had been flying around her brain like an elusive ghost only much scarier. She could be losing her mind and without her shrink to talk it through she would never know. Maybe it was time to make an appointment with Dr. Veraat's replacement. Pouring her heart out to a sympathetic stranger couldn't be worse than talking to a skeptical cop.

She jerked upright in her chair when a stack of files hit her desk. She stared stupidly at Marcia, putting a hand to her beating heart. How out of it had she been not to hear the sound of Marcia's heels hitting against the floor?

"These need to be done before you leave," Marcia said curtly. "Seeing as you have time to sit around and daydream, that shouldn't be a problem, should it?"

Anger, hot and strong, erupted so swiftly it nearly knocked her over. Summer pushed out of the chair, sending it careening back against the wall. She did *not* deserve to be treated this way.

"Why didn't I get the memo?" she demanded, her hands fisted. "If spending my lunch hour at my desk with my eyes shut is no longer allowed, I should have fucking well been told. It seems to me as my supervisor that would have been your responsibility. So until you show me that memo, I suggest you pull that fucking stick out of your fucking ass and get off of mine. How hard would it be to simply give me a stack of fucking files and tell me to work on them? But no, you have to make an issue out of it. Are you that fucking starved for attention? What's the matter? No one at home to lie and tell you how good you look in those ridiculous outfits you come to work in?" She slammed her hand down on the desk. "Of course there isn't. No friend would let you leave for work looking like you're trolling for a good fuck."

"You!" Marcia's face flooded with color. "You, shut up now! No one talks to me that way. No one."

Summer crossed her arms, getting a charge out of the tremble in Marcia's voice. "I think I just did. And if you ask me, which you didn't, someone should have said something sooner."

"Don't think I won't go to Mr. Tathum with this."

"You think I give a fuck?" she asked, tapping a finger against Marcia's chest. "I have a hell of lot more problems than you and your ridiculous outfits and misplaced superiority complex."

Marcia's mouth opened and closed like a fish drawing in oxygen. With a skin-searing look, she hurried away.

The word "tattletale" sprang to mind and Summer had to laugh. Realizing her laughter was bordering on hysteria, she covered her mouth. She didn't know what had come over her, but it felt pretty damn good to be on the other side of this equation. Her anger now burnt out, she picked up the top folder, looked at the clock and decided work could wait for the thirty minutes that was left of her lunch hour. She grabbed her wallet and hurried down the steps, pleased that the dread and queasiness were a thing of the past. Marcia was good for something after all.

Outside, she picked a direction and let the early March sun play on her face as she walked aimlessly. The downtown streets were humming with the lunch crowd, on the sidewalks and in the streets. Summer took some comfort from the normality of the scene around her. If she were losing her mind, she should enjoy this time of lucidity.

On impulse she called her mother. They hadn't talked in a few days. Her mother's way of giving her space. "Hey, Mom."

"Summer? Are you all right? Do you need me to come get you?"

"I'm good, Mom. Really I am. I have a few minutes and decided to call you for a change."

"What a lovely surprise. Your dad and I made it to Callaway Gardens. I spent a day at the spa getting buffed and scrubbed from top to bottom. I can't wait to go back."

"That's great. You deserve it. We should get together and you can tell me all about it. And I can tell you about having breakfast with Renny Jamison."

"Look at you, rubbing elbows with the stars. Are you going to show up in her next book?"

Summer laughed. "You never know. I'd better get back. Just wanted to say I love you."

"Oh, sweetie. I love you too. Why don't I come have lunch on Saturday? Better yet we could drive up to Atlanta and I could drag you through Phipps."

Summer wanted to groan. Her mother and malls had a symbiotic relationship which should not be possible for a so-called "hippie."

"Only if I have the right to limit your selection."

"Deal," Sandra said quickly. "I'll be there at nine."

"So I should expect you at eight thirty then?"

"You know me too well. Take care of my baby girl."

"I will, Mom. I will."

Her phone buzzed before she had a chance to slip it back into her pocket. "What did you forget?"

"To call you earlier?"

"Renny. Sorry. Thought you were my mother. Not that I think of you like my mom or anything," she added hastily. "I mean, you're too young. You know?"

"I think I do." Renny was clearly amused. "I called to see if we could have our dinner tonight. I know it's last minute, but I spent six solid hours writing and think that deserves a reward."

"Is eight too late? I have, uh, a thing before that." "Thing" sounded better than interrogation.

"That works. I'm thinking Stir Crazy on Roster and Second. It's all stir-fry so it can't be bad for you, right?"

"What a coincidence. I was just reading somewhere that eating stir-fry doesn't count toward daily caloric intake. Stir Crazy is perfect."

"You're very agreeable today. Too bad I don't have any more demands."

Is she flirting with me? Summer wondered. Warmth suffused her cheeks and it felt surprisingly good. "Probably comes from having four older sisters."

"To me that sounds like a reason to be disagreeable."

"Story you'd like to share?"

Renny laughed. "We'll put that in the 'to be discussed in more detail later' column. After I've had a chance to dazzle you with my charm."

"I'll hold you to that." Summer took a deep breath and held the phone to her chest. A date. The day wasn't going to be a total waste.

Kevin was sitting on her desk, checking messages on his phone, when she returned. "Hope I didn't keep you waiting long." She hesitated in the doorway, unsure of her role or his.

He looked up from his phone and smiled. "Come on in. This is your office."

"I...I shouldn't have said what I said," she blurted out.

Kevin held up a hand. "I'm not here about that. As I told Marcia, I expect the two of you to be able to work things out. If you can't, then Gar is the one who has to deal with it. Not me."

"Oh." She wasn't sure if that was good or bad. Working anything out with Marcia was bound to involve a headache. "What can I do for you?"

"Liz shared your comments on the report for the Tyler account. They're right on. Good job, Summer."

"Thanks." She ducked her head, pleased and scared at the same time. She could almost see his thoughts. See what he was working up to.

"I know how to schmooze with a client, work with the numbers. Know a little bit about graphics too. So when I say you were right on the money, you should know not only do I mean it but also that I know what I'm talking about." He gently lifted her chin. "I know I said I wouldn't push—"

"But you will," she interjected. "That's what you were going to say. I know it."

"I'd be fool on all counts not to press. I'm doing this not only for the company, Summer, but also for you. I truly believe you still have the talent. It may be buried under the surface, but with a little digging it'll shoot up through the ground, grow stronger and eventually bloom." He laughed when she rolled her eyes. "You wait. Soon you'll be bursting with fruit. Then you can thank me for fertilizing the ground."

"It's good you're a numbers man, Uncle Kevin," Summer said dryly.

"Mock me all you want. You'll eat those words. It may not be tomorrow, but it will be someday. And Summer, I can easily get someone to file. It's not so easy to find someone who has your eye for color and presentation. I'll let you have the rest of the day to file this last stack." He patted the folders that had played a part in the altercation with Marcia. "Tomorrow you switch to working under Liz. We'll start using your force for the good."

A chuckle escaped without her permission. The love of anything *Star Wars* was one of the many things Kevin shared with her dad. "Thanks, Yoda. I think."

"Tell me again when you know."

Summer paced the area in front of her desk after he left. It *was* true. No good deed went without the reward of a swift kick in the butt. You make a few simple changes to some graphs and the page layout and people go nuts. Thought you were the Second Coming, capable of performing miracles like walking on wine and making fish fly. It just wasn't reasonable.

Running her fingers through her hair, she fell back on the multiplication table. By the time she reached the twenties, oxygen was suffusing her brain, allowing for clearer thoughts. She wasn't a miracle worker. If what she produced came up short of their unrealistic expectations, she wasn't going to take the blame. She would do her best and if it wasn't enough, then so be it. That went for Kevin and Liz and for the cop she was meeting later. Her best wasn't her previous best, but it was her best now. And if she did fail, she could try channeling the kick-ass person who'd handled Marcia earlier.

CHAPTER TWELVE

"Tell me again how it happened," Carla said for the fourth time.

Summer's eyes narrowed as she looked at the veteran cop with the pissy attitude. Carla was tall and powerfully built. She wore her dark hair short and her brown eyes appeared to view the world with suspicion. Summer could understand that cops had to be wary, given what they did day in and day out. What she couldn't understand, and didn't appreciate, was the derision running underneath the suspicion. She wasn't some criminal who'd been dragged into interrogation. She had come freely and it made her mad that Carla wouldn't or couldn't give her credit for that.

"I think Summer's explained it enough times," Dani said. "Try to remember she's not one of your suspects."

"She's a potential witness," Carla said curtly. "You've obviously forgotten how important it is to nail down their story. Especially when the story is…"

"Flaky, unbelievable, a lie," Summer supplied after Carla's voice trailed off. "Take your pick, Officer Hanson." Carla's continued silence spoke volumes and Summer got the message loud and clear. "I have to go." She pulled her wallet out of her coat pocket and dropped a ten on the table. "That should cover my drink, if not the time I wasted."

Dani reached across the table and put a hand on Summer's arm. "I know it took a lot for you to come here. If it helps, I believe you."

"Thanks, I guess." She slid from the booth, walked through the dark, smoky bar, through her disappointment. It wasn't until she was outside that she felt able to breathe. Inhaling the clean night air, she told herself to put Carla and her disbelief out of her mind. She had more important things to fixate on. Things like a date. She put a hand to her chest, her heart stuttering at the thought. A date! It was a date. No accidental meeting this time. It was prearranged and mutually agreed upon. And Renny had called it a treat. Surely that had to mean date. That was a little scary considering everything she knew about dates was from books and movies. But it was thrilling too.

I must be crazy, she thought with a laugh. She should have done the nerves thing during the twenty minutes she'd spent at home after work picking out tonight's outfit—black slacks and the scooped-neck sweater which, according to her mom, brought out the blue in her eyes. She certainly hadn't dressed to impress Dani and Carla. Her usual attire would have done for them. *But not for Renny*, she admitted to herself. *Not for tonight.*

A glance at her watch showed she still had thirty minutes before the meet. She backtracked and made a right. Books and More was only a couple of blocks from Stir Crazy. She could easily spend half an hour there.

The bookstore was relatively small, but in addition to books and the coffee counter, it contained shelves crammed with cards, games, CDs and movies. She liked the fact that it was within easy walking distance of her condo and that they were willing to order any book in print.

The clerk behind the desk gave her a smile of recognition the minute she walked through the door. He'd finally stopped asking if she needed help finding anything.

Today she bypassed the fiction section in favor of books on local interest. While talking to Carla and Dani she'd gotten the idea of searching local history books for information about Brandy's disappearance. From what she'd gathered it should have been a big deal.

She quickly concluded that a search of old newspaper articles would be a better idea. The first two books she found on Seneca history made no mention of any crime and the third had only one paragraph on it—which focused more on the increase in crime due to the encroachment of Atlanta—the big city—than on the crime itself. Summer closed the book after reading the author's argument that the person responsible had to be black. According to everything she'd managed to find on child molesters, they tended to stick with their own race and kids they knew or were related to.

And just like that, she wasn't in the bookstore anymore—

The image of a little girl with blonde hair in side pigtails formed clearly as if in high definition. The girl was wearing a dingy pink coat with a black fake fur collar. Her head was down and her shoulders were slumped as if in defeat. Her too-short jeans were threadbare, as were her dingy pink and white sneakers.

"Right on time." The voice was deep and gravelly, with a touch of age. Satisfaction came through. Satisfaction laced with something dark.

And then Summer knew. She was in him. Could feel the evil. Could feel the anticipation as the girl came closer. He was so excited about what was to come. So excited about getting a new princess. His big, rough hands stroked the puppy in his arms and he waited. Waited for his target to get closer. She would stop. Puppies always overrode any cautions the girls had heard. He could take that to the bank.

"Hey, little darlin', you doing okay?"

The girl's steps faltered, then slowed to a stop as her gaze zeroed in on the puppy. She wiped a hand over her running nose. "Is that yours?"

Got you, he thought and smiled. "Well now, I found him. I'm looking for someone to take him. I already have two dogs." He set the puppy on the sidewalk and watched with glee as the girl stretched out her hand. She quickly snatched it back and put it behind her back.

"Does he bite? My granny says sometimes dogs'll bite your fingers right off."

"Not this little guy." He stroked the puppy's back. "See, he likes it. Look at that tail go."

Cautiously the girl imitated his actions. "He feels so soft." She laughed when the puppy jumped up on her and licked at her face.

"He really likes you. Maybe he should go home with you."

She shook her head. "Can't afford a dog. That's what my granny says." She gave the dog a longing look. "I gotta go. I'll get in trouble if I don't go straight home."

"Your granny's probably waiting for you, huh?"

"She's at work, but I still haveta go straight home. I shouldna stopped. I'm gonna be late."

"What if I gave you a ride?" He put on his friendliest smile. The one he knew made him look like a harmless grandfather.

"Can he sit in my lap? I promise I'll wear the seat belt."

"That's a good idea. Maybe if we stopped by a store and bought some puppy food your granny would let you keep him."

The girl scooped up the puppy. "Can we get a big bag? She might say yes if it's a great big bag."

"And a bowl for water and one for food, don't you think?"

"Yeah. Do you have enough for a collar? There's some rope around the house I could use to tie to the collar. So he won't run away when I take him for a walk. I'll take him for a walk every day. That's what you're supposed to do for dogs. I seen it on TV."

"Aren't you the smart one?" He placed a hand on her shoulder. "You know I do have enough to buy a leash to go with that collar. I'll let you pick them out."

Her face lit up. "You will? I never get to pick out nothing." When he held out a hand, she smiled up at him and slid her small hand into his. "Can I name him?"

"He'll be yours now, won't he?" He glanced around, made sure they hadn't attracted any attention before he led her down the street.

On some level of consciousness Summer knew what was going to happen, knew she had to stop it. She tried to scream. Tried to tell the girl to run, to escape. But the words wouldn't come and she could only watch as they walked off, the little girl chattering away...

A touch on her shoulder brought her back. She blinked against the warmth of tears, tasting their saltiness on her tongue, and wondered how long she'd been crying.

"Summer. It's me, Rich. Are you hurt?"

A part of her registered Rich, knew who he was. Another part of her *was* him, was back in the closet, praying the monster wouldn't find them, then smelling the acrid scent of urine when he did. Summer shook her head and stepped back, ending the physical contact the way she hadn't mastered how to do mentally. "God." She put a hand to her throbbing head and took deep breaths to soothe the churning inside her. She didn't want to add public vomiting to her repertoire. "I'm okay." She said it more for herself than for him.

"You need help getting somewhere? You don't look so good." He bent to pick up the book she had dropped.

"No." Summer wiped her face with her hands. "Thanks. I, uh, I have a thing." She forced a smile, telling herself she was okay, that she had nothing to worry about. Just another useless vision about another girl, no doubt someone who'd been taken too long ago to save. There was no need for her to wallow in the horror of another girl gone missing. No need to try and help. There was nothing she could do. Once again she hadn't seen the man, couldn't give the police the details they'd want. They wouldn't believe her in any case. But this time she'd be smart. This time she *would* keep her mouth shut. And she wouldn't feel guilty, wouldn't beat herself up—because there was no way she could help. No way at all.

"Maybe we could do something another time?" Rich pressed. "We didn't have a chance to finish our discussion this morning. And you do still have to eat, right?"

Damn, she'd forgotten about him. Summer ground her teeth when he flashed what he obviously thought was an irresistible smile. Why was he still here? Why wasn't he picking up on her clues? She exhaled loudly. No way to dodge this. She'd run from the problem this morning, hoping it would go away. Now it was time to take care of it, be more direct.

"The last time I went out with a guy, Rich, I was twelve." At least that's what her mother told her. "Then I wised up and switched to girls. I've never gone back." She watched understanding flower in his eyes, followed quickly by embarrassment.

"Oh," he said slowly, then jammed his hands into his pockets and rocked back on his heels. "That's pretty clear. Guess I'll see you around at work."

Freed by his departure Summer was able to take a deep breath, fill her lungs with air. Able to loosen the grip the latest hop had on her mind. Able to almost dispel her fear of the monster she'd been inside of.

She ignored the headache and the nausea. She was getting used to the side effects now. It was just the price she had to pay for her new skill. Grateful that Monday was a slow night in the bookstore, she made her way to the restroom and used a wet paper towel to fix some of the damage left by the tears. When she walked past the clerk with his curious gaze and out the door her skin wasn't quite as blotchy and her eyes had lost some of their puffiness.

Standing on the sidewalk she was surprised by the darkness, the coolness of the air. She automatically scanned the area but found no sign of the blonde child with the worn clothes or an older man with a puppy. Not that she'd expected to, because, like the girl on the swings, this one had been missing a long time. *All in the past*, she assured herself, setting a brisk pace to the restaurant a couple of blocks away. And yet guilt trailed her like an eager puppy.

Renny was seated in the waiting area separated from the dining room by glass doors, scribbling in a small notebook. She had removed her full-length leather coat and pushed up the sleeves of a mint-green sweater with a V-neck. Summer let herself admire the display of cleavage and was taken aback by the desire to nestle her face in it. It wasn't a bad feeling.

She cut her gaze to Renny's face when the notebook closed. "Hey. Have you been waiting long?" Her heartbeat sped up as a smile lit Renny's face. A smile that said to Summer she was worth waiting for.

"Will it sound bad if I admit to not knowing?" She tapped her notebook. "I got this great idea for a storyline and had to get it down before it slipped away."

"I'm all for great ideas and new books to read."

"Then all is good." Renny slipped her notebook into a small leather backpack. "Do you want to talk about what's bothering you or should I pretend not to notice?"

"I…" Summer fought the unexpected urge to bite her nails by admiring their current neatness. Even the pinky, which had been known to resemble a bloody mess. "It was a thing. Just a thing. I'm okay now." She withstood Renny's scrutiny, almost sighing in relief when Renny nodded, seemingly willing to let the matter drop.

Inside the eatery, the scents of cooking meat mingled with the sounds of sizzling woks and conversation. The hostess led them to a table with enough room for two and handed out menus.

Their server came almost as soon as the hostess left. "Good evening, ladies, I'm Drew. Have either of you eaten here before?" When Summer shook her head, he went through the spiel explaining the process. "What can I get you to drink?"

"Coke," Summer replied and closed the menu, which contained the same explanation Drew had just given them.

"I'll have a Diet Coke with lemon."

"I'll be right out with your drinks. Feel free to join the line at any time." Drew gathered up their menus and sped away.

"He doesn't have a bad gig," Renny said, leaning forward. "All he has to worry about are the drinks and an occasional food order. We have to do the power lifting, picking out the vegetables and meat we want cooked."

"Somehow it seems more fun for us," Summer said absently. The V-neck sweater of Renny's had plenty of power all of its own. "And you only get the vegetables you like. Plus Drew does have to take away dirty dishes if we go back for seconds."

"That's hard. I bet he's somebody's boy toy."

"What?" Summer looked up, blushing guiltily.

Renny crinkled her nose. "It's a game I like to play. A cute young thing like that is destined for boy toy in my little world."

"He wouldn't be working here if he had other means of support," she argued, giving her mind strict instructions to pay attention to their conversation. No wandering into greener pastures. "I say he's a college student paying his own way."

"Point," Renny conceded. "But if this were one of my novels his cute little butt would be that of a boy toy."

Summer tilted her head, intrigued. "Man or woman?"

"Man. Older, I think. Pillar of society type with a high-ranking job, wife and two point five kids. The wife has her own boy toy, so she doesn't care as long as he's discreet."

"Who's the central character? The pillar or the boy toy?"

"Hmm. Good question. We can discuss it over food. The stale crackers I had for lunch are a thing of the past."

Summer, who had been sure she couldn't force down a bite, had no trouble clearing her plate as they bantered back and forth over Renny's hypothetical novel.

"You have to write it now." Summer smiled her thanks as Drew replaced her empty glass with a full one. "Maybe give me and boy toy a mention on your acknowledgment page."

"What if I put you in the book? You can be the sexy secretary who doesn't understand why her boss doesn't chase her around the desk. This despite the indecently short skirts she wears."

Summer laughed. "It's funny, but my mom asked me today if I was going show up in your next book."

"Make that the sexy, but slutty secretary," Renny said with a sly smile. "She not only chases her boss, but any man with pots of money."

"She would get a kick out of that. You could call the character Rainy Day. It's different enough to protect the guilty." At Renny's blank look, she shared her full name.

"Really?"

"Hippie mom." She thought that explained it all. "She didn't start there. My sisters are Tuesday, April Storm, Winter Moon and May Flower. Add Summer Rain to that and my mom has a lot to answer for in her next life."

"You got that right."

"My dad may have saved her some grief when he finally found his backbone and insisted on naming the last baby Jonah Steven."

"And you let the kid live?"

"Jonah says he's alive because he was too fast for us girls. My mom says it's because we loved him from the get-go."

"Is it strange to be fed the majority of your memories from someone else?"

"A little," she said, thinking of the lost girls and of Rich and Marcia. Things could always be worse. "What about the siblings that made you want to be disagreeable?"

"Did I mention my mother has her sights on beating Liz Taylor's record for marriages? At least sometimes it seems that way." Renny's tone had a bite. "Number three, or was it number four? Anyway, one of them had a couple of kids. They were a few years older than me and Eve thought it was cute to leave me in their care. They weren't exactly nice or attentive unless they wanted to pick on me. Let's say I got picked on frequently. Thank God that marriage only lasted nine months. Nine long, horrible months, mind you." She drained her Diet Coke "One of the others had kids, but I never saw them. They were always with their mother. It wouldn't be so bad not to remember that."

"Uh, I don't…I don't know what to say."

"You don't have to say anything. It was one of many stories I have from life with Eve. Now there's someone who should be worried about being in my next book. Of course, Eve, being Eve, won't recognize herself. And didn't that sound catty? Let's talk about something more pleasant. You look much better than you did earlier."

Summer choked on her drink. "Thanks. I think." She matched Renny's grin. "I feel better and maybe you helped with that."

Renny arched one perfectly shaped eyebrow. "'Maybe'? I deserve more credit than that with my charming self. At least 'probably.'"

"Agreed." Summer trailed a finger through the condensation on the glass. "You *probably* helped me feel better."

"Do you feel like telling me what happened?"

"I should start by saying it's weird in a *Twilight Zone* kind of way. Another of my dad's favorites." She took a deep breath, let it out slowly. "I've been getting these what I call 'mind hopping' deals. It's happened four or five times in the past few weeks. One minute I'm having my own thoughts and then without warning I'm in somebody else's head, seeing what they see, feeling what they feel. And it's always something bad."

"I've read something about that. Are you touching the other person when this happens?"

"Not necessarily. I think both me and the other person have to be mad or scared or upset. Sometime it happens if I touch something and I'm upset. It's all new, so I don't know exactly how it works, but I think the person has to have left a strong impression for me to connect."

"Like what?" Renny propped her elbows on the table, seemingly interested.

"A swing. Remember when I asked you about the puppy? Well, I was on the swings, mad as hell, and hopped into a little girl's mind. A little girl who I've since found out has been missing for twenty years."

Renny's eyes widened. "No way! That would totally throw me off. I'd be a total basket case."

"I'm not that far from being one. The reason I was upset earlier is that I finished my meeting early and stopped by the bookstore to look up info on local history. I was looking through a book and the next thing I know I'm in this this guy's head, watching as he's convincing a young girl to let him give her a ride home. He was using a puppy as bait, just like the other time. But now that I've had a little distance I can see he knows she's starved for attention. Gave her a little bit and off she went like he was her new best friend." She rubbed her arms. "I know it happened a long time ago and the police will sneer at me again if I bring it up, but still…" She shrugged, tried to laugh it off.

"Nothing I can do except hope it goes away." *And that it takes this feeling of hopelessness with it*, she added for herself.

"If it was that long ago it sounds like the police might need your help. I've worked with a couple of cops, got friendly with them when I was doing research for a book, and I know sometimes the least little bit of info can turn a case around. Make it go from cold to solved."

"I talked to a cop earlier tonight. Which was why I was pissed off before I went into the bookstore. Keile and her friend Dani know her. Didn't matter. She didn't believe me. You could tell she thought I was making it up. And how can I really get mad since I think that too on some level? Part of me thinks I'm losing my mind. That I'm going crazy." The relief that came from telling someone was almost overwhelming. "Aren't you glad you called me now?"

"Actually, I am. For a going-crazy person you're a great date. Believe me when I tell you not all crazy people make good dates. Or so I've heard," Renny added with a wink. "But seriously have you thought the little girl is reaching out to you? You've seen her twice now. Maybe—"

"Except it wasn't the same girl. There are two others. This would make number three."

"Three?" She picked up the spoon and twined it through her fingers. "Three girls? And nobody knows anything? Do you think they're connected?"

"Maybe. Probably not," Summer admitted frowning. "There was an almost ten-year gap between two of them. I guess the third one could fit in between. And I didn't connect with the one that went missing ten years ago, but I get the sense the first one and the last one were taken by the same man. The way he was thinking I could tell he'd used the puppy trick before."

Renny took out her notebook and jotted something down. "What about the second one, who's really probably the third one? How did you find out about her? Any connection to you?"

"Through Keile. When I told her about the first girl she thought I was talking about the one from ten years ago. Ashley. Her name's Ashley."

"The one who went missing when you were in college?"

Summer nodded and took a sip of Coke to wet her dry throat. Even talking about this situation with someone who seemed to believe her was nerve-racking.

"What about the girls? Do they have anything in common? Could they be related somehow?"

"They're all blondes with blue eyes. I don't think anyone's tried to connect the two girls. From what Dani said it seemed like not many cops knew about Brandy, the first girl. Seneca didn't have its own police force back then. The County Sheriff would have been responsible for looking into the crime and the file on her seems to be missing."

"Which means the information you have is like gold. You have to go back to the police, Summer. Talk to a different person."

"And tell them what? I didn't see what kind of vehicle he was driving this time, and I couldn't swear it was the same guy. This last one was older, I think. No, I'm sure he was older."

"And again, you know more than they do. A good cop could take you through it, help you remember more than you thought you saw."

"You don't understand. Officer Hanson took me through it more times than I want to think about. And afterward she still didn't buy it. Looked at me like I was worse than crazy. Like, I don't know, that I was making it up for attention or something. Face it, Renny, those guys are long gone. Maybe dead."

"Doesn't stop the parents from wondering what happened to their little girls."

"You think I don't feel for them? Don't long for justice for those poor girls? I do. Sit through a sneering session and then come talk to me."

"Been there, done that," Renny said, picking at the scraps on her plate and then looking up at Summer apologetically. "Sorry. That sounded trite and I'm not trying to be. I was out partying, which meant I was drunk and high, when this guy grabs me. He's pulling on my clothes and I'm screaming, not so fucked up that I didn't know he was going to rape me. I was lucky some guy was sober enough to answer my cry. Full of righteous indignation, I go and fill out a report. Due to my reputation the cop didn't believe me. Thought I was asking for it."

"That's not fair. Even if you were drunk or high, he had no right to violate you."

"You know that and I know that, but the cop didn't think of it that way. At first I slunk home, telling myself maybe I did deserve it. Well, I got over that and went back and found someone who was willing to give me the benefit of a doubt. I gave them a description and they talked to some people at the party and were able to catch him. Turned out his DNA matched samples from a couple of open cases. He preyed on women who were drunk or otherwise incapacitated."

"Okay, so you do know what I'm talking about. Maybe I could pass the information on to Dani. She did follow up and find the first girl even when she didn't believe me."

"Which means she'll believe you when you tell her about the latest girl. I don't know Dani very well, but I bet she could find a cop who'll listen to her." Renny put a hand to her forehead. "I'm so slow. Officer Hanson. Carla Hanson?"

"You know her?"

"Let's say she went out of her way to let her interest be known last time I was at Eddie's. I wasn't impressed. Too pushy for my liking."

Somehow that made Summer feel better. "I can see that. What's Eddie's?"

"It's like a restaurant and club with a big room for live music. Keile and Haydn hooked me up with the lesbian band that plays there about once a month. I'll take you next time they come. Fair warning. Their shows are addicting."

"I'll take my chances." Summer sipped her Coke, happy that Renny was talking about a next time.

CHAPTER THIRTEEN

A scream, her own, interrupted Summer's sleep. She clutched at her pounding heart and blinked rapidly, wanting desperately to clear her head of the three little girls crying out for help, for justice. Justice she didn't think she could give them.

"Shit!" Summer threw back the covers and shivered as the morning chill brushed her sweaty skin. A hard workout was what she needed. A fast run would blow her head clear. Maybe then she could buy one rational thought. Could figure out why the girls were haunting her. Because if she didn't, she was very much afraid they would never go away. Never give her any peace. Afraid that she would always see three pairs of blue eyes looking at her beseechingly.

An hour and a half later, a good stretch and a hot shower decreased the level of complaints from the well-used muscles in her calves and thighs. Cream of Wheat and two bananas took care of the rumblings in her stomach.

Her mind clearer, she booted up her laptop and wrote up all she remembered from the head hop the evening before. If the guy thought he looked like a grandfather, he had to be older than the guy in the park. There had to be two abductors, she decided. But no. What if the crimes occurred at different time periods? Then it could be the same guy, only older.

"No. That doesn't make any sense."

Tapping her thumb on her laptop, she tried to come up with reasons for the time lag between abductions. The first thought that sprang to her mind chilled her blood. He was keeping the girls until they outlived their usefulness. When they got too old, he got rid of them, then went hunting for a replacement. A younger replacement.

Summer swallowed hard and forced herself to continue the thread. If he did keep them for years, he would need someplace private. A place where the houses were farther apart so a neighbor wouldn't be able to hear a child's screams or cries for help. But wouldn't it be smarter to live outside of town altogether? A country place like her parents' home—where the house next door was five acres away?

Figuring that out was all very good, but she didn't know the first thing about researching something like this. She couldn't exactly hop on her bike and ride around looking for a pervert's hideout, and the police weren't going to be any help. They didn't believe her story about the missing girl. Why should they listen to her theory about the abductor?

"Dani!" Dani was a private investigator. She worked for money and Summer had plenty of that. It would be the perfect solution to her problems to hire Dani to investigate the abductions. Dani could try to find a link between the girls, try to find a place where they could have been kept. But the first task would be to identify who the third girl was and figure out when she'd gone missing.

A glance at the clock on the screen convinced her it was too early to call Dani. But it wasn't too early to go into the office. Get in early, leave early and drop by the bookstore and see if she could get more info to pass along. Maybe go by the parking lot at the park and see if there were any vibes left. Brandy had been afraid there. Terrified the moment she realized the man wasn't who he seemed.

Summer shook her head. She needed to be focused. The more information she gathered, the quicker the case would be solved. Then she could go back to trying to reclaim "normal." A normal that did not include dropping in on other people's thoughts.

She pushed her bike out of the condo, locked the door and wheeled down the carpeted hallway. It wasn't yet seven, so she had the place to herself. In the silence she wondered about the girls, how they were picked. There had to be something more than just their blonde hair and blue eyes. Did he hang around places where little girls would be, looking for the daring ones? The ones who might go off on their own? And if he did, why didn't anyone notice him? Twenty years ago Seneca had been a small town. Strange men would have stood out.

"Hey, you're leaving early."

Summer gave a start and whirled around, taken completely off guard. Heat suffused her cheeks as she recognized the twenty-something guy who'd managed to walk up to the elevator without her noticing. He lived down the hall and had helped carry some boxes when she moved in. She'd gotten the sense he and his roommate partied a lot.

He raised his hands. "Sorry, dude. Didn't realize you didn't hear me walk up."

"My fault. Lots on my mind this morning." She wondered how long she'd been standing in front of the elevator without pressing the Down button. She pushed it now.

"I hear you. Gotta get in early so I can take some time off. Don't want them busting my balls for slacking, man."

"I hear you." She managed a smile and tried to remember his name.

"So, like, how you liking it here so far?" His accent was a mixture of the south and surfer boy.

"I like it. Good location." She pushed the Down button again.

"Dude, so true. I mean you can, like, walk around the corner, get shit-faced, then crawl back home. What's not to like about that?" He grinned.

To Summer's relief the elevator doors opened with little sound, making a reply unnecessary.

"Nice bike you got there," he said, once they were on their way down. "Prefer a motorcycle myself. Doesn't seem to hinder you from, like, getting around. I see you riding to work most days. In nasty weather too. You some kind of Amazon or something?"

She couldn't stop the laugh that bubbled up past the tightness in her belly. Her? An Amazon? "Far from it. I have the right gear, so it's not that bad."

"Be extra careful out there today." He gave her a once-over. "I know you're not a little girl, but still. Heard on the news that one turned up missing."

"What?" she said around the lump in the throat. "A girl? In Seneca?"

"Can you believe it?" He seemed almost excited. "See, her grandmother didn't notice right away. She got sick and had to go to the hospital. Nobody knew anything about the little girl being missing until last night when the grandmother was well enough to ask about her. Just before I left they said they were going to be talking to some dude who claims he saw her talking to an old guy Friday afternoon." He smirked. "He probably just wants his fifteen minutes of fame. I guess you don't watch the news. Don't blame you, man. Most of it's the same crapola over and over again."

"What did the girl look like?" she asked, though she didn't really want to know.

"Dude, it was kind of freaky 'cause she reminded me of my sister's youngest. Blond hair and big blue eyes," he said, patting his own blonde hair. "Not that it could be 'cause, hey, she's in Florida right now. Hey, what's wrong? You don't look so good. I didn't mean to scare you. I don't really think you have to worry about, you know, being snatched."

It can't be, she thought, tightening her grip on the bicycle handles. *It can't be. Please don't let it be.*

"Hey. Maybe you shouldn't, like, go in today. Stay home and chill."

She took a deep, steadying breath. "You're probably right. I thought I was better."

"Yeah," he said nodding. "You need anything later, just you know, give us a knock. Me and Jake'll just be hanging close tonight. Basketball."

It came to her. *Jay. His name is Jay.* "I appreciate the offer, Jay."

"Any time, Summer." He gave her a wave and stepped out when the doors opened to the bottom floor.

She pushed the button for her floor, then held the Close Door button until the doors shut. Only then did she give in to the trembling and allow herself to lean heavily against the wall. It couldn't be the same girl. There were plenty of girls with blonde hair and blue eyes. She'd go upstairs and turn on the TV. Then she'd see there was nothing to be concerned about. She'd see the girl was not the same one. But as the elevator ascended, her gut told her differently.

Her cell was ringing when she opened the door to her condo. Somehow she'd forgotten to put it in her bag. She propped her bike against the sofa and was able to answer the phone despite tripping over the ottoman. "Summer."

"Have you seen the news?" Renny demanded.

"No, but my neighbor told me about a missing girl. I was coming back upstairs to see if it's her." She crossed to the coffee table and used the remote to turn on the TV.

"Do you think it could be?"

"Oh my God, oh my God, oh my God." The wide screen was filled with the last school photo of Georgia Zackery. Her hair was neater and her smile brighter, but… Summer dropped onto the sofa and stared in disbelief.

"Summer? Summer, are you okay?"

"No. Really not. It's her, Renny. It's her."

"Are you sure? Take a deep breath or something and look again."

"I wish I wasn't." She closed her eyes. "I can't handle this. I swear I can't. She's going to look at me and think I did it." Fear and panic sharpened her voice.

"The grandmother?"

"Hanson. If you could have seen the way she was looking at me. If I go in, she'll throw me into a cell no questions asked. I knew I should have kept my big mouth shut. I should never have talked to the cops."

"She won't," Renny said firmly. "I promise I won't let her. We'll talk to someone else. I can be at your place in thirty. We'll go together."

"We will? Why would you do that?" she had to ask, though the thought of having someone with her, having Renny with her, brought a dizzying wave of relief.

"Friends don't let hysterical friends talk to the police alone. By yourself you'll be like one of those characters in a book who start confessing the minute the cops give them the hard-eyed look. With me there you might still confess, but I'd be able to take notes, maybe use it in a future story."

Summer's laugh bordered on hysteria. "Only if my name appears on the dedication page."

"What? Acknowledgment's not good enough for you?"

"If I'm going to be somebody's bitch in jail, I'll need that for clout."

"Deal. Probably give me some clout too. I mean, how many authors dedicate their books to hardened criminals?"

"Criminal, yes. Hardened, not so much. Misunderstood."

Renny gave a shout of laughter. "Have I talked you down yet?"

"Yes." Summer exhaled and discovered she could take a deep breath again. "Undying gratitude and all."

"In that case, expect me in forty. I know just the outfit to wear in case we get stuck with Carla."

"Is that...?" She ended the call after getting a dial tone. "I'm not guilty," she told herself, but somehow it had been easier to believe when Renny said it. Too nervous to sit, she jumped up and paced around the living room.

She hadn't done anything wrong. She was doing the police a favor. Surely they would see that? Would see that she wasn't a criminal? *Oh God, please let them see that.*

Summer hurried to the bathroom and studied her reflection in the full-length mirror. "You're not guilty," she told her reflection and finger combed her hair. The blue sweater she was wearing—the one that brought out the thin blue stripes in her slacks—worked for an innocent woman, she thought. The guilty wore white to throw off the police. A nervous laugh bubbled up. What did she know about clothes? What did she know about guilt, about killers, about any of this? But she did know something about a predator who was probably also a killer.

Panic danced up her spine and along the back of her neck. She'd been in the head of a killer. A killer who was still alive and who'd been in the bookstore less than half a mile from her condo. She barely made it to the toilet before breakfast spewed from her mouth. When the dry heaves waned, she lay down on the cold tile floor and wept.

It was unfair she had to deal with this on top of all her problems. The accident, the coma, the rehab, the not knowing who she was. All of which should have been enough to pay for whatever cosmic debt she owed. But no, she had to have psychic powers added to the mix.

There are three little girls who didn't have it so fair either, a tiny voice reminded her. She sat up and rubbed her face with her hands, then grabbed toilet paper and blew her nose. Her situation wasn't the best, but she knew where she was. She wasn't going to wake up to some old man doing things to her she didn't understand. She didn't have to worry she might never see her family again.

"So get a grip. You're still alive. You don't have it so bad." The last thing she wanted was to go to the police station with her emotions out of control. The visions occurred when she was upset. She wasn't ready to learn anyone else's deep, dark horror this morning.

When Renny rang the doorbell thirty minutes later, Summer thought she had her emotions wrapped up tight. Lust slipped past her grasp, though, provoked by the sexy beauty before her. Renny had gone for a thigh-length dress that followed her curves and displayed a generous amount of cleavage. "Wow," Summer whispered, surprising herself. She hadn't thought she could speak.

Renny's smile lit up her face. She slipped off her coat and did a quick turnaround. "I take it you like the dress?"

"'Like' is too weak. Much too weak. I know Carla won't be able to think because I can't either."

Renny dropped a kiss on her cheek. "You're so sweet."

Her senses swirling with the scent of Renny's perfume, Summer didn't say that sweet had nothing to do with it. But she thought it.

"Can I come in?"

"Uh, yeah. Yeah." She managed to back up without tripping over her tongue. "You didn't have to come, but I sure am glad you did."

"You don't have to go, but I sure am glad you are. That makes us even."

"Still, thanks." She took a deep breath. "I think I'm ready. Do you think we should call?"

"Their phones are ringing off the hook. We have a better chance of talking to a person if we go down there."

Summer's cell buzzed as they made their way to the elevator. "Yeah. On my way now…Thanks, but Renny's going with me… Sure." She slipped the phone back into her pocket. "That was Keile. She caught the news too."

"Who else did you tell about the other girl?"

"Just Dani and Carla. And Haydn."

"Good. You're going to want to insist the police leave your name out of any report before you give them anything. You don't want every kook calling you for psychic readings."

Summer pressed a hand against her stomach as the elevator descended.

"You look like you're going to the chair."

She gave Renny a wan smile. "I feel like I'm going to the chair without having had my last meal. What if they don't believe me? What if they think I'm some kind of copycat snatcher?"

Renny rolled her eyes. "I thought we settled that. What's your motivation?"

"I'm crazy, remember? Crazy people don't need motivation."

"They do. It's usually twisted and as crazy as they are, but they do have one. Where's your puppy? Where's your accomplice? You don't even drive. Did you transport that girl on the back of your bike?"

"I've been in his head. What if he's making me do it?"

"When's the last time you had a blackout?"

"A what?" Summer waited for Renny to exit the elevator before she followed suit. She was amazed they'd had the elevator to themselves considering the number of residents in the lobby. The morning rush was on in earnest.

Renny grabbed her hand as they followed the throng of people outside. "I'm up a block," she said, turning right.

Summer looked down at Renny's mile-high heels. "I didn't think. I should have let you into the garage."

"Do I look weak? A block won't kill me. So, when was the last time you woke up to find you'd lost, say, three or more hours? And I don't mean in the morning."

"The coma."

"If you kidnapped that girl because the bad guy took over your mind you'd have this gap in your memory. Unaccounted for time. You don't, so you didn't do it." She unlocked the door to her maroon BMW convertible. "I hope this isn't too small for you to ride in?"

Summer shook her head. "Riding's fine."

"Good. Seat belt," Renny ordered before she zipped into traffic. "Now—tell me why you couldn't be the kidnapper."

Summer spouted back Renny's words to her as they moved through morning rush hour traffic. The police station was on the outskirts of town, moved there two years ago to be near the new jail. A couple of bail bond establishments had popped up, but otherwise the area was underdeveloped.

Renny pulled into a visitor's parking space and turned off the ignition. "Before we go in, there's something I want you to remember." She turned to face Summer. "You're here voluntarily and you're here to help *them*. They owe you, you don't owe them."

"Yeah," Summer bobbed her head. "Okay. Gotcha." But it was still hard to open the door. Hard to think of walking into the station, enduring the stares, then the sneers once she told her story. The whispers that would spread around as she became known as the crazy woman who claimed to have seen a child abducted. She jumped when Renny's hand landed on her knee.

"You have to get out to go in, Summer."

"Yeah. Right." She zipped up to ten by ten, then opened the door and made herself get out. If she expected the walk to the front door to be easier, she was wrong. The sidewalk seemed to lengthen until the door looked miles away. "Courage," she mumbled. There was a little girl out there who was more scared than she was, she reminded herself. If anything she said helped the police find the girl sooner, then she'd bear the embarrassment. Suddenly the distance to the door shortened.

Renny reached for Summer's hand and interlaced their fingers. "Here to help them, remember?"

"If I forget, promise to remind me."

"You don't even have to ask."

"Help you?" The Hispanic cop leaning against the receptionist's desk straightened. He didn't look old enough to shave.

"Is Officer Hanson available?" Renny asked, unbuttoning her coat and flashing him a big smile.

"Uh, she's, uh, out in the field," he stammered, blushing. "I can help you." He cleared his throat. "What's this about?"

"I hate to be a bother, but is there anyone...else we could speak with? It's a complicated situation." Renny put her hands on his desk and leaned forward, giving him an unrestricted view of her cleavage.

Summer was surprised she could feel amusement. But she did catching the look of wonderment that took over the young cop's face. She figured Renny had shown him a glimpse of his Valhalla. "That was mean," she said once he'd bounded away. "You're lucky he didn't pass out."

"He did turn an interesting shade of red. He's greener than grass. Wouldn't be surprised if this was his first day on the job."

The young cop, his blush still visible, returned with an older man. The other cop was wearing street clothes, which said to Summer he was higher up. The look he sent them had her going through the multiplication table and still her heart raced. She could tell he wasn't going to as much as sample a word she said, let along buy. Not from the top of his comb-over to the belly that strained against the less than crisp white shirt, to the blue slacks and scuffed black shoes.

"This is Detective Kohner with CIU," the young cop said.

"I'm Renny Jamison and this is Summer Baxby. Is there somewhere we can go that's more private?"

Detective Kohner crossed his arms, resting them on the bulk of his protruding middle. "What's this about? We're real busy around here."

"We—Summer, that is—may have some information about the missing girl."

Summer could almost feel his gaze pierce her flesh. In her mind she could see blue rays shooting out of his dark eyes, striking her down.

"May?" he said, throwing back his shoulders. "Either you do or you don't. I don't have time to play games with you. That little girl doesn't have time for me to play games with you."

"This is not a game." Renny matched his terse tone. "Now is there somewhere we can sit down and discuss this? If not, then I'm sorry we wasted your precious time."

He gave her a look as if taking her measure, then jerked his head toward a small conference room. It was made smaller by the big round table and six chairs it contained.

As Summer followed Kohner and Renny into the room, both of them stiff with self-righteous indignation, she worried she and the young cop would get taken down in the cross fire.

"Maybe now you can share what you may or may not know," Detective Kohner said as he pulled out a chair and motioned for them to sit.

Summer swallowed hard. "I have these what you might call visions. I saw the little girl in a vision. I saw Georgia Zackery."

"What are you, like, psychic?" he asked and leaned back to prop his feet on another chair. "I guess it's too much to ask what I'm thinking now, huh?" He smiled. "When did you have this," he made quotation marks in the air, "vision?"

"Yesterday evening. Right before eight." Summer wondered why she'd been worried she'd be found guilty. How could she be, when Kohner was having a good time not believing her?

"Tell me about these, uh, what do you call them? Yeah, visions. Do you have to be in a trance?"

"No. I was in the bookstore on Second and Auburn, looking for books on local history when it happened. She was walking down the sidewalk and saw a puppy. The man said—"

"What man? I thought you said you saw the girl."

"I didn't see the man. It was more like I could see what he was seeing."

"So you really can't tell me anything about this pervert, can you?"

Renny squeezed her knee and the panic subsided. "He was older and white. He had his own vehicle."

"Along with everybody else in this city." He frowned and looked at his watch. "Go on."

"He told her he needed to give the puppy away because he had two dogs already. She told him her granny said they couldn't afford one."

"Are you trying to say her granny was there too?"

"Why don't you let her finish?" Renny said heatedly.

"Because he doesn't believe a word I'm saying," Summer said quietly.

"Didn't say that," Kohner said. "How many of these *visions* have you had?"

"Uh, three. There were three others." Summer looked away from his gaze, feeling naked, exposed.

His smile bordered on a smirk. "You see any other kidnappings we should know about? Preferably ones where you *actually* caught a glimpse of the perp."

"Like you give a damn!" Renny pushed back her chair, braced her arms on the table and glared at the detective. "I convinced Summer to come forward thinking you people would be happy to have more information. Obviously she knew you better. Thanks for nothing."

Summer had to scramble to keep up as Renny stormed out.

"You were right." Renny pulled on her coat and removed her keys from her pocket. "Asshole. Detective Asshole." She blew out a sharp breath. "I'm sorry I dragged you down here for nothing. God, can you believe him? He didn't bother to write down a damn thing. Didn't have the goddamn courtesy to pretend he believed you enough to hear the whole story."

Summer listened with one ear to Renny's rant. A headache was trying to creep up the back of her skull. Georgia had been gone for three days. Summer wondered if she'd given up hope of being rescued by now. "I should get to work. Make this day count for something."

"Again, I'm really sorry. You want to be dropped at home or work?"

"Work," she said quickly, knowing if she went to the condo she might never leave. At work she'd have something to do. Something to take her mind off this nightmare she was trapped in. "Thanks for standing up for me. For believing me. For dragging me down here. I know he didn't hear a word I said, but I said them. One day I think that's going to make me feel better about myself."

"I wish that day was today." Renny slid behind the steering wheel, put the key in the ignition, then hesitated. "Hey. I have this crazy idea. Not sure you'll like it."

"I'm crazy, remember?"

Renny gave her a ghost of a smile. "I think we should go back to the bookstore and try to find the book you touched. Maybe with me there to, I don't know, anchor you, you could see more."

Summer's mind stuttered at the thought of actively seeking a mind hop. She looked at her hands, surprised to see they were clenched into fists as if readying for an assault. When she'd had the same idea earlier, she hadn't known the old guy was alive. Hadn't known he was so close and still hunting. Could she do it? Could she willingly open herself up to the ugliness?

The school photo of Georgia Zackery flashed behind her eyes. She couldn't be any kind of decent person if she didn't try with everything she had to connect with that little girl, to find her. Hadn't she felt frustration at not being able to do anything for Brandy? This was her chance to perhaps balance the scales. "Six work for you?"

"Perfect." Renny rubbed Summer's arm, exhaled, then zoomed out of the parking lot. "Maybe grab a nice low-fat salad afterward?"

Summer's smile was shaky around the edges. "On the condition you promise you'll write Detective Kohner into one of your books. And not in a good way."

Renny's grin was almost feral. "Already ahead of you. He'll be the first victim of a cop-killing psycho. He won't go easy or fast."

"Is it mean to want Carla to go next?"

"'Mean' can be your friend." Renny came to a stop at a red light and patted Summer's thigh. "Working together we'll find more information. Then we'll go back to the cop shop and show them our mean. Blow their asses out of the water with our mean until we find someone to listen to you."

Summer raced through five times five as the beating of her heart echoed the beating in her head. Her idea of mean was... She didn't know what her idea of mean was. Not really. What she did know was it probably wouldn't blow out anybody's ass. If there was a goddess, her job would be to stand behind Renny and try to look mean. With practice it could be done. She flipped down the visor and began practicing.

Renny gave her a quick glance. "What are you doing?"

"I, you know..." She shrugged. "I'm practicing my mean."

"Oh," Renny said slowly. She made a left and pulled up in front of Summer's office building. "Uh, let's not quit the day job, okay?"

"You just wait, *okay*? I'll blow your ass out of the water when I'm done." She opened the door, repressing a smile in response to the amusement Renny was doing an awful job of disguising. "Bookstore at six. Prepare to be impressed."

CHAPTER FOURTEEN

Inside the office building Summer looked at the bank of elevators, then headed for the stairs. No more elevator conversations for her today. Maybe she should take Stu up on his offer to build her some muscles. Then she wouldn't need to use an elevator ever again.

She considered it bad luck when she spotted Marcia standing next to Fiona's desk. Judging by Marcia's expression, the feeling was mutual.

"You okay?" Fiona asked, her eyes wide with concern. "You sounded real shaky on the message."

"Yeah, uh. I had a, uh, a thing come up. It was important."

"A 'thing'?" Marcia questioned, her eyebrows raised. "You're late for work because of a 'thing'? You'll have to do better than that."

"I'm taking the time, so back off." She stifled the urge to show her mean. "You're no longer the boss of me." The expression on Marcia's face was priceless. Taking the high road, Summer waited until she was in her office to give in to laughter.

"Someone's in a good mood." Liz stuck her head around the doorjamb.

"Only a little. Just got one in on M&M."

"That'll do it." Liz plopped her butt on Summer's desk. "I could say I stopped by to see if you need any clarification on the work I left in your in-box, but I won't. Are you okay? Fiona forwarded your message and you sounded kind of...No, you sounded distraught. You're not having any repercussions from the head trauma, are you?"

"In a way. Short version. I thought I might have some information for the police about an ongoing case. After talking to them, turns out they don't think I do."

"Am I correct in assuming you're not ready to give me the long version?"

She nodded. "Maybe some time when it's not so fresh." *When I know I'll stay in control*, she thought, shying away from the concern in Liz's eyes. Concern that could be her undoing.

"Good enough. My door's open if you need or want to talk. Whatever you say stays between us."

"Thanks. Don't complain when I take you up on that offer."

Liz winked. "I'm made of sterner stuff. If at some point you feel you need to get out of here, do it. Work will get done."

"I need the work, the focus."

That proved to be true—Summer was able to work steadily until one, when hunger struck. The early March sun was weak at best, still the need to be away from her desk, to move, got her up and out. She walked the crowded sidewalks, passing restaurant after restaurant without being able to decide where to stop. Without thought, she found herself in front of the bookstore.

Her heart hammered as she wondered if the kidnapper could be in there now, browsing through books and looking normal. After a moment's hesitation, she opened the door and stepped inside. The clerk behind the desk was unfamiliar, but she smiled a welcome.

Feeling foolish, Summer walked the few aisles, scanning the patrons while maintaining a safe distance from the local section. More relieved than disappointed when none of them matched the limited description she carried in her head, she browsed through the fiction section until she spotted a book she'd enjoyed before. She made small talk with the clerk while buying it, then clutching it to her chest, she retraced her steps back to the office. She couldn't say why, but some part of her felt the book was a protective shield. Maybe it was because the author was Renny Jamison.

* * *

At four thirty Renny wrapped up another excellent writing session. She stretched her back, pleased with her progress and her ability to put the events of the morning on the back burner. If her readers didn't like her new offering, it wouldn't be due to lack of effort on her part.

A grumble at her feet drew her attention. "I hear you. I'll bet you're ready for a walk?" She got her face bathed by a frisky Chazz.

Once she extracted herself, she sent him for his leash and took herself to the bedroom. Chazz sat, leash in mouth, staring at the front door when she returned. "Come on. I didn't take that long." His bark seemed to say otherwise. "Whatever."

The walk to the park was brisk, fueled by Chazz's impatience. He stopped to water a couple of bushes, but mostly kept to the path leading to the park. The sounds of other dogs reached them before they arrived and Renny had to tighten her hold on his leash to keep from being dragged.

"You'd think there was free food," she muttered, slightly winded. "No picking up smaller dogs, Chazz," she admonished, unclipping his leash. She took his quiet "woof" as agreement and gave him a two-handed rub. "That's my sweet baby. Go play."

"Sounds like someone's besotted with their newest family member."

Renny turned to see Keile and Can entering the gate. "You're here early and without the kids. How'd you manage that?"

"The rest of the family got sucked in by the swings. I came over hoping to run into you."

"What's up?"

"Shouldn't I be asking that question? How did it go with the police this morning?"

"Oh, that." She blew out a sharp breath, having managed to put it aside until now. "Disaster's the appropriate word. The detective we spoke to was such an ass. He didn't bother to hide the fact he thought Summer was full of shit. There's a girl missing, for God's sake. I thought they'd at least hear her out. Try to check out her version of events. But no, that asswipe sat there smirking, interrupting her with stupid questions. Not only was it a waste of time, but it made Summer feel worse than she already felt."

"And you."

"Pissed me off. I was the one who convinced her they would listen."

"What about Carla? You try to talk to her?"

"Wasn't there." Renny grimaced. "And I was sporting plenty of cleavage for the occasion."

Keile laughed. "You thought your girls would sway her?"

"By any means necessary. Come on, it's not like she wasn't all over me that last time at Eddie's. I figured the girls might be enough to persuade her to listen to what Summer had to say. Maybe do some follow-up."

"Hail to the power of the bust."

"More like it *was* a bust. That fat-ass detective must have been gay. He didn't even give them a good look. Didn't trip over himself trying to do my bidding like the young cop we first talked to."

"The bastard."

"Damn straight. If you could have seen him sitting there like a big blob, judging her. Ugh." She shook her head. "He was everything she thought he would be."

Keile stroked her arm. "Not your fault. What's next?"

"We're supposed to go back to the bookstore. See if Summer can get more…I guess you'd call it information. But now I'm not so sure that's the right thing to do. What do you think?"

"Bookstore? What does that have to do with anything?"

"You know. Where she saw the girl, felt the guy."

Keile scratched her forehead. "What exactly are you talking about? I thought it was the swings. In fact, I know it was the swings because it brought back memories of pushing Kyle on the swings and falling a bit in like."

"I'm talking about the girl that's missing now, not the one from twenty years ago. I thought if she touched the book again she might get more information about the bad guy."

"You mean she saw the girl that's missing now?"

Renny leaned back. She didn't think she'd ever heard Keile's voice as high as it was now. "Well, yeah. I thought that's why you called this morning."

"No. I knew she'd seen the other girl from before and thought she could help in some kind of way. Wait." Keile ran her fingers through her hair. "You're telling me she saw the girl who went missing Friday and the cops still blew her off?"

"Exactly! That's why I'm so pissed. That's why I practically insisted Summer go talk to the police in the first place."

"Okay. Start from the beginning."

Renny laid it out, from the meeting with Dani and Carla, to the vision at the bookstore, to convincing Summer to go back to the cops over dinner.

"Dinner, huh? You making a move that way, Renny?"

"I don't know. Maybe." She thought about how her heart had done a little flip when she'd looked up and seen Summer watching her and how angry she'd been at Kohner on Summer's behalf. "Yes. But as you know, it's…complicated," she said, falling back on Summer's terminology. "She told me about the accident and the memory loss. I can see for myself that she's very unsure of herself, quick to think she's not quite right. In spite of that, or maybe because of that, I think she's fun, interesting. And, well, you've seen her, she's gorgeous, with those big blue-gray eyes and shy smile."

"I guess you do understand about losing a part of yourself. Just be careful. She's fragile."

"I know. Don't worry, Mama Bear, I'm going to take it slow for Summer, for me. I've fucked up plenty of relationships in the past. I don't want this to be one of them. So yeah, I'm proceeding with caution."

"Good. That's good. Sorry, didn't mean to give you the full-court press."

"That's okay." Renny put a hand on Keile's shoulder. "I wouldn't like you nearly as much if you weren't worried about her. I'm worried about her too. Which is why I'm having second thoughts about exposing her to this guy again. What if she connects and it's too much for her?"

"What if it isn't? Did she agree to do it?"

"Well, yeah, but only after I suggested it."

"She probably would have eventually thought of doing the same thing. This way she has you there to catch her if she falls."

"Maybe. Or maybe we don't go and she doesn't have anything to make her fall."

"Summer won't do nothing. She told me about the other girl, made it through a grilling with Dani, then Carla and then she *still* went with you to the police. She obviously feels the need to help. She may not remember, but the Summer I knew was always the first to reach out with whatever was needed. Said she'd learned it from her parents. I doubt not remembering changed that."

Renny exhaled slowly. "That makes me feel better. Much better."

"Feel free to call if for some reason things go south."

"Done." Renny whistled for Chazz. "I'll call you either way. I know you'll be worried."

CHAPTER FIFTEEN

"How do you want to do this?" Renny asked. They were standing in front of the bookstore, observing the last remnants of rush hour traffic streaming by.

"Maybe the first thing to do is go inside." Summer's smile wasn't bright, but it was a smile. She considered that a major achievement, considering what she was expected to do. "I wish I knew more about what triggered this head hopping deal. Usually I'm mad or upset when it happens. Not that I'm not really nervous right now. Just not sure that's enough."

"Only one way to find out. In our favor, the place is practically empty." Renny opened the door and motioned for Summer to enter. She smiled at the clerk, who gave her a long look, then glanced away.

"He's probably wondering if you're Renny Jamison," Summer whispered. "Maybe you should sign some books while you're here. They have yours in the local talent section."

"Maybe I will. After you quit stalling."

Summer grimaced. "That obvious, huh?"

"Not really. It's more that I'd be doing the same thing if I had to do what you're about to. We can put this off. Go grab something to eat first. Get you hyped up on caffeine."

"I couldn't eat a thing." Her stomach was empty and it was better it stayed that way until she knew how she'd react. She flew through the multiplication table to ten, took a deep breath and let it out slowly. "Let's do this."

"Wait." Renny took her hand and entwined their fingers.

The section was, of course, where it'd been yesterday. Maybe it was neater, with the books by author in alphabetical order. Summer ran a finger along the bindings, hoping it'd be enough to make contact. It wasn't. She had to let go of Renny's hand to pull the book off the shelf. "This is the one," she said unnecessarily. "I looked at it and thought the conclusion was all wrong. How the guy was most likely white because Brandy was white. And though stranger abductions get lots of attention, they're rare."

"What did you do then?" Renny prompted, putting a hand on Summer's shoulder.

"Let me think. I must have replaced it. No. That's not right. It fell on the floor afterward. I must have been holding it when it happened."

"Then maybe you should flip through the pages. Look at the ones you looked at before."

Summer complied, going so far as to run her fingers over each page. "I'm getting nothing."

"You're positive it's the same book?"

"Yes. See?" She pointed to the last paragraph on the page. "Here's where he's essentially saying the perp drove the hour it takes to get here from Atlanta to snatch the girl. What kind of sense does that make? What? There were no white girls in Atlanta at the time?" Summer looked up in disgust and—

she wasn't in the bookstore. Wasn't standing next to Renny. She was sitting at a table with a dusty, what-used-to-be white tablecloth, listening to a girl's screams and a puppy's howls.

"Damnit!" He hurled an empty beer can, clipping the puppy in the head. "Shut the hell up. Should have thrown you out the truck when I had the chance." He pushed back from the table, stood and wobbled before grabbing hold of the back of the chair. Damn girls always cried the first night. He'd give her that, then he'd teach her how to behave. He only hoped she learned faster than the last one.

He slowly made his way across the room, crowded with bits of old furniture, kicking aside empty beer cans when he needed to. Outside the girl's room he paused briefly and walked on without opening the locked door. He was tired. Too tired to deal with her tonight. But tomorrow. Tomorrow he'd start training her...

The pounding in her head was the first thing Summer noticed. The comfort of Renny's hand on her shoulder was the second. "He still has her and she's not his first. Oh God, Renny. She's not his first."

"Did you see him?" Renny gripped her arms.

She shook her head and immediately regretted it. "Wherever he lives is cluttered with furniture and Busch beer cans. He was sitting at a table that had a fake flower arrangement in the center. There was a dark wood china cabinet with chipped dishes. A stack of papers about knee high, no, two stacks to the right of the table. And none of this helps Georgia." She sighed. "They could be anywhere. Miles from here."

Renny rubbed her back. "It's more than we had before."

"He's going to start 'training' her tomorrow. Which could be today or yesterday or the day before. Oh, God." Summer dropped the book and covered her face with her hands. "She's not a girl anymore. He's probably already raped her and they won't listen to me. What can I do to make them listen to me?" She leaned into Renny, felt arms enfold her and gave in to the tears burning her eyes.

"Oh, Summer. Don't do this to yourself. Don't take on the blame for other people's actions." Tears welled in Renny's eyes. "I'm so sorry I asked you to do this. It's too much."

Summer took a shuddering breath. "Not your fault. It had to be done." She nestled her face in the crook of Renny's neck. "Thanks for being here. It's easier to take with you here."

"Where else would I be? You ready to go?"

"Yeah." She wiped her face, exhaled and dared to scan the store. As expected, she and Renny seemed to be the sole focus of attention. "I've embarrassed us enough."

"This is nothing." Renny dug around in her backpack, then handed Summer a tissue and removed one for herself. "Compared to some of the stunts I've pulled this isn't even a blip. The trick is to walk out with your head held high." She demonstrated, drawing a watery smile from Summer. They walked out of the bookstore, heads held high.

Summer's phone buzzed as soon as they hit the sidewalk. It was Dani. "Summer."

"How you holding up?"

"I've been better."

"I bet. Carla's looking for you."

"Carla wants to talk to me? Why?"

"Apparently your name came up at the station house. Carla got volunteered to feel you out, see what you might know."

"Why bother? They won't believe a word I say."

"She doesn't have much choice. This came from higher up."

"Great. Now she'll have resentment to add to disdain."

"Believe me, she'll do a better job of hiding it. So, can I give her your number?"

Reciting the multiplication table was so easy and Summer was up to five times five before she caught herself. "Would it just be Carla?"

"In the room. There could be others observing."

"It'd be like an interrogation?" Panic bit at her throat as her earlier fears returned. "I…" She looked at Renny, seeking comfort. Seeking reassurance.

Renny held out a hand for the phone. "This is Renny. What's this about seeing Carla?"

"The deputy chief got wind that Summer might have some info pertinent to the abduction. To say he wasn't very happy to hear Detective Kohner's report on his meeting with Summer is a big understatement. The department's feeling some pressure. They don't have a lead, the press has gotten word that there may be two earlier abductions linked to this latest one, so they need something. Plus the GBI, that's the Georgia Bureau of Investigation, is threatening to come take a look. Could be a big mess."

"And what? Summer's supposed to ride in on her white horse and save their sorry asses? She's done that twice and got shot down both times."

Dani snorted. "It's not that bad. The deputy chief is a good guy. I can vouch for him."

"If she agrees to this, they're not talking to her without me," Renny said firmly. "That's nonnegotiable. And we walk at the first snide remark."

"I don't have the authority to negotiate, but I'd be willing to give Vincent a call. Let him know the terms and let him be the one to get the word to Carla."

"And I assume this Vincent is the deputy chief?"

"That would be Vincent Chapman and, like I said, he's a good guy."

"Summer and I'll talk it over and get back with you."

"It'd be good if it could happen tonight."

"Don't push." Renny ended the call and returned the phone to Summer. "And that was totally heavy-handed. I'm sorry I completely took over. That was rude."

Summer slid the phone into her coat pocket. "That was more saving me than rude. I froze. I don't think I could have forced a word out of my mouth." She bumped Renny's shoulder. "Thanks for coming in on your white horse. That's the third time today."

"A record," Renny said and smiled. "I don't know about you, but I'm starving and a salad's not going to cut it."

"There's this place, Mac's. It's not that far and they have good burgers."

"Sounds like a plan. Promise you won't let me eat all the fries. They go straight to my butt."

Summer thought that was a good thing. She resisted the urge to look at said butt. "I can do that, and if you'll be there, I think I can talk to Carla too."

"It's entirely up to you," Renny said, pushing the Walk button. "If it was me, I'd do it. Maybe insist this Vincent guy is there. It's a chance to get in a dig at Carla. I image she's steamed at being commanded to talk to you."

"That sounds like a good reason *not* to talk to her." The Walk signal turned green and they crossed the six lanes of traffic.

"You're looking at this the wrong way. This is your chance to say whatever you want to say and she has to listen. Most importantly she has to do it without sneering. I, for one, would enjoy that."

Summer slowed down, pursed her lips in thought. "You may have something." She pulled open the door to Mac's and the smell of burgers ramped up her appetite. "Can I use my mean face?"

"Meat," Renny moaned. "This smells heavenly. Pardon my drool."

Summer smiled. Whatever happened with the police would happen. And maybe that was okay. "Still want me to police your fries?"

"Why don't we forget about police and abductors for now? I feel I need to focus my thoughts on burgers."

"Agreed." She nodded when the hostess asked if there were two for dinner. The restaurant wasn't as busy as it had been at lunchtime, so they were shown to a booth.

The hostess placed a menu in front of them, saying, "Your server will be with you shortly."

"Any chance you want to share spinach artichoke dip?" Renny asked.

"I'm game."

"Hello, ladies. My name's Mark. I'll be taking care of you tonight. What can I get you to drink?" Mark was barely over five feet and that was with some heel on his boots. His hair was bleached blond and worn in a mullet.

Summer wondered if his neon green shirt was worn for safety reasons. "I'll have a Coke."

"Diet Coke for me," Renny said. "And we'll start with the spinach artichoke dip."

He smiled, showing white teeth. "Fabulous choice. I'll be right back with your drinks."

"Should we tell him the eighties called and wants its hairstyle back?" Renny joked. "You don't see that every day, and I for one am grateful."

"What's wrong with his hair?"

"It only went out of style when we were children. Some things are not meant to be repeated. Mullets fit firmly in that category. And big, puffy hair. Take my word on this." Renny closed her menu. "It occurs to me we've never talked about what you do. I know you and Keile work in the same building, but that's it."

"I'm a gofer more than anything. My boss is good friends with my dad, so when I decided it was time to get back to the real world, he offered me a job. Entry level to match my skill set."

"So what do you do?"

"Started out filing under a supervisor who hated my guts from Day One. We'll call her M&M to protect the guilty."

"Seems kind of harsh to name her after the candy. For the candy that is."

"She's the anti-M&M. Bitter. She has issues, but if Kevin's willing to overlook them, so am I. Besides, I don't work under her anymore. Not sure if she's relieved or upset about that." Summer smiled. "I'm hoping upset. Now I review reports and presentations, make comments on the graphics. Hoping to prod my dormant artistic skills."

Mark returned with their drinks. "The dip should be out shortly. You ready to order?" He took their orders, then hurried to a summons at a nearby table.

"What's this about artistic talent?" Renny took a sip of her soda.

"I used to paint. Mostly portraits. Lost the ability when my brain was wiped clean," she added the information matter-of-factly and was proud of it.

"Confession time. I know very little about art."

"That makes two of us." Summer removed her straw from its wrapper and dunked it in her drink. "I don't think I'm an art snob. Hope I never was. Speaking of artistic talent, tell me about your book. How's it coming?"

"Great. I should be finished with the first draft in a couple of weeks."

"I hope I haven't been keeping you from it with all of this? I didn't think."

"Don't worry about it." Renny waved a hand. "I had plenty of time to write today. Plenty of words leaping from my brain so fast I had to struggle to type fast enough to keep up."

"Is that usual for you?"

"Not like this. I usually have a couple of days where it flows smoothly, but more days where I poke and prod along. Maybe get through a scene, then step back to figure out where to go next. Not this puppy. It's been off the leash. I think I needed to write about it. The abuse, the partying, all to cover the feelings of failure. I see it so clearly now. Like writing it out helps put it away. I'll always be an addict. No getting around that."

"Aren't you afraid readers will see the main character as you?"

Renny shrugged. "I can live with the comparisons that are sure to be made."

"Then I can't wait to read the book and come up with some comparisons of my own."

"Cheers." Renny lifted her glass and tapped it against Summer's. "Another reason the interruption doesn't bother me is that I get the pleasure of enjoying your company."

Summer's cheeks warmed with her own pleasure. "Is your agent still giving you grief?"

"Not after I told her she'd have something solid to look at in a month. She won't say, but I'd bet she's accepted I need to spread my literary wings. And my past success should catch me if I stumble."

"Does that…?" She chewed on her lip, wondering if she was asking too much.

"Go on," Renny prompted. "I don't mind answering questions. At least not your questions."

"Are you…afraid you'll stumble?"

"I feel that way every time I start a new project. People can be fickle. I always wonder what will happen if they don't like it. What will I do with my life? That's my version of the tortured soul creative people are supposed to have. Is fear of stumbling holding *you* back?"

"Maybe a little. Last week I saw this little boy. Redhead with freckles for days and I wished so badly for pencil and paper." She rubbed her fingertips. "Haven't had the urge since. Later I did try to draw his face. Didn't work. I didn't feel it inside. So I guess that's my version of the tortured soul. My shrink thinks I'll get the urge back, but I wonder if it's possible anymore."

"I'm sorry you lost so much." Renny shook her head when Mark delivered the dip and asked if they needed anything else. She scooped out some dip and put it on a little plate. "'Sorry' has to be the sorriest word in the dictionary. You'd think by now someone would have come up with a better word because 'sorry' doesn't really cut it. Not in this situation. Not when you've lost something so vital."

Summer nibbled on a tortilla chip. "Appreciate the sentiment. But you know about starting over, right? I mean, after the rehab. That seems like it's a start-over to me."

"Only if you do it right. The first time I did it the wrong way. Did the same things I'd done before, and so, of course, I ended right back where I started."

"Why, uh, how did you start on drugs?"

"It started after the show began to lose viewers. Once the ratings fall, you know cancellation is around the corner. And it was. Then I hit puberty hard. Bad acne, weight gain, you name it, I had it. Couldn't buy a role. Or rather, my mother couldn't buy me a role. After a couple of years of frustration, I went wild." Renny played with the condensation on her glass. "First it was drinking, then drugs, then sex. I'm lucky in that regard. I had sex with boys, girls, strangers and all without thought of protecting myself or them." She shrugged. "That's what happens when you're high. You don't think, you don't care, you're invincible. And deep down I got off on the fact that the negative press really pissed Eve off. I went into rehab the first time because she made me. Threatened to withhold the funds."

"How old were you?"

"Just shy of eighteen. When I got out, I was clean for probably eight months. Then I learned to hide it better. I wasn't as wild, wasn't as public. Fooling Eve was such a rush it took me a few years to realize the only person I was fooling was myself. One day I wake up and I have no idea where I am, I mean none, how I got there or who the naked bodies surrounding me are. Scared me shitless, so I checked myself into rehab and with a lot of work, it took."

"Is that when you moved here?"

"That was five years ago. I stayed in LA because I felt like I had something to prove to all of those who'd written me off as a loser. I had to be clean and productive where the paparazzi could take note. Dumb. I should have come here sooner. Stayed with my grandmother and taken advantage of the opportunity to really get to know her. Or stayed with my father in Atlanta. He wanted me to come live with him after the first rehab stint. I didn't go because I was afraid he'd compare me with DeAmber. She's my half-sister and from all he'd told me, she was the perfect daughter."

"Look at the Borg. Perfection's overrated."

"*Star Trek*? You a fan?"

"My dad is. He's a sci-fi nut and, like I told you, we've watched a lot of movies together."

"That's right. His way of helping you after the coma."

"You remember that, huh?" Summer smiled, grabbed another chip.

"I remember everything you've told me," Renny said, her tone serious. "I hope I have the chance to learn more."

Summer felt her cheeks heat up and had to look away from the intensity of Renny's gaze, suddenly shy. "Well, yeah. Oh good. Here comes our food."

CHAPTER SIXTEEN

Summer looked up too late to avoid a collision with Rich. She was trying to enter the elevator and he was trying to leave. They held onto each other a brief moment, absorbing the shock. "Sorry," she said and took a step back. "I wasn't watching where I was going."

"My fault." Rich stepped back and punched the button to hold the door open. "I'm not getting off here. Got on a damn up elevator by mistake."

Against her better judgment, Summer entered. She saw the button for the lobby was lit and moved to the opposite corner, away from any possible contact with Rich. As pissed off as she was from another confrontation with Marcia, she was afraid of hopping into his head again.

"You getting out of here early?" Rich said.

"Outside appointment." She switched her bag to her other hand, wondering why the elevator was going so slow. They should have been to the ground floor by now.

"I got fired," Rich announced, seeming to need to tell someone. "Fucking unfair. I do the damn job better than anyone there. Should have been a manager by now. Bastards."

"Uh, sorry." She was tempted to press the lobby button again, but that would mean getting closer to Rich and the anger shimmering around him.

"Me too. Sorry I wasted my time with that lame-ass company. I can do better," he boasted, looking at Summer. "Go someplace better where they'll recognize my talent for what it is. My supervisor will be the sorry one when she realizes how much she needs me. Fucking bitch!"

"I'm sure she will," she said, placating him in hopes he'd lower his voice and unclench his fingers. In hopes he'd get himself under control because Lord knew she didn't have any extra to give. Not when she was on her way to get grilled by the police. Possible third strike.

"Damn right!" He smashed a fist against the wall. "Thinks she's so damn smart, superior. She'll see when I have a damn job that's better than hers."

But Summer didn't hear, wasn't able to pay attention—

Her head jerked back from the hard slap. Tears welled in her eyes and she tried not to scream.

"I told you to shut up," the man said, his face as red as his shirt. "Don't make me show you again what I do to bad little girls."

She shrank back, still feeling the soreness between her legs. "I'll be good," she said. "I promise, mister." His smile scared her almost as much as his frown. She trembled, but she didn't back up when he patted her on the head. He didn't like it when she backed away from him...

"Hey. You're not going to faint, are you?"

Summer blinked her eyes, clearing them and found herself looking into Rich's light blue eyes. They were filled with concern. "I'm okay," she said, despite the steel drums being banged against the inside of her skull. She swallowed hard and tasted bile in the back of her throat. She'd seen him. Oh God, she'd seen him.

Aware of Rich's scrutiny, Summer managed to keep it together. Managed to stay on her feet when all she wanted was to slide to the floor and put her head between her knees. She bit her bottom lip hard to stave off tears. What had just happened? Was he taking over her mind, jumping into her head whenever he wanted? But no. It hadn't been him. If it had been him she wouldn't know what he looked like. Wouldn't be able to describe him to the police.

"You need a lift?" Rich put a hand to her shoulder, interrupting her thoughts.

Summer tried to step back, but there was no place to go. "I…I have a ride," she said slowly, fighting being dragged back into the closet. She shrugged away from his touch. "I'll be okay."

"Only trying to help," he said, clearly offended. "I wasn't going to hurt you. I don't hit women."

Summer looked up and focused her attention on the floor number illuminated there, staring at it as if her life depended on it. She would not make eye contact. His hurt feelings were nothing when compared against the reactions his presence invoked. She didn't have time for this or him. Didn't have time to fall apart.

She blew out a breath when the door opened at the lobby level and strode out, intent on reaching the front door and fresh air. Stepping outside, she filled her lungs and the pieces of her began to solidify. Renny and her convertible were waiting out front, blocking a lane in spite of the honks and gestures of fellow motorists. She hurried over. "I hope you haven't been waiting long."

Renny was dressed more conservatively today. Her blue pants and long-sleeved white sweater didn't make the same statement as the red dress. "What's wrong?"

Summer fastened her seat belt and leaned back into the comfort of the leather seat. "What didn't go wrong? Huge fight with Marcia, who thinks I'm taking advantage of the company by asking for time off two days in a row. You'd think she owned the place and not Kevin. After we shouted each other down, I had the misfortune to get on the elevator with Rich." She rubbed her throbbing temples. "If I didn't know better I'd swear it was some kind of sign."

"The Apocalypse?" Renny asked, her tone mild. "Should I be wondering who this Rich is?"

"The person who started it all."

"The guy you got stuck in the elevator with the first day?"

"Yup. He got fired today and apparently wanted to make sure I knew it wasn't his fault. Like I care." She took a deep breath. "So while he's practically foaming at the mouth, all of a sudden I see him. Our guy. Clear as day."

"No!" Renny shot her a quick glance. "He's been in your building?"

Her heart stuttered. "No! God, I hope not." She put a hand to her chest and took another deep breath, then another. "What a scary thought."

"Don't listen to me. Not enough sleep. Go on."

"At first I thought he'd taken over my brain again. Then I realized it was her. Georgia. She was looking at him, scared beyond belief. He raped her," she said softly and let the tears fall. She didn't have to pretend with Renny.

"Oh, Summer." Renny rubbed Summer's leg as her face hardened. "I'm sorry you have to know that. I'm sorry and sick that Georgia has to know that. If Carla doesn't listen to you today, I swear I'll beat her bloody. She'll see my mean," she added with a snarl.

"Can I say I'm glad you're on my team? Your mean is very impressive."

"Yes, you may," Renny said primly. "Pull down the mirror and practice your own mean. We're closing in on that prick today." She pressed harder on the gas and they shot through traffic.

Too soon for Summer, they pulled into the station parking lot. Knowing she had something concrete to share now didn't make getting out of the car any easier. Maybe it even made it harder, she mused as she undid her seat belt. This time it would be much worse if they didn't believe what she had to say. Because now she had a face. She knew what he looked like. Now she really had to make them believe her. If they did, his image would be blasted all over. Someone had to know him. Someone had to come forward in time to save Georgia from any more "lessons."

"'You're doing them a favor' still applies," Renny said and gave Summer's knee a gentle squeeze. "First sneer and we're through with them, remember? I'll make a scene like they've never seen. Then we'll go higher up if need be."

"My shero." She nodded and threw back her shoulders. "Let's get this over with."

They were met by Carla and a good-looking gentleman with salt-and-pepper hair and keen brown eyes. He was tall and fit and looked like he could take care of himself out on the streets.

"Hi, I'm Vincent Chapman, deputy chief. I want to thank both of you for coming in."

Summer took the proffered hand, liking his style, his smile. "Summer Baxby and this is Renny Jamison."

"Pleasure, Ms. Jamison. Enjoy your work." He exchanged a firm shake with Renny. "I hope you don't mind, but I'd thought I'd sit in on your session with Carla."

Summer exchanged glances with Renny. Now she wouldn't have to ask. "That would be okay." From the expression that flickered over Carla's face, it appeared she wasn't in agreement.

He led them past the room they'd been in the day before, to a larger room with a smaller table and more comfortable chairs. "Ms. Baxby, I'm going to want to record our session. I find it helpful to go back over information at a later date, see if I can come at things from a different angle. Is that going to be okay with you?"

"Uh, sure. Call me Summer."

Vincent stated his name for the record, then named the other people present. "Summer, I'd like you to tell me what you know in your own words."

"I know what he looks like," she said. "What he looks like now."

"What? That's not what you said Monday," Carla said, halfway out of her chair. "If I had known that—"

"You would have what? Treated her better?" Renny interjected. "She didn't know about Georgia on Monday. She didn't even know last night when she talked to you what the guy looks like now."

"She should have called me as soon as she knew," Carla retorted.

"Carla," Vincent said mildly but with a foundation of steel. "Summer, would you be willing to work with a sketch artist?"

"Of course."

"Carla, why don't you see when we can get Patrick in here to work with Summer?"

Carla gave a stiff nod and left the room, followed by a trail of resentment.

"While we wait for word maybe you could tell me what you tried to tell Detective Kohner yesterday." Vincent opened his notepad. Unlike Kohner, he let Summer tell the whole story, then asked questions, pressing her in a way that got him more information. "Any thoughts on what might have triggered the last episode?"

"None. I didn't touch anything in the elevator, and I was concentrating on not hopping into Rich's head. I was already upset and I don't have much control when I'm upset."

"Who's Rich?" Vincent's tone was mild, but his eyes were suddenly sharp, focused.

"He used to work in the same building that I do. Same floor. He...he's the first person I ever had the mind hop deal with."

"Got a last name?"

"Uh, Slator, I think. You can't believe he's part of this? He was just upset, that's all. And so was I. I mean, it wasn't about this. Not for either of us."

"He may have information that's relevant to this case. At this point we need to follow every lead." Vincent pulled an evidence bag from his pocket. "I have to ask one more favor. This is one of Georgia's toys."

Summer looked at the miniature rainbow pony, exhaled and held out her hand.

"It's better if you handle it," Vince said gently and placed the bag on her hand.

After a moment's hesitation, she pulled the pony from the bag and felt a guilty relief when her mind stayed clear. She concentrated harder with the same results. "Nothing. I'm getting nothing." She stroked the pony's mane before gently placing it back in the bag.

"It was a long shot."

"I'm sorry."

"Don't be," he said quickly. "I don't expect you to work on command."

Carla stuck her head in the door. "He won't be available until later this afternoon. Prior commitment in Athens."

"I...I could come back," Summer found herself saying. "I don't mind."

"We certainly would appreciate it," Vincent said. "I have your contact information. Why don't I give you a call, set up a place to meet. It doesn't have to be here."

"My, uh, my cell will work."

"Good deal." Vincent held out his hand. "I want to thank you again for coming in. You've been a big help."

Summer felt a glow of pride that lasted even when they were back in Renny's car. "He seems like a decent guy. Smart."

Renny smiled slyly and eased into traffic. "Somehow I don't think Carla thought so. He kept her on a tight leash. She needed it."

"I thought you did a good job of that. Somehow I don't think she's infatuated with you anymore."

"Breaks my heart. You need a ride this afternoon?"

"I don't want to take up any more of your time. I'll make him meet me somewhere downtown."

"I thought we settled the issue of you taking up my time."

"It's not that I don't appreciate the offer, but this one's easy. I want to save you for the heavy lifting."

"I'll take that as a compliment."

"It was. I couldn't have gotten through this morning without you. The way you shut Carla down helped. A lot. Let me focus on what I had to say."

"That was a perk. About that guy Rich. Maybe you should watch your back when he's around. At least until the police have checked him out."

"He's harmless, but if it makes you feel better…"

"It does. I'd hate for anything bad to happen to you."

The warm feeling in her center rose and suffused Summer's cheeks with heat. "Thanks. I, uh, I feel the same way. About you, I mean. Uh, any chance you might want to, uh, go out Friday night? Dinner, maybe a movie, something like that?"

"Yes" was the enthusiastic reply.

"Okay. Well…you know I can't, uh, pick you up, right? I mean I should since I asked, but…"

"And here I was looking forward to riding on your handlebar." Renny zipped over two lanes and pulled up in front of Summer's office building. "What if I picked you up at six thirty?"

"What if you came to my condo at six thirty and I walk you to dinner," Summer countered. "And I'm paying, unlike the last two times."

Renny smiled. "If it makes you feel all macho who am I to argue." She leaned forward and gave Summer a quick kiss. "Until Friday."

"Was that like a teaser?" She put a hand to her tingling lips. "If so, it hit the mark." She carried the feeling up eight flights of stairs.

"The big man's here," Fiona whispered with a furtive glance over her shoulder as soon as Summer entered the suite. "Marcia started running her mouth the minute he arrived. I'm sorry, but he left word for you to come see him as soon as you came back."

She managed a smile. The waves of sympathy pouring off of Fiona were very strong. "Then I'd better get to it." She dropped off her coat and bag, then proceeded to Kevin's office. His door was shut and she hesitated a moment before knocking.

"Not so brave now."

Summer turned with resignation to face Marcia. "Can you for once leave me alone? Just once I'd like to not hear your vindictive comments."

Marcia lifted her chin, sneer firmly in place. "You are not the boss of me," she threw out as she walked away.

Kevin's door opened before Summer had a chance to knock. He studied Summer's face before stepping back and beckoning her with his finger.

"I'm sorry," she said once she was seated in front of his desk with the door closed. "I know I said it before, but I'll try harder to ignore her. This hasn't been my best week."

"Do you think I can't see that on your face? Liz has been in here asking me if I know what's wrong and, I'm sorry to say, I had to tell her I didn't know what she was talking about. As I said before, your spats with Marcia don't much concern me unless they get in the way of work getting done. Having known you all your life I am, however, concerned about you and your health and wellbeing."

She couldn't look away from the concern etched in his eyes, on his face. She might not remember his past caring, but it was coming through loud and clear in the now. "Sorry I worried you."

He waved off her apology. "Tell me what I can do to help. Your mother will come after my ass if anything happens to you."

Chewing on her bottom lip, she debated how much to share, how much to trust. In the end, she decided he was probably better able to deal with what she had to say than her mother would be. "It started the first day I came here to work." She was grateful he heard her out without interruption. For both their sakes she kept Marcia's trauma to herself.

"Is there any danger this psycho could find you?"

She shook her head, surprised at his first question. "The police agreed to keep my name out of it. And even if there was, I couldn't do nothing, Uncle Kevin."

He smiled. "Of course you couldn't. Not the protector of the underdog. Will you tell your parents? Better yet, when will you tell them?"

"I don't want to. They've already been through so much because of me. I don't want Mom to have to worry any more than she already does."

"Your mom is a lot tougher than you give her credit for. She also knows you well enough to take one look at you and know something's wrong. Do you plan to evade her for the foreseeable future?"

Summer groaned. "We're supposed to go shopping Saturday."

"You need to tell them. Despite your confidence in the ability of the police to keep your name out of this, people talk. It may not be a cop, but there are other people who work at the station. People who can be easily swayed or who can't keep their mouth shut. You don't want either one of them to find out that way. Your mom especially."

"I'll call her at lunch. I find work steadies me and I need to be more in control before I talk to her. But I guess no matter what I'll say she'll be worried." She sighed. "God, I wish I hadn't gotten on that elevator."

"Probably wouldn't have made much difference." Kevin stroked his chin. "The ability's in you, not that poor kid you were stuck with. Something else would have triggered it eventually. When was the last time you spoke with Dr. Veraat?"

"She's been away," she admitted reluctantly. "Family emergency. I'm trying to, uh, wait for her to get back."

"Doesn't she have someone covering for her?"

She squirmed in her seat. "It's some guy I don't know. But if it gets too bad, I'll go see him. Promise." She met his gaze unflinching.

"It's your mother you need to be concerned about. Remember 'pride goes before the fall.' It's a cliché for a reason."

"I don't plan to fall before she comes back."

* * *

Summer's next stop was Liz's office, where she proceeded to give her the long version alluded to on Monday. Liz's look of surprise was almost comical.

"Remember, I warned you."

"That you did." Liz tucked her hair behind her ears. "Obviously it didn't take. Damn, I'm sorry you have to go through all of this. And from Day One. On the other hand, let me say I'm glad you'll be able to help. I have a niece and I know my sister would go crazy if she disappeared one day never to be heard from again. What you're doing is good stuff, Summer."

"Okay, you're the second person today I've told this to who's treated my ability like it's an everyday thing. Kevin I can understand. Loyalty to my dad, fear of my mother. But I can't understand why you're not yelling 'Bullshit!' or running for the hills like a normal person would."

"Never said I was normal. I had an aunt who had what the family called second sight. If you lost something or wanted to know if your boyfriend was cheating on you she was the one to go to. I grew up thinking her gift was another part of her, like her leg or her singing voice. That it was so cool."

"So I haven't entered the *Twilight Zone*. But I have to admit I find the initial police response more reassuring."

"If you want me to say 'bullshit' I will," Liz said with a sly grin. "But I'm not running. Face it, Summer, you're like a superhero."

"Next thing you'll be getting me a cape."

"Don't tempt me. But seriously, take whatever time you need to. I'll deal with Marcia."

"Thanks for the offer, but slapping at her bitchiness is kind of a guilty pleasure. Sick, I know, but there you have it."

"We all have to get our jollies where we can. Anything I can do to help, ask. Don't bother offering a disclaimer," Liz added when Summer made as if to reply. "They don't work. And since you're here, we might as well do some work." She opened one of the many folders on her desk.

CHAPTER SEVENTEEN

"Despite what your conscience is telling you, you don't have to go." Sandra Baxby pulled the keys from the ignition. They were parked in the lot of the building where the police sketch artist had his studio.

Summer took one of her mother's hands and held it to her cheek. Her mother had insisted on picking her up from work, on bringing her here. "Yes, I do. This will be the easy part."

"What if talking about it, thinking about it, makes you see him again? Makes you see that poor little girl again? How can either of those possibilities be easy?"

"Mom, I have to do this. I know all of this is difficult for you to take. I really do. I would have spared you from knowing if I thought I could get away with it."

Sandra's lips twitched. "That is so you. 'If I thought I could get away with it.'" She shook her head. "I wish I could spare you knowing that monster. But I can't." She exhaled. "Then we have to nail him to the ground so hard he'll never be able to get up."

Once her mother made up her mind, she was all about the action. Summer had to pick up her pace to keep up with her mother. Upon entering the loft she could see Patrick's taste was eclectic. Old and new styles merged, from Andy Warhol to Georgia O'Keeffe to Vincent Van Gogh. She liked it. Liked it a lot.

"Be right with you," a voice called down from upstairs.

She looked up and was struck dumb. The light coming from an upstairs window bathed the speaker's head in light. For a moment Summer thought she was speaking to an angel. An angel with light brown eyes in a beautiful face framed by blond, curly hair.

"You must be Summer. Carla described you perfectly."

"Wow," Sandra whispered. "He's beautiful. For a second I thought—"

"He was an angel," Summer finished. When the angel came rushing down the stairs in a dingy white T-shirt and ripped jeans, she could see he was at best a down-to-earth angel.

He crossed to the door and turned the sign to read closed. "I'm Patrick. I hope coming here wasn't an inconvenience, but I do better work here than at the station."

"I can understand that. As you figured, I'm Summer and this is Sandra Baxby." She pointed to her mother.

Patrick studied Sandra for a moment. "Mom I would say. You have the same eye shape, brows. Good to meet both of you. I have a workspace back here we can use."

The workspace was the opposite of the front room. It was stark white on all sides and dominated by a drafting table, three easels and a big set of drawers filled with supplies. Patrick directed Sandra to the comfortable-looking oversized chair, then patted one of the two stools near the drafting table. "Have you ever done anything like this before?"

Summer looked at her mom before shaking her head.

Though Patrick looked intrigued by the response, all he said was, "It's simple and hopefully painless. You tell me what you saw and I draw it."

As Summer settled on the stool, someone banged on the front door hard enough to have the pane in the door rattle.

Patrick sighed. "Be right back. Someone can't read."

"Not an angel, but still wow," Sandra said, fanning her face. "Hope his art is as good as his looks."

When Patrick returned with an irritated-looking Carla in tow, Summer's stomach dropped to her knees. Had she said this would be easy? Politeness had her giving Carla a perfunctory nod.

"Who are you?" Carla stopped in front of Sandra, looking like she was prepping for an attack. "I don't remember there being another witness."

"Sandra Baxby," she said with cool distain. "I'm here as Summer's representative."

Carla's lip curled in a sneer as she looked at Summer. "Always in need of protection."

"Carla, you're free to observe, but I'm going to have to insist you leave my witness alone," Patrick said firmly. "I need her relaxed."

"Chapman said I had to be here. Take it up with him." Carla took the remaining chair, a sulky look on her face.

"Summer, I need you to close your eyes and visualize the suspect." Patrick put a hand on her shoulder and gave it a gentle squeeze. "Open and tell me about him. We'll start with the shape of his face."

They worked for an hour. "It's, well, it's close," Summer said with a frown.

"What do you mean 'close'?" Carla demanded, coming to stand over Summer.

"The eyes aren't quite right." She massaged her stiff shoulders. She could practically see the defensive shields surrounding Patrick get stronger. Maybe she should concede, she thought, when he raised a blond brow.

"You think you can do better?"

"Break time," Sandra declared. "Summer could use a fifteen-minute break."

"And I can't?" Patrick demanded, very un-angel-like.

"Fine." Carla huffed. "Then maybe Ms. Perfection can do a better job of explaining exactly what she saw."

"You're going to want to back off," Sandra warned, every bit the protective mama bear. "When you've experienced what Summer's experienced then you will have earned the right to be snide."

"I need air." Patrick threw down his pen and left the room. He was followed by Carla.

"Don't let them get you down, sweetie." Sandra pushed Summer's hands aside and began to massage her daughter's shoulders.

"Maybe I'm being too picky." Now that she wasn't concentrating, Summer could hear the sound of traffic—horns honking, trucks rumbling. It seemed so normal and helped put things in perspective. She could almost hear Renny reminding her that she was helping them.

"You're doing fine. I'm going to run up the street and get us some drinks. You probably need a snack. What did you have for lunch?"

She squirmed under her mother's knowing look. "I…"

"As I thought. I'll be back. Don't let them start without me." Sandra grabbed her suitcase-sized pocketbook and hurried off.

Summer heard the rumblings of voices, but she couldn't make out the words. She guessed her mother was demanding Patrick not start without her. Her mother was nothing if not protective. Sometimes overly so. They would have to work on that once this nightmare was over. Her mother probably needed the return to normal as much as she did. "Something else to talk to Dr. Veraat about," she said and absently pulled the drawing closer. The eyes were too small, too close together. And the nose was a little bit off. She hated to think what Patrick would say when she pointed this out. At the rate they were going, she'd be stuck here until well into the evening.

Chewing on her bottom lip, she flipped the page and grabbed a pencil. With a few quick strokes she outlined the kidnapper's face, then played around with the eyes until she was satisfied. She added the lips, the lines in his forehead and around his mouth, the beard. A shiver went down her spine. It was him. She dropped the pad, her heart beating staccato in her chest.

"Look, I apologize for losing my cool. Hey, what's wrong?" Patrick quickly crossed to Summer, took her hand. "Did you have another vision?"

She pointed to the pad.

Patrick's eyes widened. "Is this him? Well, duh, of course it's him. This is awesome. Man, you have skills." The last part was added with admiration, bordering on awe. He switched back to his drawing. "The differences are subtle and yet they add up. Forced again to say 'job well and truly done.' Let me get Carla. She can run this by the station, saving me a trip."

To Summer, Patrick's words were background noise. She was busy trying to figure out how she'd managed to put pencil to paper now when she'd failed so many times before. How was it that a monster had unlocked her creativity? What did that say about her? About her relationship with him?

Hugging her midsection, she rocked back and forth, needing the comfort. Needing to believe when they captured him there would be no more connection between them. No more connections to the girls whose childhoods he stole. She dropped her arms, stood up straight when Patrick returned with Carla.

"You sure this is him?" Carla demanded, thrusting the sketch in front of Summer's face. "I need you to be absolutely sure before we release this."

"I'm sure," she said, looking away from his face. She didn't need the drawing to know what he looked like. He was already in her head. Wasn't that enough? "Contrary to what you might think I don't get any satisfaction from providing false information."

"I'm the one who has to pay if you're wrong about this. How am I supposed to believe you when you can't even look at him?"

Summer glared at Carla. "Don't you get it? He's in my fucking head! Why the hell would I need to look at that?"

"What's going on here?" Sandra demanded as she advanced into the room to stand by her daughter. "You were supposed to wait for me." She shot Carla an accusing look.

"It's okay, Mom. Carla was just leaving. She got what she came for."

"Thank you for your cooperation," Carla said, less than gracious. "Deputy Chief Chapman might need to speak with you."

"Not today," Sandra said firmly. "She's done more than enough for today. Time for the police to do their own work."

Summer reached for her mother's hand. "It's okay. If Mr. Chapman needs to speak with me today, he knows how to reach me."

Carla left with a curt nod.

"We should go too." Summer stood. "Hopefully I won't have to use your services again," she said to Patrick.

"Not likely. Not after what you did." The admiration was still visible on his face, still audible in his voice. "You ever do any showings? You're a professional, right?"

Summer managed a smile at his enthusiasm. "A lifetime ago."

"What was that about?" Sandra asked once they were back in her purple VW Bug with the rainbow peace sign on top and a line of daisies on every door.

Summer looked at her hands. "I drew my own rendering of the kidnapper."

"Oh, baby." Sandra's face lit up. "That's wonderful. How did that happen?"

"I was looking at Patrick's sketch, trying to figure out what was wrong and suddenly I'm drawing. I'm correcting the eyes, then the nose, adding the other features and then I'm finished. It looked exactly like him." Summer turned to look at her mom, tears in her eyes. "Oh, Mom, what if I was only able to draw because we're linked? What if I can't draw anything else?"

Sandra pulled her into her arms as best she could. "Let's not think that way. Dr. Veraat said the skills would come back. You're the one responsible for capturing his image. Only you." She let Summer go, fumbled with the bag she placed on the backseat and withdrew a bottle of orange juice. "Here, sweetie. Drink this. We'll go buy you some real food. Once you eat something, you'll be able to think more clearly."

Summer downed half the bottle. She didn't know what to think. Didn't want to say anything else that would worry her mother. "I could eat," she finally said, more due to guilt than hunger.

"You *will* eat," Sandra declared as she pulled out of the parking lot. "The only choice you have is what to eat."

She sighed. She knew that tone. Had heard it plenty of times over the past two years to know what it meant. "Spaghetti and garlic bread."

"House of Pasta." Sandra made a quick right, then another to take them in the opposite direction. "Then we'll stop by your place and see what you need from the grocery store. I swear you've lost five pounds since I last saw you. You don't have any to spare."

"I don't mean to worry you, Mom. I've been eating. It's all this…" She shrugged.

"And you didn't think to tell me about this earlier? It shouldn't have taken Kevin to make you come clean."

"We've already been through this. I told you I didn't expect it to get to this. I thought it would go away. And you've already suffered through enough because of me. God, Mom, I didn't want to add more. I *don't* want to add more. Seems I can't help it." She wiped at tears.

"As your mother it's my right to worry about you. I worry about all of my children." Sandra patted her blonde tresses. "Why do you think I have to color the gray?"

Summer snorted. "You don't."

"I think about it."

"Anyway. I don't see the rest of your kids combined worrying you as much as I do all by myself." She blew out a breath and watched the passing scenery as they left downtown behind and headed to an Italian restaurant located on the northern outskirts of town. Before she moved downtown, Summer had managed to convince her parents to take her there once a week.

"Listen and listen good. I give thanks every day that I have you to worry about. It beats mourning your loss every day." Sandra blinked rapidly. "Frankly, you were due some worrying about. For the most part you were always my good girl."

"Rose-colored glasses will do that."

"No, my little Summer Rain, you were always sweet, always looking out for everyone else. Even from the beginning. Of all my kids you were the only one considerate enough to be born on your due date. Not one of your sisters or your brother can say that. You slept through the night sooner and, best of all, you sailed through your teen years without turning into a little bitch who felt the need to fight me every step of the way. No way you have a connection to a monster. Your sweet heart wouldn't let you. If there's any connection, it's to those girls."

The band around Summer's chest loosened. "It's strange to hear things about myself that I can't remember. I wonder if I ever will."

Sandra beat out a yellow light and made a left onto Highway 101. "One day you will. Until then listen to the woman who's known you all your life." She pulled into a parking space and turned off the ignition before patting Summer's thigh. "I know it doesn't seem like it, but you've come so far in only two years. Try to remember that the next time you're faced with a challenge. You've beat so many already, and you're going to beat more."

CHAPTER EIGHTEEN

The ringing of her phone brought Summer out of a tortured dream. Without thought she answered it. "Yeah," she mumbled, her voice thick with sleep.

"This is Vincent Chapman. Sorry to wake you, Summer, but we think he's snatched another girl."

"No!" She sat up and exhaled. Another girl missing could only mean Georgia was dead. Could only mean her efforts hadn't been enough. "Please, no. There was supposed to be more time. Why would he kill her already? He hasn't had her a week!"

"We might never know. What we do know is Corey Smith didn't make it home from school. We've talked to her friends, searched along the route from school to home, searched her hangouts and nothing. I'm hoping you'll be able to help."

"But I don't know a Corey Smith and I haven't seen anything since this morning. How can I help?"

"Would you be willing to handle something of hers? See if her disappearance is connected to the others? I know it didn't work before, but frankly we're running on empty."

"And if this thing with Corey is connected? What then?" *That won't put you any closer to him,* she thought. *No closer to putting him behind bars.*

"The chief's going to need to call in the GBI. This guy's escalating at an alarming rate. Please, Summer, I wouldn't ask if it weren't important."

"Okay. Okay." She took a shaky breath. "I need someone to pick me up. I don't drive."

"I can bring it to you."

"No! I don't want that here. Don't want him anywhere near here." The condo might not be home, but she felt safe from him here. "I'll come to you."

"I'll send two officers. Is thirty minutes enough time for you to get ready?"

"Twenty. I can be ready in twenty. They can buzz me from downstairs. I'll come down."

"Thanks for this, Summer. It means a lot."

She rattled off her address before disconnecting the call. When the trembling started, she brought to mind her mother's words. The connection was to the girls. They were the ones reaching out to her. This was just another challenge. She'd gotten through others, she would get through this one. If she made contact, she could use it to get to him, to keep him from harming any more innocents.

Once dressed, she decided to go down to the lobby. Waiting down there would help keep this mess out of her condo. Keep this a place where she didn't have visions or mind hops. Grabbing her bag, she went downstairs and paced until her police escort arrived.

At the station, they were met at the door by Vincent. With him was the young cop Renny had tormented. Despite the hour, his uniform looked fresh.

"Thanks for coming, Summer. You remember Juan Griego. If anyone's to blame for your being here it's him. He convinced me to call you."

Juan blushed bright red.

"Thanks for the vote of confidence," Summer said, thinking again he had to be new to the job. He was as fresh as his uniform.

"I thought we could do this in my office," Vincent said. "This place is a madhouse as you can see. Every officer on active status has been called in to help."

Inside Vincent's office with the door shut, the noise dropped to a manageable level. "Can I get you anything to drink, Summer?" Vincent asked, gesturing to the chair beside his desk.

"Water would be good," she said, a mass of nerves and uncertainty. What if she couldn't do it? Would another little girl lose her life? She couldn't answer that now any more than she could on the ride over. She missed the motion of Vincent's head that sent Juan for water. Missed it because she was too busy reciting the multiplication table as if it were a benediction.

Juan was back quickly with a bottle of water and two Cokes. He smiled shyly at Summer as he handed her the water. "It will be okay," he said softly.

Looking into his dark brown eyes, Summer almost believed him. She took a drink to soothe her dry throat. "Is there some sort of procedure for this? This is the second time. Should I be read my rights or something?"

Vincent's lips twitched as if he wanted to smile. "You're not under suspicion. First, I'd like you to look at this photo."

Summer concentrated on the little girl's face. There was no big smile, no joy in the girl's eyes. "Is this her? Is this Corey?"

"Yes. Anything?"

"I'm sorry. I…I don't recognize her."

"No need to apologize. Next we'd like to give you the item we received from the girl's mother. If that's okay with you."

She chewed on her lip. "Okay." She wiped her sweaty palms on her jeans.

Juan handed her a plastic bag with a stuffed bear that had seen better days. "She sleeps with this bear every night, her mother said. Can't sleep without him." She reached in to touch it and—

she was at an unfamiliar park, sitting under a tree and trying to ignore the pain between her legs. Her mama said she had to let him do it. That she was being a good girl. She didn't think so. Letting him touch her down there was being a bad girl. Her teacher said so.

She wiped her cheeks with the back of her hands and wished she could make herself disappear like the girl in her favorite book. Go to that special place where everything was good. The place where mamas loved their little girls all the time.

Closing her eyes, she prayed. The man with the Bible in front of the beer store said if you prayed hard enough God would answer. She didn't really believe him 'cause hadn't she prayed hard enough to get the man to stop? But what else could she do? God was her only hope. The police wouldn't help. They'd think she wanted that man to do that to her. That she'd asked him do it. She would be the one to go to jail.

"Corey, are you okay?"

She opened her eyes and looked in Benjy's scared face. At first she'd been afraid of Benjy. Now she knew he would never hurt her because he was the nicest person ever. "I'm okay," she said.

"Don't look that way to me." He settled his bulk beside her and held out a candy bar. "Maybe this'll help," he said in that deep, slow way of his and patted her shoulder. His touch never hurt even though his hands were huge like the rest of him.

She sniffed. It was her favorite kind. Just like Benjy to remember that. "Thanks." She took a big bite and she did feel better. Benjy was her best friend in the whole world. Some of the other kids called him names like "retard" behind his back. But only when she wasn't around. She didn't let them talk about her friend like that. But Benjy, he didn't care what they said. He just kept smiling and being nice.

"You wanna do something? What you wanna do?"

"I don't know. I don't wanna go back home. I don't want that man to touch me again. It hurts and he slaps me if I scream."

"He shouldn't ought to be doing that." Benjy shook his head. "That ain't right. We'll go to the police, Corey. They'll stop him. The police help you when you're in trouble. That's what they're supposed to do."

"No, Benjy. Mama would kill me if I went to the police. Besides she said they'd blame me and lock me up. I don't want to go to prison."

He scratched his head. "That can't be right, Corey. I don't think your mama's right. They'll lock that man up. That's what they do on TV. I seen them do it."

"Benjy, that's just make-believe stuff. In the real world the cops don't care nothing about poor people. Mama says that they want to put all of us in jail so the rich people don't have to see us."

"Then you can't go back there. That ain't right."

"Maybe I could go home with you again. Stay a little while until I feel better. I won't be no trouble."

"Okay. You can lay down on my bed and I'll sit in the chair and watch over you. Then I can walk home with you and tell that man to leave you alone."

She frowned. Benjy was big enough and he could probably beat up that man her mama called a friend, but her mama would pitch a fit. Probably call the police and make them arrest Benjy. "That's not so good, Benjy. My mama would get both of us in trouble."

"Okay. Let's go to my place. I could fix you some food. I went to the grocery store. Do you like macaroni and cheese? I can make it good." He stood, then held out a hand and helped her up.

Corey put her arms around one of his thick legs and squeezed hard. Maybe she could stay with Benjy forever. "I love you, Benjy."

The smile stretched his wide face. "I love you, Corey. You stay at my place as long as you want. I'll take good care of you. Promise..."

Summer blinked as the scene faded and the throbbing in her head began. She was back at the cop station again and being watched closely by Juan and Vincent. "It's not the same," she said and pressed her fingers against her temples. "It's not the same."

"Can you give us anything?" Vincent Chapman handed her a tissue.

It was then that she felt the wetness on her cheeks, noticed the wet spot on her shirt. "She's somewhere near a small park. The park is near her home and she goes there a lot. She's hiding out with a tall white man with scars on his face." She wiped her face even as more tears fell. "She's getting abused by her mother's friend." Summer blew out a sharp breath that did nothing to subdue the anger building inside her. "The mother knows, tells Corey she has to go along."

"Tell us more about the guy she's with now. Are you sure he didn't molest her?"

"His name is Benjy and all he wants to do is protect her. Oh, God." Summer pressed the tissue hard against her eyes and took a deep breath. "He's a little slow. You know, mentally challenged. He wanted to call the police, but Corey wouldn't let him. Her mother's convinced her she'll be the one put in jail. You should go back to her friends. They'll know who Benjy is. Can probably tell you where he lives."

"Thank you," Juan said gently. "You've been a great help."

Summer handed Vincent the teddy bear, suddenly drained of energy. "You'll understand if I don't say 'Anytime.'"

"Understood," Vincent said. "I'd like to echo Officer Griego's thanks and add that you saved us a lot of manpower better used finding Georgia Zackery. I'll have the officers escort you back home."

"If I could have a minute in the restroom…?" Summer cleared her throat as her voice broke.

"Take all the time you need. Juan will show you the way."

In the restroom Summer gave in to tears. What kind of world did she live in where mothers let their kids be abused? Where men stalked girls to use, then discard? Maybe she'd been better off when she didn't know anything. When she lived in the cocoon that was her parents' house. The need to call her mother was very strong.

A knock on the door had her scrambling to her feet.

"Ms. Baxby? Summer, are you all right?"

She recognized Juan's voice. "I'll just be a minute."

"Take your time. As long as you're okay."

Summer sluiced cold water over her face until she felt chilled. It didn't do much to hide the damage from the crying spell. But she shouldn't care, she thought, looking into eyes that seemed too big for her face. She'd done them a favor, so if they couldn't deal with her tears, with her sorrow, then that was on them.

Juan was standing by the door as if on guard. She could see the compassion and worry etched on his face and wondered how long he'd last in law enforcement. Wondered whether he would toughen up or move on. "I'm ready," she said.

In the back of the squad car, Summer tried to balance her heartache over Corey's abuse with the hope Georgia was still alive. The scales weren't level when the officers escorted her to the lobby and waited until she was on the elevator. They weren't level when she unlocked the door to her condo, stepped inside and felt some of the unease smooth away. Maybe she'd never get there. Maybe she wasn't meant to get there.

Knowing she was too wired to sleep, Summer searched the guest room for the pad and the set of charcoal pencils with her name engraved on them that her father had given her when she was released from the hospital. His gentle reminder of what she'd been before. She'd used them a couple of times before putting them away, frustrated by her sophomoric efforts.

She found them in the trunk along with other pieces of her former life and vowed she'd eventually go through each item and find them a new home in the open. But now she wanted to see if she could draw something that wasn't steeped in darkness. Wanted to assure herself she was in control of her talent.

After settling on the sofa, she quickly flipped past her previous efforts to a clean sheet. At first the whiteness of the page seemed to mock her. Gradually she remembered Corey and the simple love she and Benjy shared. The pencil flew across the page as she tried to capture what might have been the expression on Corey's face when Benjy offered her the candy bar. When Corey realized there was someone who paid attention to her.

It took five pages for Summer to be satisfied. As she studied the drawing a memory surfaced. Her mother holding back her hair while she blew out seven candles on a cake in the shape of Wonder Woman. Her family had clapped and cheered. After cake, she got to open her presents. She grabbed the big box first, ripping off paper in abandon. The child's easel on the front of the box sent her into a frenzy. She knew it was going to be the best present ever.

Smiling in wonder, Summer set the pad aside and leaned back. A memory. One that she recalled all by herself. And what a wonderful memory to have now when she was feeling so down. She hugged herself and brought back the feelings—the love she felt from having her mother protect her hair from getting burned, the enthusiasm shown her by the rest of her family because she blew out all the candles. She'd been loved then as she was loved now. How lucky was that? She snuggled into the thickness of the sofa and replayed the memory again and again—

The dream started with rain. She was standing at the window watching drops roll down the windowpane and disappear. The rain was good. The rain meant he'd come home late.

"Dinner's ready, sweetie."

Summer turned to see a woman smiling at her. Somehow she knew this woman, who looked nothing like her real mother, was her dream mother. She approached her slowly, taking in the tired eyes, the bruise on her cheek, the black eye and she was afraid. But she didn't fear this woman, rather she was afraid for her.

"Have a seat. I made your favorite."

Summer sat in the chair to the right of the head of the table and wondered when beanie-weenies had become her favorite. Since the mother had gone to the trouble to fix the food, she forked some into her mouth. The force of the front door hitting the wall stopped her heart. She dropped the fork and ran to the mother, who looked as terrified as she felt. The monster was back early.

"You're right on time for dinner," the mother said.

The man stalked to the table and swept the pot of beanie-weenies onto the floor. "You call this food?"

Summer put her hands to her ears, but couldn't block out the sound of his hard voice.

"It's all we have left," the mother said softly, wringing her hands. "There's an opening at the diner. Earl said he could use me. It would give us extra money."

"You trying to say I can't support my family?" He smiled when she shrank from his raised fist. "That's what I thought. You're the problem. Probably spent my money on that sniveling brat. Come here, boy."

Boy? She wasn't a boy. Trembling, Summer tried to press herself into the woman's back, make herself invisible. She didn't like the man. Didn't like how mean he sounded. But she especially didn't want to look at him with his red eyes and big teeth that might bite your arm off.

"Don't you hear your daddy talking to you?" The man grabbed Summer's arm and pulled her to stand in front of him. "Look at you, you little sissy. Acting like a scaredy-cat and hiding behind a woman when you should be standing up to me like a man. You're worthless."

"Leave him be, Stan." The mother raised her chin when Stan glared at her, meeting him eye to eye. "Richard's not at fault here."

Summer watched in horror as the backhand seemed to come from nowhere, sending the mother to the floor. "No!" She twisted from the man's grip and ran to the mother. She didn't know what she was going to do, but she had to do something to stop the man before he made the mother go away forever...

Once again, the insistent ringing of the phone interrupted Summer's sleep. And once again she was grateful for the reprieve. She rubbed her gritty eyes, reached for the bedside table and came up empty. For a second she was afraid she was still in the other house, still on the floor with her mother. "No!" When she reopened her eyes, she realized she'd fallen asleep on the sofa. It had only been a dream. Before she gave in to relief, Summer grabbed the cell phone off of the coffee table in front of her and answered on the fourth ring. "Hello."

"I woke you," Sandra said. "I'm sorry."

She squinted at the clock on the mantel. Six thirty! She'd overslept two days in a row. "Don't worry about it. I seem to be running late. Again."

"I hate to sound like a broken record, but are you sure you're okay? It's not like you to sleep late during the week."

"I got called down to the police station around two. Another girl went missing."

Sandra's gasp came through loud and clear. "Maybe it's time for you to come back home. At least until they catch this madman. Maybe then the police will decide to do their own work."

Though the same thought had run through her mind earlier, coming from her mother it sounded cowardly. "It wasn't the same guy. And the police can find me there too."

"If that was supposed to make me feel better you failed miserably. If you were here I could be with you when the police decide they want to talk to you. I don't like the idea of you going through something like that alone."

"Mom." Summer closed her eyes and sighed. "I was called because it was important. With what I told them a little girl will be better off. That has to count for something."

"Which one of us are you trying to convince?"

"You. Maybe me too. I must be tired."

"Take the day off. Do something frivolous, something fun."

"I don't know what that is yet." Now she knew she was tired. She hadn't meant to say that out loud. "Work's not so bad. It gets me out of the condo and I enjoy what I'm doing now. But you can't tell Uncle Kevin I said that. He might gloat."

"Your secret's safe with me. Promise me you'll be careful going to work. People seem to forget how to drive when it rains."

How lucky was she to have someone who watched out for her, who did the right thing. "I will. I promise. I probably don't say this enough, but I really do love you."

"You say it plenty."

Summer decided if she hurried, she could squeeze in a thirty-minute run and still get to work on time. On the treadmill she woke up enough to worry about the dream. The way she figured it should be enough she picked up on Rich's childhood traumas when she was in his presence. But, no. Now she was letting him invade her dreams, making up stories of what his life might have been like. This could not go on.

She ramped up the speed, channeling her frustration with every footstep that slapped against the pad. But she couldn't outrun her thoughts. Couldn't knock down the niggling fear that by reaching out to Rich on the elevator she'd created the connection. Why else would she be dreaming about him? He wasn't involved with the missing girls or Corey and yet... She blew out a sharp breath. "No 'yet,'" she said firmly. It was only a dream, her interpretation of something that could have happened. "But didn't. Didn't happen."

CHAPTER NINETEEN

By the time she reached the reception area at work, she'd convinced herself the dream was a fluke. That it wouldn't happen again. She took the absence of Fiona and Marcia at the front desk as an affirmation of her theory.

The box on her chair drove all thoughts of flukes out of her head. *Christmas in March*, she thought as she opened the box to find the graphics software she'd requested. Exactly what she needed, something fun to immerse herself in. After installing the program on her computer, she got lost in exploring it.

"Your pay form is late."

"Huh?" Marcia didn't warrant a glance.

"Your pay form was due to me by twelve. It's officially late."

And you're getting such pleasure in letting me know that, Summer thought and looked at the clock on the bottom of her screen. Twelve thirty! Already? "I'll do it right now."

"Too late. I've already sent them to Gar for approval. You'll have to wait for the next pay period. Of course I'm sure your *mommy* will be happy to advance you your allowance. Just like she was happy to come to work yesterday and rescue you."

"Shut up already." Summer waved her hand around her head as if swatting a pesky fly. "Find someone else's shit to eat."

"Aren't we brave now that Mommy's not here to protect you. I'm surprised she didn't come in with you today."

Summer, who had as yet to turn around, did so then. "I don't know about you, but I have work to do. Why don't you run along and freshen that goop you call makeup. I'm sure there's some clown out there waiting to make you his soul mate." She crossed her arms and leaned back. "FYI, my mommy doesn't give me an allowance. I have two big old trust funds to take care of my needs." She laughed as, with a shake of her head, Marcia flounced off.

Still in a good mood, she pulled her sketchpad from her bike bag and drew a caricature of Marcia. She squinted, turning the finished project right, then left. Color. It needed color. She knew just the place to get color pencils, and since it was the noon hour, now would be the perfect time to go there. "You won't think I need my mommy to fight my battles much longer," she told the sketch and grabbed her wallet.

She literally ran into Gar on the way out of her office. "Sorry." She put a hand on his arm to steady him. "You okay?"

He nodded. "For someone who can't weigh more than a hundred you pack a strong punch. I have to admire that." He straightened his tie. "I didn't realize you were here. I was coming to leave you a note that Liz signed your pay form along with the hours charged to personal leave. But since you're here I have to wonder why you didn't sign your own form and why Marcia didn't remind you to sign your form."

"It's my fault. I lost track of time and then it was too late. I don't expect Liz to cover for me."

"Wait." Gar put his fingers to his temples. "I'm sensing another Summer versus Marcia moment. Yes, and I see that Marcia thinks she won this round." He grinned. "How did I do?"

She put her fingers to her temples and closed her eyes. "Wait for it. Yes, I see the circus in your future." She joined in his laughter.

"How do you put up with her?"

"I have my ways." She retrieved the sketch from her desk. "Wait till I get my hands on some colored pencils."

"Wow. She'd kill me if she heard this, but it's so her. This is good, Summer. Much better than the guy at the flea market."

"Thanks. I think."

He looked chagrined. "You know what I mean." He handed her the pad. "I guess we won't have you around here much longer."

"I'm getting the pink slip for forgetting to sign my payroll form?"

"No. I thought with your talent returning you'd go back to what you did before."

"It's yet to be seen that my talent has returned. Kevin did me a big favor by giving me a job. I'll stick around a while and return it."

"Cool. I probably shouldn't ask, but could that sticking around include looking at updating our logo? I mean, just kind of look at it and see if it could use some improvement. It's my task, but…"

He looked so hopeful she couldn't disappoint him. "I'll work it in with Liz's stuff."

Gar raised a fist in victory. "Great. I gotta go tackle the gym. Oh." He retraced his steps. "Here's the number of leave hours we charged."

She watched him practically dance out the door and wondered what she'd gotten herself into. Whatever it was, it was better than worrying about other things.

When she returned from lunch with two new sets of pencils and, as a concession to her mother, food, Dani was waiting for her. All thoughts of downing the veggie wrap and pita chips vanished. "Hey."

"Sorry to bother you at work, but I wanted you to hear it from me first."

Summer took a deep breath, ignoring the quizzical looks from Fiona. "We, uh, we should go back to my office." She led the way there, though it was the last thing she wanted to do. It was never good news when someone felt it had to come from them.

"I found more girls," Dani said once the door was closed. She straddled the chair beside Summer's desk. "Most weren't from here. The GBI and the FBI are coming in, so it's going to be all over the media."

"But not me, right? They promised to keep my name a secret."

Dani nodded. "I've done some checking and I haven't heard even a whisper of your name. Despite what you did last night."

"That's something. Have you heard if there's been any positive response to the, uh, the sketch? Aside from the guy who already confirmed he saw him with Georgia."

"Last I heard there was nothing that positively ID'd the perp. These things take time. A lot of effort's spent tracking down bogus leads because you never know when you'll hit the right one. Someone will see it and know who he is. If not in here, then from surrounding states."

"Okay. So don't expect it soon." She frowned, pressing her fist against the tightness in her chest. "Will they want to talk to me?"

"If you mean the GBI or the FBI, the answer's no. Vincent wants to keep a tight lid on his source of information. He knows he can trust his guys, and while he hasn't had much interaction with the GBI, he knows the feds like to muscle their way in and take over from the locals."

"That's a huge relief. Thanks for, you know, coming by. It's, uh, nice to be in the loop."

"You deserve it, Summer. Listen, Vince called in a favor. I'm going to be working closely with the department on this one. If you have any questions or concerns give me a call."

She waited until Dani was almost at the door to ask the question that had been burning in her brain. "How many girls?" When Dani turned Summer could see she wasn't going to like the answer.

"I was hoping you wouldn't ask. Possibly as many as twenty-five who fit the profile. Won't know for sure until he's caught. And only then if he talks."

As the door closed behind Dani, Summer rested her forehead against the desk, wishing she hadn't felt the need to ask the question. Hadn't felt the need to know how many innocents had been destroyed. It took everything she had, but she put it behind her and returned to the graphics program. Unfortunately the day had lost its luster.

* * *

The sun was shining brightly when Summer wheeled her bike away from the office building. The temperature was warm enough to fool her into believing spring might come early. Thoughts of the twenty-five girls fueled her legs as she peddled. Twenty-five girls gone, never to be seen again. She veered left onto Fifth, ignoring the road that would take her home. The park. She'd go to the park, see little girls who were happy, little girls who were loved like she'd been. There had to be good to balance the bad she was being inundated with. If there wasn't... "No 'if,'" she shouted. The balance was there and she would find it.

As she'd expected, the warmer weather had drawn out parents and kids. The playground was a hive of activity. Summer locked her bike to a pole and settled under a tree to watch the kids lose themselves in play.

"Hey, remember me?" The young boy gave her a big smile. "I'm Kyle and you're Mama Kee's friend with the bike. You came to our house for the party and then you came back for dinner."

Kyle's smile begged for one in return. She was struck again at how much he resembled Keile. "I'm Summer. Do your mothers know where you are?"

"Yeah, they know I'm at the park," he replied and gave her a look that said he questioned her intelligence. "Why are you sitting here?"

"I like watching kids play."

"Kyle! I told you to wait for me." Clearly exasperated, Haydn pushed a stroller over to where they were sitting.

"I'm waiting right here with Summer. Can I go on the swings now?"

Haydn sighed. "Yes. But next time you need to walk the whole way beside me, not in front of me, not behind me. Are we clear? Okay, go," she said after he nodded. "Hi, Summer. How are you holding up?"

"As well as can be expected, I guess." Summer stood to get a look at Chelsea. "Sounds like I should be asking you how you're doing. Kyle seems, uh, well…"

"He's an armful. That's beyond a handful." Haydn removed Chelsea from the stroller. "So far this one hasn't displayed the same wandering spirit."

"She's a beauty." Summer took Chelsea's outstretched hand. "And friendly."

"Only if Keile and I are nearby." Haydn smiled. "She was taking a walk with Renny and hissed at this elderly woman who'd stopped to admire her. Poor Renny was mortified. Told us we needed to take Chelsea to the vet and have the cat exorcised out of her."

Summer laughed. "That sounds like Renny. Do you think I could, uh, hold her?"

"Sure. We did have her declawed."

"She's making up stories about you, isn't she?" Summer rested her cheek against the top of Chelsea's head, breathing in the scent of shampoo and hope. Here was a little girl who'd only known love. She blinked against the burn of tears.

"You okay?" Haydn put a hand on Summer's arm, her hazel eyes warm with concern.

"Better than." She sniffed. "This is what I need. After, you know, all I've seen this week it's good to hold a little girl who's only known love."

"I'm sorry you're having to go through that on top of everything else. Kyle, sit down!" Haydn dashed over to the swings where Kyle was hastily plopping his bottom onto the swing.

"Could have been worse," Summer told Chelsea. "He could have jumped." As soon as the words left her mouth a memory surfaced. She was the one on the swing, soaring high. Her sisters, May and Winter, were egging her to jump. Summer remembered letting go of the ropes and having momentum carry her through the air. Before she could do it again, her mother was there, full of worry. Summer had denied accusations that her sisters had put her up to jumping and later they bought her an ice cream cone as a reward. Two scoops.

Summer hugged Chelsea and the memory close as she spun around, laughing.

"Somebody looks happy."

"Keile! Hey, I didn't realize you were here too. I remembered another childhood incident. It feels great." She did another quick spin and squealed along with Chelsea. "I feel great. Oops. Somebody wants her mama."

"Can and I were at the dog park." Keile adjusted Chelsea on her hip while Can stretched out beside the stroller. "I don't have to ask how you're holding up."

"I owe it to your daughter." She stroked Chelsea's smooth cheek and earned a grin. "And you and Haydn. Thanks to you, I can feel the love, the innocence in Chelsea. It's giving me hope."

"Sounds like that's something you needed."

"Desperately," she readily admitted. "Dani thinks this guy could be responsible for snatching twenty-five girls. Twenty-five. I came here to see a different side."

Keile whistled softly. "That's a lot of baggage to carry around. I'm glad my little sunshine could help. But you should also feel good about your part in this, Summer. They wouldn't have been able to put it together without you. That's not too shabby."

"They have to catch him first. He's been doing this for twenty years, so he's good at hiding. Probably in plain sight. I wish…I wish I could do more for Georgia." She sighed, willing away tears.

"You know what? You're coming over to our house this weekend. You can kick back and hang out with the kids."

"That's a great idea," Haydn said as she joined them. She snaked an arm around Keile's waist, then leaned in. "The weather's supposed to be more of the same. Between us we can convince Keile to throw something on the grill. It'll be fun."

"Sunday? Would Sunday work?"

"Come at one," Haydn said. "We can eat at four and get you home not too long after dark. I'll ask Renny and we'll double team her for more deets about her new book."

Summer nodded. It sounded like exactly what she needed. "Could I...would it be okay if I tried to sketch the kids?"

"You're drawing again?" Keile gave her a big smile. "Summer, that's awesome."

Summer shrugged. "I'm trying."

"As long as Kyle isn't required to sit still for long periods of time, I say go for it. Kyle!" Haydn put her hands on her hips.

"Chelsea and I got this." Keile jogged over to where Kyle was once again standing on the swing.

"Isn't she great?" Haydn said, her gaze fixed on Keile.

She nodded. "I used to have such a crush on her. Oh. I, uh, I—"

"Doesn't bother me," Haydn said with a wave of her hand. "I know she's all mine now."

"It looks good on her. Good on you too. I'll, uh, see you Sunday." She walked off, then turned. "I can't tell you how glad I am to have run into you guys."

CHAPTER TWENTY

Renny held the phone away from her ear and gave it a good glare. When it didn't disintegrate, she put it back to her ear and continued to listen to her mother rant about her latest crisis. That was her mother's definition, of course. In Renny's book, "crisis" was far too strong a word. She glanced at the clock on the microwave and swallowed a groan. If this story didn't get wrapped up soon she was going to be late picking up Summer.

Sudden silence clued her in that she might have missed a question. "I'm sorry, what did you say?…He's fine…No, I haven't seen him since his birthday…I don't know when we'll get together again…She's nice and they seem happy…Your name didn't come up once…Eve, I need to go. I have an appointment and I don't want to be late…No, I'm not interested in that role, either. Bye." Renny ended the call and finally gave in to the scream that had been threatening since she'd answered it. "Sorry, Chazz." She stroked his back. "Wait until you meet Eve, you'll be screaming along with me."

She slipped on her coat and grabbed the small purse made necessary by the lack of pockets in the little black number she was wearing. Attaching the gate that theoretically closed Chazz in the kitchen—they both knew he could jump it in a heartbeat—she headed for the garage.

As Renny fought her way through traffic, she realized this was her first trip downtown on a Friday night. She'd heard about the popular happy hour specials, but being a non drinker now it had never had a pull. The volume was akin to some weekend mornings, but the atmosphere was different—younger, edgier, with night lights and neon signs. It seemed more like a big city and fun.

She waited out pedestrian traffic before turning into the parking deck under Summer's condo. After punching in the code Summer had given, she drove around until she found the reserved spots.

"Consider this the Bat Signal," Renny said, holding the phone on her shoulder with her ear while she locked the car door. "Lobby. Gotcha."

Her heels clicked against concrete as she made her way to the elevator, only to discover she needed a key card to get through the door leading to the elevator. "I need you to come down here and let me in. The door needs a key card...No problem."

Summer emerged from an elevator not a minute later. "Can you tell I haven't been down here in a while?" She held the door open for Renny to enter. "Sorry."

"Like I said, no worries tonight." Renny tugged on Summer's jacket. "What's this? This is the first time I've seen you in a suit. Nice."

"You sure I don't look like a scarecrow?"

"No straw, ergo no scarecrow. You look really nice, Summer."

A blush stole up her cheeks. "Thanks. I want this to be a good time for you. Nothing about the other stuff tonight. Just you and me. If that's okay?"

Renny hooked her arm through Summer's as they entered the elevator. "That sounds perfect. Should I ask where you're taking me?"

"The Bistro."

"Whoa. How did you manage to get reservations so quickly? I've been told the wait time can be four months."

"I have connections." Summer pushed the Open Door button and motioned for Renny to precede her. "A co-worker is distantly related to the owner. When I asked her for suggestions, she offered to hook me up."

"I hear the food is well worth the wait. Keile took Haydn there for their last anniversary. Said she earned major points, which I think was a euphemism for sex." She gave Summer a sly sideways glance. "So watch out."

Summer's face burned red. "Uh, I…Yeah." She cleared her throat and opened the door that led outside. The noise of the streets surrounded them—the sounds of traffic and revelry from the growing crowds.

"I'm teasing. I know you would never take me out to dinner because you expect sex. Because I'm thinking you've never thought about sex. Well, in the last two years."

"I'm taking the Fifth," Summer said, rubbing her cheeks. "Either way I go is embarrassing."

Renny laughed. "God, you're adorable. Okay. I'll stop teasing. What's this I hear about you sketching Keile's kids? Sounds like something's changed since we had dinner."

"It's kind of a pisser that to some extent I owe it to Marcia. We exchanged words Wednesday and before I know it I'm drawing a caricature of her and thinking about colored pencils. Felt like the safe that holds my brain opened enough for me to think I'll get it all the way open."

Renny gave Summer's hand a quick tug. "That's great! No, that's fantastic. Are you still scared?"

Summer put a hand against her stomach. "More excited. Maybe I gave 'existing' a shove and turned the corner to 'living.' A little scary, but mostly not. I feel like I can keep on going if I have some paper and something to draw with."

"I know exactly what you mean. Control. Gives you a measure of control."

"That's it. Someone pisses me off, I can make them a caricature. Something makes me sad, I can turn it around and find something positive to draw. Something that makes me feel better. Something that gives me a little power."

Renny caught the flicker of pain in Summer's eye. "What are you thinking about?"

"A little girl who found comfort, a true friend when she needed it."

"Tell me."

"I got a call late Wednesday. Another girl gone missing. Only it wasn't the same. The mother…She was pimping her daughter. Knowing my mother and all she's gone through for me it's hard to understand. Anyway, Corey had a friend. And even in her misery she felt better because he knew what her favorite candy bar was. Later I was able to get that moment on paper. It helped."

"You've had a turbulent couple of days. Are you sure you're up for going out?"

"Positive. Doing this, going out, is what I need. This is normal. If that isn't enough, I'll have tonight to look back on when my mother's dragging me from store to store tomorrow."

"You say that like it's a bad thing."

"Only because it is. When it comes to shopping that woman is like the Terminator. She can't be stopped. Crying and begging don't work."

Renny threw back her head, laughing. "I have got to meet your mother. She sounds wonderful."

"Except for the shopping thing, she is."

"Then treasure her. She could be like mine. Eve doesn't drag me shopping, she drags me down." She frowned. "Scratch that. I shouldn't have said anything. She called as I was getting ready to leave. Supposedly to tell me about a new part that's perfect for me, that will get my name back in the headlines, but really she just wanted dirt on my father and his wife."

"I'm confused. Your name's already in the headlines. Does she not realize how popular your novels are?"

"But it's not for a starring role," Renny said, biting down on bitterness. "For Eve it's all about Hollywood. Television was okay, but according to her, to really be successful you must be in the movies. Like her. My little hobby is fine and well, but 'darling you really should come back to civilization and be seen.' And although she's quit adding the bit about 'now that you've dealt with the weight and acne problem,' it's there like the elephant in the room."

"I'm sorry she can't appreciate your genius. I know if you were my daughter, not that I want you to be, but if, I'd be talking you up all over the place. You're great."

"You're hired as my press agent. With you behind me this new book will be on the bestsellers list in no time."

"I'd need to read it before it came out. For the right spin, of course."

"Good one, but you'll have to wait like the rest of the eager masses. All two of you."

"There's bound to be five at least. Don't sell yourself short."

Renny couldn't stop a smile. "Okay, five. Eve will buy one even if she won't read it."

"Could…do you think she's jealous of your success? Maybe she doesn't want you to be more famous than her."

"I put nothing past Eve. Being maternal was never her strong suit. I'm sure she had me so she could look beautiful with a baby in her arms, play the role of the loving mother in public. I stopped trying to figure her out the second time I was in rehab. My counselor said it was in my best interest. And in the time between her calls I do a good job of remembering all I've accomplished despite her. Eve is Eve. She's never going to change. And enough about my mother. You didn't ask me out to hear about her."

"That's right. I asked you out to make points." She came to a stop halfway down the block. The Bistro had opened three years ago and, due to excellent food and service, had expanded to take over empty neighboring space. The owner had grown up in Seneca and after spending most of her life working in restaurants on the northeast coast had come back to her roots to open her own restaurant.

On the inside, the impression was of understated elegance. Sounds were muted and the staff moved with hurried purpose. Due to the early hour, the place was only half full.

"Very nice," Renny murmured, removing her coat. She enjoyed the way Summer's eyes widened, then narrowed in focus.

"Wow. You look…Wow."

"You like?" She preened.

Summer nodded.

The maître d' cleared his throat. "May I help you?"

"Uh, Baxby. Reservation for Baxby."

"Ah, yes. I'll be happy to take care of your coat, ma'am." He motioned for a young woman, then carefully draped the coat over her arm. "If you'll follow me."

They were shown to a table for two that looked out over the street. Their austere-looking waiter seemed to materialize from nowhere. He spouted off the specials and took their drink orders.

"Classy joint," Renny said, after he was gone. "I bet they don't get a lot of patrons ordering soft drinks with their meals. He probably thinks we're cheapskates. Which to me is a step down from being considered a recovering alcoholic."

"Does it bother you that people know that about you? About the drugs and alcohol?"

"Don't forget the wild parties and promiscuous behavior. It gives me character and character helps sell books," she said loftily. "Seriously, I freely admit to the mistakes I made in the past. But that was then. Now I want people to see me and know I'm not that party animal who didn't give a damn about anybody or anything anymore. That I've grown up. Some will and some won't. I can't control those who don't, so I stopped worrying about them. Makes me a happier person." She opened the menu. "Speaking of happy. This place might be more dangerous than the bakery."

"That depends on your viewpoint," Summer said, studying the menu intently. "I, uh, personally haven't noticed any damage to your, uh, posterior."

"You looked, huh?"

"Pleading the Fifth again. Here come our unsophisticated drinks."

Simon served them their drinks with the same aplomb with which he would have served champagne. "Are you ready to order?"

"We need a few more minutes," Renny said, sending him on his way. "Now what were we talking about?" She tapped a finger against her chin and pretended to think. "Oh, yeah. Point of view. Your point of view."

"Funny, I thought we were discussing the menu. The filet mignon stuffed with lobster sauce sounds good."

Renny ran a finger over the back of Summer's hand. "That's okay. Your eyes gave you away. And Summer, I'm thrilled you like your point of view. I know I'm finding mine well worth the ticket." She returned her attention to the menu. "Decisions, decisions."

* * *

"Told you he assumed we were cheapskates," Renny said as she slipped on her coat. "The expression on his face when he saw the generous size of your tip was priceless. It wasn't there for long, but I did see it."

Summer shoved her hands into her jacket pockets. "He deserved every penny. And now he thinks we're recovering alcoholics. That should make you happy."

Renny grinned. "It does. More points for you. Do you mind if we walk around, take in the sights? I need to work off some of that beef stew."

Summer gave a quick glance over her shoulder. "Do you want us to get banned?" she whispered. "'Beef stew'? Maybe we should run before the chef hunts us down for that insult."

"I didn't say it wasn't excellently prepared. The beef practically melted in my mouth and the sauce was perfect. But despite the fancy name..." She shrugged. "Beef stew."

"Heathen. McDonalds for you next time."

"I had an addiction to Big Macs when I was eleven, almost twelve. Had to sneak them because they weren't on Eve's approved list. I was already starting to fill out."

"Sorry." Summer dipped her head. "I should keep my mouth shut around you. I can't seem to say anything that doesn't bring back bad memories."

"What are you talking about? I have fond memories of sneaking Big Macs past Eve's eagle eyes, using mouthwash to hide the smell on my breath. I tried one when I was older. Didn't have the same appeal. By then I'd stopped blaming Eve for everything that went wrong in my life and accepted that the forbidden was a temptation I had to be leery of. And that's the last time I talk about my mother tonight. Let's talk about something else before I lose any more date points."

As Summer was learning about Renny as well as her mother she didn't mind. "No points lost with me. But okay. I'm sort of backing out of my promise. You already know I went to the park yesterday. What you don't know is why. Because of the stuff we're not talking about I needed to see girls who were alive and well. Who hadn't had their childhood snatched away too soon. Then I held Chelsea, felt all the love Keile and Haydn have poured into her, all the love she's holding inside and suddenly I was remembering an incident with my sisters. I didn't snitch on them and in return they bought me ice cream. That's sisterly love for you." Summer smiled, remembering how good the ice cream tasted. "You should have seen me yesterday. I was so giddy with happiness. Can't wait for more presents like that. Because that's what it was—a gift."

"Sounds wonderful."

"It was. I had another one a couple of days ago. My seventh birthday. I got this huge easel. One I could stand at and paint on like a real artist. But the best part was remembering how happy my family was for me. How much they loved me. Of course the seven-year-old me was just ecstatic about the easel."

"Did you start painting right away?"

"The memory didn't extend that far, but I imagine I probably ripped through the other presents and waited till later to start my masterpiece."

"I'd bet your mother has it stashed safely in the attic."

She heard the wistfulness in Renny's voice. "Hey, what's the very first thing you ever wrote?"

"This horrible plot for a television show. Starring yours truly. I was about thirteen and desperately seeking work. So I thought, hey, I can write something for myself. Can't be that hard. Wrong."

"Horrible?"

"Stank worse than ten skunks and filled with all the melodrama of a teenage girl. Luckily I got a few bit parts and put it away. I take it out now and then when I need a good laugh."

"You still have it? Can I read it?"

"That would be a big no," Renny said firmly. "Some things aren't meant to be shared."

"Not even if I ask my mom to dig out my old masterpiece?"

"Tempting, but not really. I've never willingly let anyone read it. Never will."

"Okay. Fine." Summer gave a playful pout. "Wait. Did you say willingly? That means someone else read it. Is that why you don't share?"

"Slip of the tongue," Renny muttered. "Forget it."

"I'm sorry. They had no right."

"It was years ago. No big deal. I'm over it."

No, you're not, Summer thought, angry for a teenage girl who'd probably thought her life was over. "I'm still willing to show you my early etchings."

"It was Eve. She read it and laughed. Said it was absurd."

"Then I feel sad for her. Sorry she couldn't see what that script meant to you. Sorry she can't see you today."

"That confirms something for me. You have a good heart, Summer Baxby. Maybe that's why those girls reached out to you. They knew your heart was big enough to feel for them. To see them."

She was surprised by the rush of pride she felt. "That's the nicest thing you could have said to me." She stopped and reached for Renny's arm, oblivious to the disruption that caused in the flow of foot traffic. "Renny, that helps me flip this whole thing. I've been so afraid that I was connected to him. That he was getting inside of my head. But it's not him. It's his victims. No."

Summer pulled at her hair as her theory fizzled like a balloon stuck by a pin. "That doesn't make sense. When he grabbed Georgia I saw it through his eyes. I was connected with him, not her."

"Let's step to the side." Renny moved them out of the way of the swell of pedestrians. "It doesn't matter who you connected with. Didn't we just talk about your good heart?" She grabbed Summer's arms and gave her a little shake. "Come on, there is no way he can get inside your head and take you over. It wouldn't happen, Summer. Your heart wouldn't let him."

"I want to be as sure of that as you are." She rested her head on Renny's shoulder, drinking in the scent that was a mixture of Renny and perfume.

"Summer? What's going on?"

Not him, not now. She sighed and lifted her head up and forced a smile. "Rich. Hey. Uh, how are you?" As he was dressed for an evening out, she figured he was on the prowl. No doubt looking to practice what he considered his wiles on some unsuspecting woman.

"I'm good. Sorry about the thing in the elevator. Didn't mean to freak you out."

"That's okay." When he looked from her to Renny, then back to her, Summer could tell he was remembering their conversation in the bookstore. She could see him adding the sums, followed by the widening of his eyes when he came up with four. "This is my friend Renny. Renny, this is Rich." She nodded a "yes, Rich from the elevator" in response to Renny's inquiring look.

He smiled, flashing white teeth, and held out a hand. "Nice to meet you."

Summer wanted to scream, wanted to tell Renny not to touch him. Not to get sucked into the horrors not buried deeply enough behind the good looks. She held her breath, then exhaled when she remembered he didn't have that effect on anyone but her.

"Well, I'll let you two get back to doing whatever it is you two do." Rich's eyes were bright with innuendo as he gave them a nod and turned to leave.

"Wait." Summer dared to touch his shoulder. "It's…Do you know a Georgia Zackery?"

"You mean that girl that's missing?"

"Yeah, her. I mean did you know her before she was missing?"

"Why would I?" He pulled at the lapels of his sports coat, gave his practiced smile. "I have my pick of the ladies. No need to deal with the kindergarten set."

"That's what I thought. Uh, listen, the police might uh, come talk to you. I told them you didn't know anything," she added quickly as he lost his smile. "It's complicated. But it's not like you're in trouble or anything."

"What the hell are you talking about?" He took a step toward her, his eyes narrowed to slits. "You told the police *I* had something to do with that girl going missing?"

Summer took a step back but feared even that distance wouldn't be enough to block him out. Wouldn't be enough to block his thoughts, his fears from invading her brain. "No. I didn't. I swear I didn't. It's just…on the elevator I had a thing and you were there." She covered her face with her hands and didn't stop reciting the multiplication table until Renny's arm encircled her. "He's not in any trouble," she whispered. "I wasn't trying to get him in trouble."

"I think you want to back off," Renny said firmly. "It's obvious the police are grasping at straws to find the girl. And if they haven't contacted you already, it means they've already eliminated you as a person who can help them."

"I don't see why my name should have come up at all." He puffed himself up, clearly not wanting Renny to think she could intimidate him. "What if it was your name? Wouldn't you be pissed if the police were looking at you for something like this because of her?"

"I'm smart enough to hear and understand what's being said," Renny replied with a sneer. "Not once did Summer say the police were looking at you as a suspect. In fact, she clearly stated you weren't in trouble."

"Like I can take her word," he all but spat out, pointing a finger at Summer. "I don't even know her. And she sure as hell doesn't know me. I'm sick of women getting me in trouble. Getting me fired and in trouble with the police—"

Summer was back in the closet, hidden real good this time. This time his mother had made sure the raving monster wouldn't find him. If Rich opened his eyes he could see the monster through the small hole in the comforter that covered him. He could see the red eyes shining out of a face twisted and ugly and evil. He kept his eyes closed and shivered, hoping the monster would stop the yelling and go away. Go away before using his big hands on Rich's mother. Go away and never come back.

He jerked when he heard a thump, heard his mother cry out for the monster to stop, to leave them alone. "Please, make him disappear," he prayed quietly, rocking back and forth, sucking his thumb even though the monster would hit him if he saw. "I'll be real good this time. I promise I won't pee on myself. I promise."

But the only response was the sound of grunts, fist hitting skin and his mother's cries of pain. Rich knew those sounds. Had heard them too many times in his young life to not be afraid. He put his hands over his ears and hummed, but the sounds wouldn't go away. Wouldn't stop.

In desperation, he threw off the comforter and looked for something that would stop the monster. Would make him go away for good. In the book, the boy had found a magic sword, but Rich knew there was no such thing in real life. In real life monsters were your father and there was no magic to protect you from that.

"Boy! Get out here and take your punishment like a man."

For a second Rich was too scared to move. He could hear the monster, but he couldn't hear his mother. Couldn't hear the soft cries that usually came after a beating. Something was wrong. Really wrong. When the monster called him again, he scrambled back to the hiding place his mother had made, pulled the comforter over his head and with his heart beating in his throat, he could only mumble the Lord's Prayer like his mother had taught him. He did not, however, pee on himself as he listened to the monster rage…

"Summer? Summer?"

When she came back her head was throbbing so hard she felt nauseous. She tried holding her breath, but that only made the throbbing worse. "Give me a minute." Pushing away from Renny, she headed to the side of the nearest building and lost the contents of her stomach. With the worst of the spasms gone, she leaned against the building and cried.

"Is she drunk?" Rich demanded to know. "Shit. You mean I'm in trouble on the word of a drunk?"

"She's more sober than you are. I think it would be better if you left," Renny said, crossing her arms over her chest.

"I'm not going anywhere until I get a damn good explanation." Rich jutted his chin, glaring at Renny. "Last I heard being on an elevator with someone was not grounds for having the cops consider you a person of interest. Look at her. If the police saw her now they wouldn't buy a damn thing she had to say." He whipped out his cell phone and took a few shots of Summer's misery.

"Hey!" Renny held her hand in front of the phone. "How big an asshole are you? Show a little compassion. She's had a tough week."

"Tough week?" he scoffed and flung out his arms, barely missing hitting Renny. "I got your tough week. Did she lose her job because some asshole was jealous of her? Did she get a ten thousand dollar past-due tax bill for property she didn't know she owned? Well? What? Let me guess. They were out of her favorite cocktail? No drug candy to put up her nose? Boo-fucking-h—"

"Shut up! You shut the hell up," Renny said, stabbing a finger in his direction. "You don't know what the hell you're talking about, so shut the hell up. You think Summer's over there crying because of some alcohol? You're wrong. Dead wrong. More likely she's crying over something she sensed about your stupid ass."

"Get real. The two of you must think I'm going to believe anything. Like I'm some kind of moron."

"The worst kind," Renny shot back. "And, hey. Maybe calling you a moron is an insult to morons. You're a starfish. I hear they don't have any brains."

"Like you would know, bitch."

"Stop," Summer said weakly, the ache in her heart almost unbearable as she made her way back to them. "Please stop." She took a couple of deep breaths, tried to get back some control. "Rich, I'm sorry your name got pulled into this mess. But the police aren't looking at you for this. What they are looking for is a seven-year-old girl. All I did was tell the truth to help them do their job. If you feel you need to rip me up for it, be my guest. Renny, you ready to go?"

"Been there." She hooked her arm through Summer's, taking a lot of her weight. "I'm sorry for whatever you saw."

"Me too." Though she didn't look back, Summer could feel Rich's stare. "Do me a favor. If I ever try to have another conversation with him, slap me silly."

"What if I just pull you in the opposite direction? I wouldn't want to break my hand on your hard head. The book would never get finished."

Summer managed a wan smile. "Can't have that. Not after you yet again rode in on your trusty steed to defend my honor."

"What else was I going to do? Prick. Him I wouldn't mind slapping silly. Oh, wait. He already is. Care to tell me what you saw?" she asked gently.

"His father really was a monster. I think he beat Rich's mother to death, tuned Rich up regularly for not being manly enough." She swiped at the tear, unaware of the attention she was drawing. "He was so scared and so helpless. Kids should never have to feel that way. It breaks my heart. God, I wish Dr. Veraat was back. I don't know if I can handle this. I don't know."

"Have you thought anymore about seeing someone else? Another woman maybe? I have some contacts through AA."

"I probably should. I feel so…" She sighed and was quiet the rest of the way, fighting back images of a terrified boy and lost girls.

When they approached her building, she realized how unfair she was being. Poor Renny hadn't bargained for hysteria and vomit with her gourmet dinner. "Some date I've been, huh? I understand if you don't want to suffer through this wonderful experience again. It's okay if you want to leave, try to salvage what's left of the evening."

"I hope you don't think a little bit of vomit is going to discourage me. Used to be a party girl, remember? I've seen worse and lived to tell the tale," Renny boasted and lightly squeezed Summer's arm. "Hell, I've done worse. Not that it's a good thing, mind you. I'm just saying."

"How can you joke?"

"How can I not? I'm not trying to make light of what happened. But neither will I blame you for it. What you're dealing with is…I don't even have words. What you won't have to deal with is me thinking any less of you because you had a normal reaction to a young boy's hell. In fact, it's the opposite. I think more of you. The strength to take it all in and still care is incredible. How could I not want to go out with you again?"

"Okay." She nodded, taking a deep breath, then used her key card to get them through the door leading to the elevators. "Any chance you want to come up and catch a movie? My dad has me well stocked."

"It has to be a comedy. I demand to laugh my fat ass off."

Summer smiled. "That'll be kind of hard, don't you think? Not that I've been checking it out or anything, but your ass is not fat. No winning the fat ass contest for you."

Renny put a hand to her chest, looking affronted. "I'm hurt, I say, hurt. That you would crush my hopes like that, well, I just don't know what to say."

"Anyone ever tell you your Southern accent stinks?" she asked and jabbed the Up button.

CHAPTER TWENTY-ONE

Summer jerked awake, a scream lodged in the back of her throat and the remnants of a nightmare wedged in her brain. Looking around she was glad to find herself on the sofa in her apartment. *Must have fallen asleep during the movie*, she thought and cringed. Yet another bad mark on her date card. "Sorry about flaking out," she mumbled, wiping her spitless mouth.

"I was almost there myself," Renny said around a yawn. "Bad dream?"

"Two for one. The missing girls, all twenty-five of them, on top of Rich and his loving father. The only good thing is that I think Georgia's still alive." She rubbed her eyes. "I have got to get that guy out of my head."

"Rich or the monster?"

"If Rich goes, his monster goes with him."

"Not Rich's. I'm talking about Georgia's monster…"

Summer leaned back and closed her eyes. "When she's found, he'll go. I hope. If only she'd give me better clues about where he's keeping her." She exhaled. "That's too easy, I know."

"What if you sketched what you do know? Sometimes if I'm blocked, I try to type without thinking about it. Most of it ends up being garbage, but the tiny piece I keep is usually pivotal. Could be your eyes took in more than your brain's telling you."

"Worth a try." She turned off the TV and DVD, then retrieved her pad and pencils. After staring at the blank page a moment she smiled. "This reminds me of when I used to paint with a blindfold. Drove Cyn crazy that whatever I came up was better than anything she could do with her eyes open." She closed her eyes. "I'll start with the table..." She blinked and looked at Renny with dawning wonder. "Oh, God. Oh, my God, Renny." Summer grabbed her head, squeezed. "Cyn. Oh, Cyn. How could I forget her?" Her shoulders slumped under the weight of guilt.

Renny reached for Summer's hand and held it between hers. "Not just her, Summer. You forgot everything and everyone. But you remembered her now. That's what's important. Who is she?"

"Eighteen. We met when I was eighteen. My grandmother gave me a trip to New York City for my birthday. May twenty-sixth. I know my birthday now. Really know it." She exhaled. "The memories are falling over themselves. It's almost too much."

"Then tell me about Cyn. Focus on her."

"I met her at MoMA the first day I was there. The first thing I noticed was her hair. Cyn had lots of red, red hair. And she was tiny, but you didn't notice because she had so much energy. She was twenty-three, just out of college, and had all these grand plans to take on the sculpting world. Swept me off my feet. By January I'd transferred to NYU and we were sharing an apartment near Central Park. She was in the car with me when...She didn't make it, Mom said."

"That's tough. You were together over ten years," Renny commented after a protracted silence.

"Why can't it be simple?" She rubbed her temples, exhaled. "It wasn't all good. She could be moody, up one minute, down

the next. More so after I started having some success. Damn."
She covered her face with her hands.

"What's wrong?"

"That night. We weren't talking. Big blowup. Shit." Summer
took shallow breaths, rocking back and forth, then she pushed
off the couch and paced. Holding her head, she muttered "No"
over and over as the events of that night played out like a
B-grade movie. "It needs to stop. Make it stop." She grabbed at
her hair as tears beaded in her eyes. "Why can't it ever be easy?
Why the hell can't it be easy?"

"Summer, are you here?"

She exhaled, faced Renny and noticed she was now standing,
confusion riddling her face. "I have to be the worst date ever,"
she said with a sad smile. "You should run. Fast and far."

Renny crossed to stand at an arm's length. "Not going to
happen," she said firmly. "Do I need to get you to a hospital?"

Her laugh was closer to a sob. "Don't worry. I'm not having
a breakdown. Not yet." She wiped her eyes, then dried her hands
on her pants, heedless of the tears still falling. "I remembered
what I think my subconscious wanted me to forget. Damn, I
wish I hadn't."

"Do I need to call your mother, anyone? Tell me what I can
do to help."

"You're still here. That helps. It's just I can't…" She took a
deep breath, trying to get enough air to tamp down the panic
threatening to raise its powerful head.

"Calm down." Renny ran her hand up and down Summer's
back. "Whatever it is, we'll deal. And if we can't, then we'll find
someone who can."

"She was so angry. The rage on her face when she looked
at me. It's true. Oh, God." She covered her mouth and hurried
to the bathroom. All the water Renny had practically poured
down her throat since they'd been back from dinner came back
with force, overshooting the toilet and hitting the wall. Even
after she was empty dry heaves wracked her body. She held on
tight when Renny wrapped an arm around her waist and patted

her heated face with a cold rag. It said a lot about her misery that she wasn't embarrassed for Renny to see her like this. She leaned into Renny's shoulders and gave into the sobs.

"You're going to be okay," Renny murmured, holding Summer tight. "I know it doesn't seem like it now, but you're going to be okay. You'll see. This is part of your recovery." She continued to hold Summer long after the trembling stopped.

"No wonder my mind went blank," Summer said eventually, her voice raspy. She was tired. So tired. "I didn't see it coming. I knew her—well, thought I knew her—and still didn't see it coming. I found out she was screwing one of our friends and we had this huge fight. Accusations were flying, and then she slapped me. Tried to do it again, but I pushed her back. Took me a minute to get over the shock and I left. Wandered around the park, trying to make sense of what had happened. Eventually I found myself at a friend's house. I couldn't go back home. Not with my eye swelling." She exhaled slowly, took a deep breath. "I dodged her for two days. Had to think, decide how to proceed. I didn't know what to say to her, you know?"

"Of course. She changed the game plan. Not only cheating, but violence."

"Yeah. Anyway, she convinced me to meet her to talk it out, said I owed her that for all the years we'd been together. Dumb."

"No. It wasn't. You had a lot of years invested. I'm sure you wanted an explanation."

"That and to have my say. We met at this little bistro not far from where I was staying. It was crowded, loud, so when she begged me to go for a drive I thought, sure, why not? I wanted to be sure she heard what I had to say."

"You were going to end it?"

"The moods were bad enough, but cheating? Final nail in the coffin for me. I expected more respect for me, for what we had. She'd tried to throw the blame on me before, so I was thinking, private is better. We get in the car and she starts right away pinning the blame on me. How I haven't been there for her, blah, blah, blah. The kind of things they teach at Cheaters-R-Us."

"Bullshit, in other words," Renny said dryly.

"That's what I said. That if she couldn't deal in truth we had nothing to say to each other." Summer closed her eyes. She'd been too full of indignation to pay enough attention to the maniacal look that had come over Cyn's face.

"Finish it. You need to get it all out, then you can put it away and maybe one day forget."

"Put it away, maybe. Forget? Never. Where was I? Oh yeah, calling her on her bullshit. Told her to take me back to the restaurant. We were done. I had nothing more to say. She had plenty. Built-up resentment from years before. The more she talked, the more erratically she drove. At one point, I asked her to pull over, let me out. She laughed and sped up instead, then started weaving across the center lane. The words that were coming out of her mouth. That look on her face." She shivered. "All I could do was cover my eyes and beg her to stop. I think I felt the impact, heard Cyn scream and the windshield shatter. I'm not sure what happened then, but I was ejected from the car at some point. Faulty seat belt they said later, but…"

"Don't think about that." Renny's voice was scratchy, her eyes drenched with tears. "You already remembered enough for now. Come on, I think you should be lying down. This on top of the other is too much. You need to lie down, try to sleep."

Summer drew back and brushed a hand over the wetness on Renny's cheeks. "I need to clean up, brush my teeth. Then I'll feel better. That'll make me feel better."

"You brush, I clean. And before you try to argue, let me point out how easily I could take you down," Renny said with a scowl more comical than threatening.

She gave in. Maybe she wasn't the only one who needed something to do. "I'll owe you. Dinner and a movie. But this time minus the melodrama, okay?"

Renny ran her fingers over Summer's hair. "For your sake I hope it is."

* * *

For the first time since she checked into rehab for the second stint, Renny woke up snuggled to another body. She'd dated, had sex with a few women, but never spent the night. It was comforting to open her eyes without wondering who the other person might be or what she'd done to get herself in her current situation. There was something to be said for sobriety, for having all her senses intact.

She looked at Summer, noting the furrowed brow on an otherwise smooth face, and itched to smooth out the wrinkle as much as the underlying cause. That was a new role for her—caregiver. After thinking it over, she decided it was one that she liked. One that she was ready to assume. Unable to resist, she dropped a light kiss on that brow. She wasn't disappointed when Summer's eyes opened.

"Hey," Summer said softly and smiled. "You're still here. Seems I owe you more than dinner and a movie."

Renny chuckled, glad the intimacy of last night was still there. She'd been a little concerned that Summer would wake up and regret asking her to stay. "I hear diamonds are a girl's best friend." She wiggled her ringless fingers.

"A small price to pay for the services rendered," Summer said seriously. "For my continued sanity."

"You know I'm kidding, right?"

"Of course. It's still a small price to pay." Summer propped herself up on her elbow. "What I can't understand is why you're single."

"Obviously I was waiting for you."

"I should be so lucky." Summer bent and dropped a kiss on Renny's lips. "Thanks."

Renny threaded her arms around Summer's shoulders and tugged. "You're being stingy with the thanks."

"Can't have that." This time Summer's lips met Renny's with intent and purpose. Without breaking the kiss she shifted her body until she was on top of Renny. Tongue met tongue as their passion ignited.

"Better," Renny said, dragging air into her lungs. She slid her hands down the back of Summer's sleep shirt until she gripped her behind. "Surely your sanity is worth more than that. I'm thinking bare skin might up the ante."

Summer sat up, reached for the hem of her shirt and hesitated.

"Off."

Her face suffused with color, Summer complied. "Don't complain if it isn't up to standards."

"Oh, but it is." Renny ripped off the shirt and reached for Summer's milky white body. "Beach for you this summer." She nibbled on Summer's bottom lip. "Food too."

"Anything else?" Summer asked with arched brows.

"I don't know. Do you remember how to dance?" She sucked in a breath when Summer pressed against her center. "Silly me." She cupped one of Summer's small breasts and squeezed a taut nipple. "What was that?"

"Me moaning."

"No, that," she whispered. "I heard a noise out front."

"You do know burglars do their thing at night, right?" Summer's eyes widened at the sound of keys meeting table. "Shit!" She glanced at her alarm clock. "My mom!"

"No!" Renny shoved Summer away, slid from the bed and grabbed her clothes.

"Summer? Don't tell me you're still in bed. It's nine."

They looked at each other as Sandra's footsteps came closer. "Say something," Renny hissed.

"Just a sec, Mom. I, uh, I got a late start." She motioned for Renny to go into the bathroom.

"Take your time, dear." Sandra sounded amused. "And tell your friend she doesn't have to sneak out the window. Why don't I walk to that bagel shop and pick us up some breakfast?"

"That would be good."

"Had to be my shoes." Renny had gotten over her embarrassment and was working on amusement when Summer joined her in the bathroom, wearing a robe. "They're right there by the sofa and obviously not something you'd wear."

Summer covered her cheeks. "What's better than diamonds? I'm going to owe you the world before this date is over."

She opened the cabinet above the sink and pulled out a new toothbrush. "Will you consider this a down payment?"

"This is so TV sitcomish. I could have written the script. Of course there would have to be righteous indignation in the mother's voice after discovering her young virginal daughter in bed with an experienced older woman. Maybe an inhuman scream."

Summer's lips twitched. "You're going to make me laugh. How can I laugh in a situation like this?"

"How can you not? I bet your mother's laughing as we speak. Come on." She gave Summer a poke. "You know you want to laugh."

Summer slapped Renny's hand away. "Do not. My mom almost walked in on us, remember?"

Renny grinned and reached for the toothpaste. "Hey, she was real cool. Has this happened before?"

Summer looked horrified. "God, no. I think." She put a hand to her chest, exhaled. "No, I'm sure. That I would have remembered. And before you say it, yes, I did forget she was coming over to drag me out shopping."

"Considering the evening you had, it's a wonder you remember your name. If I'm not upset, then you don't get to be upset. And after you buy me the world, I won't be," she added with a sly smile, then brushed her teeth.

Summer seemed to stew a minute. "But that means you're upset now. If you're upset, then by your rules, I get to be upset."

Renny rinsed her mouth. "How can I possibly be upset knowing you're going to buy me the world?" She sluiced water over her face. "Can't." She grabbed a towel and wiped her face. "Set and match."

"That makes no sense."

"And therein lies the beauty."

"That doesn't make any sense either. I don't suppose you want to come with us, run interference?"

"I'd love to meet your mom, but not like this. I'd better hurry before she comes back."

"Okay, but you're going to miss the reward she's picking up now that she's stopped laughing."

"Like I need pastries after the dinner I devoured last night."

"Pastries? I'm talking about the gold plaque for going out with her daughter."

Renny laughed. "Good one, but I already got my reward." She struggled into her clothes, thinking this was the wildest date ever. And she didn't have to suffer through a hangover.

"So I'll see you tomorrow at Keile's," Summer said as she trailed Renny to the living room.

"I'll probably take Chazz to the park, say around ten, if someone wanted to meet me there." Her heart did a little flip when Summer's face lit up.

"Someone would love to meet you there."

"Good." Renny slipped on her coat and pulled Summer close for a kiss. "Tomorrow."

On the elevator, Renny ignored the knowing looks. After all, she did look like she was going home after a sleepover. Next time they'd go to her place, then Summer could be the object of amusement.

* * *

"She's gone?" Sandra asked as she hung up her coat. "I'm sorry, baby. I didn't mean to scare her off. I should have called first." She picked up the bag of pastries and the cardboard container with three cups of coffee.

"Don't worry. Your arrival was a fitting end to a disastrous date. I can't believe she actually wants to see me again. Crazy, huh?"

"Not from where I'm standing." Sandra deposited the bag and the coffee on the dining room table and pulled out a chair. "I told myself I wasn't going to pry. That you're a big girl now and I should wait until you felt like sharing." She took a sip of coffee. "But the hell with that. Who is she?"

"Tell you later." She sat next to her mom and brought one of her mom's hands to her cheek. "I remember Cyn." Then, taking a deep breath, she added, "And most of the accident."

"Oh, Summer." Tears beaded in Sandra's eyes. "I wish you could remember one without the other."

"Me too." She had already decided no one else except Dr. Veraat needed to know the circumstances surrounding the accident. Cyn had already received her punishment. Telling her family would only hurt them. "It's not as bad as it could be. I remember the noise from the collision, screaming, then pretty much nothing else. But get this. I also remembered my seventh birthday. Sitting at the picnic table in the backyard, blowing out the candles, and the stack of presents. Would it be okay if instead of going shopping we went home? I want to see the house again now that I have my own memories of it."

"Of course." Sandra dabbed at her eyes with a napkin. "Your dad will be so happy. He doesn't show it, but he's been worried about you, about what's happening. We all have."

"You all can stop. Especially you. You've done way more than your fair share."

"My prerogative." Sandra opened the bag, pulled out a cinnamon twist, broke it in half and thrust one half at Summer. "I'll always worry about my kids. Wait until you have some of your own."

"That's not going to happen."

"There's plenty of time for you to find the perfect woman, make a withdrawal from a sperm bank and give me grandkids."

She thought about Cyn, about the betrayal, and wondered if she'd have been open to a relationship with Renny if she'd gotten her memory back before they met. Maybe she would have eventually learned to trust again. As an adult, not as the girl she'd been when she and Cyn met.

"No comment?"

She took a healthy bite of the pastry and settled for a noncommittal shrug. To please her mother, she finished the rest of the twist. "Shall we go? I'm eager to see the place, explore old haunts. Knock more memories loose."

Once they were on the road, Summer shared bits and pieces of her evening, including the name of her date.

"You'll be in her book for sure now."

"Mom!"

"Just saying…" Sandra laughed.

"If I was a writer she'd be in my book. You should have seen the way she took on Rich."

"Rich?"

Summer smothered a groan. She hadn't meant to bring that up.

"Well?"

She gave her the bare minimum, downplaying her reaction.

"That poor boy." Sandra pursed her lips, cocked her head to the side. "I haven't thought about that in forever. As I recall, they lived in that little house off of Winslow. Kind of set back in the woods. The mother seemed nice, but she never had much to say about herself or anything, for that matter. If I remember correctly the boy was a few years younger than you and close to seven or eight when it happened. He went into the system after that. I don't remember hearing anything about him."

"What happened to the father?"

"Once they found him, they threw his sorry butt into jail."

"Would he still be there now?"

"I have no idea. I think I remember they moved the trial out of the county, further south. After that, the story died down. Most likely he served his time for manslaughter and moved. Why the interest?"

"Just curious," Summer said, but she made a note to do some research. There had to be a reason he was on Rich's mind lately. "For Rich's sake, I hope he never has to see that man again. It has to be hard knowing someone you thought you knew, thought you could trust, could be that cruel."

"Are we still talking about Rich?"

"Of course. Who else would I be talking about? You know I'm surprised you haven't made more comments about the identity of my date."

"I thought I caused you enough embarrassment for one day. I have to admit I am impressed by your choice. So, you had *the* Renny Jamison in your bed? Will it be in the tabloids?"

Summer rolled her eyes. Her mother was getting too much enjoyment out of this. "No. And the bed part was only a technicality." A technicality only because her mother showed up, but that was strictly need to know. "I told you she only stayed because of the upset about Cyn."

"So you don't know her in the Biblical sense?"

"Mom!" Despite the teasing in her mother's voice, her cheeks burned. "Don't ask, I won't tell."

Sandra laughed and turned on the radio. Classic rock poured forth from the surround sound speakers. "Never believed in that. Check the Constitution. It's a mother's right—no, duty— to ask."

"And right under that in fine print you'll find that it's a child's right to change the subject in this type of situation," Summer said primly. "I forgot to tell you—I bought drawing pencils this week. You were right. My ability to draw is not linked to anyone but me."

"Excellent change of subject. One you knew would make me swallow the bait." Sandra shot her daughter a quick sideways glance. "Which is why I won't question why your cheeks are so red on a mere technicality." She cleared her throat. "Tell me. What brought this on?"

"More like who. Your fault really. Marcia made disparaging remarks about you."

"Bitch."

Summer laughed. "Exactly. What could I do but put her likeness on paper."

"I can see why you would have needed color pencils to do justice to the makeup." Sandra nodded her head. "Makes me proud. You took the high road. Still taking the high road."

Summer barely heard. Her breath quickened as her mother made a right and drove up the long driveway. They crested the hill and the sprawling three-story house came in to view. She knew this house, not from the year and a half it had been her sanctuary. No, she knew it from roaming its halls with her siblings, searching every nook and cranny for hidden treasure.

From growing up with the love and security that had given her freedom to explore, to expect to find something different and great. Her parents had done that for her, for her brother and sisters.

The house was located twenty miles outside of town on ten acres. The property had been a working farm before her parents bought it and added on sections. Sandra kept the large garden, but most of the fields had been left alone to revert to grassland. There were other houses in the area, most on five-acre lots and most owned by people who wanted the semi-rural life.

When the Bug came to a stop, she sat for a moment, taking in the mature trees surrounding the house. They were bare now, but in a few weeks the buds would form and from there bloom to keep the house cool in the summer. She'd once earned a trip to a timeout for taking a dare and climbing one of the trees until her sister said "Stop!" Looking down and realizing how high she was, she had started crying, too scared to climb back down.

"I remember it." She turned to her mother. "There's no place like home." That thought brought back another memory. "Oh God, I was thinking, no, I was seriously considering moving back here from New York. Not here with you and Dad, but definitely to the South." She put her hands to her head and squeezed. Other fights with Cyn also came back—the screaming, the shouting, the threats, all ending in betrayal. Summer opened the door and got out of the car, but she couldn't leave the ugliness behind.

Taking in the scent of home, she stared at the house and willed thoughts of Cyn, of New York away. She was here for other memories. Like the time they used duct tape to attach Jonah to a wall or sleeping out in the backyard, pretending to be settlers heading for the Western frontier. Cyn had never been in this house. There was nothing of her here.

Sandra slipped an arm around Summer's waist. "However you got here, I'm glad to have you close by now. I would have preferred the other way."

Summer leaned into her mom, dropped a kiss on her soft cheek. "Come on. Let's surprise Dad. Maybe break out the croquet set he gave me for my tenth birthday."

CHAPTER TWENTY-TWO

Summer awakened before daylight the next morning. There was no gasping for breath, no lingering unease from bad dreams. She sat up, stretched and did a mental scan of body and mind. She felt good. No, she felt great. Spending a day playing with her parents had been a good thing. Getting back huge chunks of her memory had been an even better thing. She'd thought about spending the night with them and in the end decided to come back to her new home. Decided that despite all the things that were going on, she didn't need the crutch of her childhood bedroom anymore.

Splashing her face with cold water, she changed into workout clothes and hit her treadmill. As her shoes slapped against the rubber pad, she continued her self-assessment. Having the memories made her feel solid, on firmer ground. More like a real person. Not the Summer she'd been before the accident—maybe she'd never be that Summer again—but also not the Summer she'd been yesterday morning.

As she picked up her speed, she thought not being the old Summer was probably a good thing. She could start new, somewhat fresh and without the weight of dealing with Cyn. Looking back, it was clear to her how much effort she'd put into the relationship with little return. The constant ups and downs, the arguments she never saw coming had slowly worn her down to the point where getting out and moving back home seemed the only way to survive. She'd wanted, needed to be closer to her family and the steadiness they'd given her throughout her life.

She never got a chance to share her plans with Cyn. They'd had that horrible fight over Cyn's infidelity and then... She exhaled. But somehow, she thought Cyn had known. Had probably sensed her withdrawal, her losing herself in her art. Her unwillingness to fix everything by shouldering the blame.

Whether Cyn knew or not, she wasn't going to take any of the blame for Cyn's behavior. Nothing she'd done had driven Cyn to break their vows. Nothing she'd done had caused that last desperate attempt to keep her chained to Cyn. None of it was her fault. None of it.

Her breathing ragged, Summer slowed her pace and attempted to get a grip on her emotions. She hadn't realized how angry she was—at Cyn, at herself. She should have faced the issue with Cyn years ago. So what if she'd been young when they first got together? Hadn't she figured out over the years that their relationship wasn't what it was supposed to be? Was nothing like the one her parents had? But she'd stuck it out, managing to convince herself time and time again that Cyn would change. That Cyn would get over her jealousy at Summer's growing acclaim in the art world. That the upswings and downswings weren't getting worse.

"Boy, was I wrong." Time to admit her failings and put them away. Hopefully, even learn something from it. Learn that she couldn't help someone by absolving her of all responsibility. That's essentially what she'd allowed Cyn to do. No, she decided with a wince, she'd enabled that. Enabling had to be worse.

"History," she muttered. "Do not repeat." She lowered the speed on the treadmill for a cool-down walk. Enough with the thinking. Time for doing. She'd hit the shower and fuel up, then find something to occupy her time until it was time to go to the park. Time to see Renny and pray there were no more mishaps. No mind hopping, no remembering dark events and no interruption by mothers. Just her and Renny and Chazz.

* * *

By nine thirty Renny couldn't stand it anymore. She sent Chazz for his leash and pulled on a thick hoodie. If she took the long way and encouraged Chazz to dawdle they would only be fifteen minutes early.

Outside she breathed in the crisp morning air, looking for and finding the first signs of spring—the offshoot of buds on tree limbs. She loved this time of year when everything began waking up from winter's slumber. Not a bad way to think of her romance with Summer, she thought. They were both waking up from a period of slumber, thickening the branches of their lives by being willing to give the relationship a chance.

She looked at her hands, imagined buds sprouting on them and laughed, drawing Chazz's attention. "It's nothing you would understand," she told him, rubbing behind his left ear before continuing forward.

The playground was getting a workout, she noted, enjoying the shrieks and cries that signaled kids having fun. It was easier to think of them having fun than it was to think about the images Summer carried around in her head. And, knowing Summer, in her heart.

Chazz pulled on his leash, obviously eager to get to his playmates.

"Slave driver," Renny grumbled as she let him increase their pace. Then it was she, and her heartbeat, who sped up when she spotted Summer leaning against the fence surrounding the dog park.

Looking well rested, Summer's face lit up with a smile. "Hey, you." She gave Renny a quick hug, then Chazz a two-handed rub.

"Shopping with your mom looks good on you." Renny opened the gate and set Chazz free. "You should do it more often." She shielded her eyes from the sun and watched as Chazz raced up and down the field at full speed.

"We skipped shopping. I spent most of the day at my parents' place instead. It was great. Beat my dad at croquet."

Seeing the carefree smile on Summer's face, Renny almost wished she'd been there to see it. "Croquet? I didn't think anyone still played that."

"We haven't in a long time. My dad gave me the set when I was ten and the two of us used to play most weekends, weather permitting. We always fought over who got the blue ball. He always won the coin toss till I wised up to his use of a two-headed coin."

Renny thought of the father she barely knew and couldn't imagine him unbending enough to try to sneak one by her. "Sounds like an interesting guy. Why blue?"

"It's our favorite color. For me and Dad 'having the blues' is a good thing."

"Interesting way to look at it. The two of you are close, I guess?"

"He got tears in his eyes when Mom told him I'd already called dibs for croquet. Then he tried to squeeze the life out of me all the while claiming my dibs wasn't valid."

"That's close," Renny declared. "I can be happy for you and envy that closeness at the same time."

"I'm lucky. I know that now and I hope I never forget again. Will you look at that?" Summer laughed and pointed to where Chazz stood patiently as his leg was being humped by an overweight Chihuahua. "He really is sweet."

"That's my baby." As they watched, Chazz shook off the Chihuahua and returned to playing tag with an Irish setter. "Have you had breakfast?"

"Cream of Wheat. Breakfast of champions." Summer flexed her arms. "But it was hours ago. I was up early."

"Nightmares?"

"Not a one. Best sleep I've had in forever. I conked out early because I spent most of the day trying to keep up with my dad. He insisted we go to the arcade like we used to do, then practically made me play every game."

"I've got to meet this guy. So not only does he have a two-sided coin, he's a gamer?"

Summer grinned. "From way back. He designs video games. Mom claims she married him because she knew he was never going to grow up."

"Why did he marry her?"

"Because she's beautiful and she didn't take herself or her money too seriously."

"Definitely have to meet them now."

"I'd love for you to. We could go to their place and I could show you all the good hiding places."

"Better people than me have tried to resist that, I'm sure. But back to breakfast. You want to come back to my place? I actually have food. And beverages."

"Better people than me have tried to resist that, I'm sure," Summer parroted, earning an elbow jab to the ribs. "I would be happy to eat your food."

"Better," Renny said with a mock scowl. "If you want you could hang out till it's time to go over to Keile's," she said with studied casualness.

Summer nodded. "That would be great. And not because it would save me a trip back over here."

Renny tilted her head to the side, her smile deliberately flirtatious. "Should I be flattered that you showed up early and you want to spend more time with me?"

"I don't know. Is the truth flattering or is it fact?"

Renny shook her head. "No philosophical questions until I've had at least another cup of coffee. Maybe two."

"Where's the fun in that? The best philosophical discussions take place in the realm of pre-wakefulness. You know, when you're not asleep and yet not fully awake, so your mind is freer to consider the impossible."

"I haven't visited that realm since I became sober. Looking back, I don't think the impossible is all it's cracked up to be."

"You haven't been doing it right."

"I'm not touching that one." Renny whistled for Chazz. "I'd need at least three cups of coffee for that."

Summer retrieved her bike and fell into step with Renny and Chazz. "Was that a challenge?"

She pursed her lips, gave Summer a sideways glance. "You're different. More confident. I like it."

"My foundation's been shored up. I'm not so afraid a misstep will lead to a complete collapse. Changes everything."

"Not who you are underneath, I bet," Renny said, getting a firmer grip of Chazz's collar as they approached a couple walking a black Lab. "Bet it didn't change your heart."

"Okay, maybe not everything," Summer conceded. "Can I assume you've recovered from the date from hell?"

"Enough to finish the book."

"Renny, that's wonderful! Here I am going on and on about me and you have this great news. You should have said something sooner. You must feel great."

"It's only the first draft," she cautioned. "I'll let it sit, then give it a good edit. But yeah, it feels effing great to have pumped it out and way ahead of schedule."

Summer gave Renny's hand a quick squeeze. "I should be taking you out to breakfast to celebrate. We'll do dinner one day this week. Toast it with sparkling grape juice."

"You know they don't sell that in restaurants, right?"

"I'll bring my own. In a discreet brown paper bag."

"Please don't think you have to abstain from drinking alcohol around me. I can handle it."

"Not drinking isn't a problem for me. I haven't touched alcohol in three years. I never was much of a drinker anyway."

"Just know it doesn't bother me." As they made the left onto her street, Chazz picked up his pace. "He always does this. Like all of sudden he realizes he's been away from home."

"Wow, a purple door," Summer said as they walked up the driveway. "Do you use that as a landmark?"

"Courtesy of my grandmother." Renny unlocked the front door and motioned for Summer to enter. "As you can see, she liked the colorful." She pointed to the bright yellow walls of the foyer. "I haven't had to do much to the house. She kept it in great shape. For me, I guess."

Summer took off her jacket and handed it to Renny. "Love the hardwood floors."

"Feel free to look around while I go throw something together for brunch."

In the kitchen, Renny arranged the foodstuffs on the table. She'd stopped by the store yesterday on the way home from Summer's place with this occasion in mind. Because of that, she put more effort into making the small kitchen table look like something she'd seen in a magazine.

"I like your house." Summer entered the kitchen with Chazz at her heels.

"Again, most of the credit goes to my grandmother." Renny motioned at the table. "Please join me."

"This looks nice." Summer pulled out a chair.

"If you're not hungry at least eat the doughnuts and spare my ass. If it gets any bigger it'll need its own zip code."

"Leave your ass alone. I happen to like it." Summer transferred two chocolate-covered doughnuts to her plate. "The little bit that I managed to see," she added, then took a big bite.

"Are you trying to tell me something?" Bagel temporarily forgotten, Renny propped her elbows on the table, cradled her chin. "I get it. You woke up Summer, didn't you?"

"More Summer than I've been and possibly less Summer than I will be."

Summer's tone was matter-of-fact, but Renny wondered what emotional price the new discovery carried. She studied Summer's eyes, found them clear and decided the price must have been just right. "I think that deserves champagne more than me finishing my first draft."

A smile played at Summer's lips. "You would. But once again we're talking about me. How many people show up to your book signings more interested in Renny the child star than Renny the author?"

"More and more they're interested in the author." While they ate, Renny shared some of the funnier stories from her book signings.

When Summer stood to take her empty dishes to the sink, Renny waved her back down. "Nope. You get the first-timer's pass. Next time, though…" She mimed washing dishes.

"Am I allowed to let Chazz out?" Summer motioned with her head to where Chazz was sitting patiently by the back door.

"That you may do." She put away the food, then loaded the dishwasher. "It might actually get warm enough to cook out later," she said, watching Chazz find a spot to sun himself. "Maybe sit on Keile's deck."

"I can entertain myself if you have things you need to do."

"And here I was thinking you were going to entertain me."

"Yeah?" Summer put her arms around Renny's waist and rested her cheek against Renny's back. "I guess I owe you for feeding me. Not sure what my bill is up to now. What's more than a diamond?"

She laughed, enjoying the warmth Summer's body was generating in a certain area. "A whole diamond mine. And no blood diamonds."

"Gotcha." Summer nipped at Renny's neck. "But what can I do until then? For entertainment purposes, I mean."

Renny turned so they were face-to-face. "I seem to remember getting interrupted yesterday. Any chance you remember where we were?"

The kiss started slow and easy, a gentle reminder of the morning before. Then deepened as tongue met tongue in a duel of need. All Renny felt was the softness of Summer's lips and the heat of their combined fire. It was intoxicating. But more, it was arousing.

"I think I remember," Summer huffed and sucked in a breath. She rested her forehead against Renny's. "If I promise my mom won't drop by, will you help me take off my clothes again?"

Renny gave her a quick hard kiss. "Maybe. For future reference, 'Mom' and 'taking off clothes' should not be mentioned in the same sentence."

"Scout's honor."

"Then follow me." Renny led her out of the kitchen, down the hall that separated the dining room from the living room and up the stairs with the natural wood banisters. Renny's room was in the back—a master suite with a large bathroom and a walk-in closet that could easily have been a guest room.

"This takes up half the floor. Nice." Summer's gaze moved from the books overflowing the small bookcase to the Georgia O'Keefe paintings adorning the walls and stopped at the huge bed. "Your grandmother had good taste."

"Not important." Renny tugged on Summer's jeans. "Okay, now you need to strip."

Summer kicked off her shoes and wiggled out of her jeans. "Hey, you too."

She shook a finger. "I watch you, then you watch me. Win-win."

After a moment's hesitation, Summer removed her polo shirt. "I'm not dancing around a pole." She stood in matching panties and bra with her hands on her bony hips, tall and thin and, in Renny's eyes, a beautiful survivor.

"Smartass." Renny pushed her back onto the bed and straddled her. "I thought I was in charge." She undid the front clasp on Summer's bra and squeezed her breasts, watching the pink nipples harden as she rolled them between her fingers.

"You're breaking the rules." Summer's complaint was half-hearted at best. She sucked in a breath and raised her hips when Renny's mouth found a nipple. "You get a pass this time."

"Yeah?" She kissed her way to the other nipple, licked, then sucked before she sat up and pulled off her sweatshirt. She stood and quickly removed the rest of her clothes.

For a moment, Summer could only stare. Renny's body was lush, the epitome of femininity. To her eyes, no diet was needed. She exhaled and only then did oxygen get to her brain. "Turn around," she ordered, her voice husky. "That's definitely not big enough for a zip code, but it does deserve an award. Best in show."

"You just won the bonus round," Renny declared and rejoined Summer on the bed.

"Wrong." Summer ran the back of her hand along the side of Renny's face. "I won the grand prize."

"I'm the writer here." Renny brought Summer's hand to her lips. "You can't go stealing my lines," she added, punctuating each word with a kiss until she made her way to Summer's lips.

"You're the writer," Summer agreed and threaded her fingers through Renny's hair, bringing their lips back together. They shared kiss after kiss, stroke for stroke, taking their time in this new dance.

"I want to touch you." Renny rolled to her side and trailed her hand down Summer's body to the top of the brown curls, then back up to play with her nipples.

"What a tease." The touch of Renny's long fingers was like liquid fire that burned, but didn't hurt. "Touch me." She gasped when Renny complied and lifted her hips to get closer to pleasure. It had been so long. Too long since she'd felt the boiling of her blood, the rush as it coursed through her body. "Harder." Reaching out blindly, she closed her hand over Renny's to deepen the pressure, to bask in the bombardment of sensations. At Renny's request, she opened her legs wider and could only shake her head from side to side as Renny slipped inside. In and out and at the same time keeping the pressure on the center of her desire.

"Yes," she said as the pressure inside her spiraled around her, tighter and tighter until it was almost unbearable. Until every nerve called to her, louder and louder. She came on a sob of pleasure, riding the waves as ripples of release shook her body and filled her mind. Struggling for breath, she snuggled against the luscious curves of Renny's breasts and waited for her heartbeat to return to normal. "Wow," she finally managed. "Just wow."

"Yeah, wow. Despite being pale and skinny, you're not so bad."

Summer managed a smile. "Overwhelm me with compliments, why don't you?"

"I try my best." Renny ran her fingers through Summer's hair. "Probably not the right time, but the streak...Natural?"

"If something coma-induced is natural. Would you throw me over if it was dyed?"

"Probably not. Just wondering what it might look like someplace else."

Summer opened her eyes. "Kiss me, you romantic fool." The amusement died away at the touch of Renny's lips against hers, the feel of Renny's body stretched on top of hers, skin against skin. She smoothed her hands down Renny's back and cupped her behind, pressing center against center.

"Yes," Renny moaned against the side of Summer's neck. "Yes."

Summer angled a thigh between Renny's legs, felt the wetness as Renny pressed against her thigh. She remembered this dance, this give and take. Reaching up, she brought Renny's mouth to hers, exchanging slow, intoxicating kisses, made sweeter by the movement of Renny's hips.

Eventually it wasn't enough for Summer. Not nearly enough. "On your back," she whispered and maneuvered until Renny was where she wanted her to be. "I want to see you when I touch you, when you come."

With her mouth, she loved Renny's breast and trailed a hand past the stomach and through her glistening curls. Renny's sigh was music to her ears. As she stroked, she felt the silkiness against her fingers, watched Renny's eyes narrow, darken and saw the beauty of pleasure arrayed on Renny's face. "Beautiful," she whispered as Renny fell over the cliff with a quiet gasp.

Summer rested her head against Renny's chest, listened to the drumming of her heart and felt satisfaction.

"You get an A-plus for entertainment."

"Didn't do it by myself." Summer sat up, took a deep breath and let it out slowly. "Ditto on the A-plus. Hey, where're you going? I'm not finished."

Renny walked to the closet and took a robe off the hook on the door. "I could use some liquid refreshments and I need to let Chazz in. Coke okay for you?"

"Water. I need to rehydrate before I go at you again." She wiggled her eyebrows. "Plenty of water. I plan to take my time with you."

"Be right back."

CHAPTER TWENTY-THREE

Later that evening Summer collapsed in a heap, letting Chelsea catch her before she reached the finish line. She was working off the huge dinner she'd consumed by having crawling races with Chelsea. Kyle had declared himself too old to participate, so he and Renny were playing with Legos.

"I think we have another babysitter," Keile said. She was sitting on sofa snuggled next to Haydn. They were admiring Summer's sketches of their children.

"She has plenty of energy and enthusiasm," Renny said with an innocent smile.

"Why do I get the feeling she's talking about something else?" Haydn put a finger to her chin, looking like she was giving the thought considerable consideration.

"Could it be the redness of Summer's cheeks?" Keile asked.

Summer considered her ringing phone a lifesaver. She frowned at the caller ID, but answered anyway. "Summer… Yeah…But—…Okay. Twenty minutes." She gave Chelsea a squeeze and breathed in her baby scents to remind herself there were some innocents left. That some girls did get a childhood. "I..." She cleared her throat and tried again. "Looks like my reprieve is over. They need me at the police station." She tried to smile, seeing the worry in Renny's eyes.

"I'll take you." Renny stood as if to signify it was a foregone conclusion.

"Do they have something new?" Keile asked after a quick glance at Kyle.

"They, uh, they want me to try something again."

"Is that safe?" Haydn crossed to take Chelsea. "Seems like you've been through a lot this weekend."

"Maybe this isn't the best time," Renny said, reaching for Summer's hand. "Can't it wait until tomorrow?"

"I'll be fine." She gave Renny's hand a squeeze. "And Dani will be there to keep the cops in line." Summer wondered if her smile looked as plastic as it felt. She didn't want to go, but couldn't not go. Not when there was a chance she might pick up something off of Georgia's toy.

"I'm still going."

This time Summer's smile was real. Renny looked cute in her bulldog stance. "Figured. What's bigger than a whole diamond mine?" At Keile's and Haydn's puzzled expressions, she said, "Long story." Then, "I'll be okay. Really," she added, and this time she sounded sure. "There's a little girl out there waiting to be rescued. I have to handle this."

"What is it you didn't want to say in front of them?" Renny asked once they were in her house. They stopped off so Chazz could be fed and, at Renny's insistence, to get coats.

"The dogs found something in the wooded area near Constitution. A body. They've identified the remains as a girl who went missing in Florida about six months ago. She fits his type." She shook her head. "Oh God, Renny. There are other remains, bones, they haven't identified yet. Bone structure suggests they're all young females."

Renny put her hands on her hips. "What do they want you to do? I know you're not going there to link with a dead body. No fucking way. Over *my* dead body."

"No, Renny. No. They want me to try to link with Georgia again. I know it didn't work last time, but they're desperate. They haven't had any hits off the sketch and the multiagency team they pulled together is getting a lot of pressure. And the feds are here now that it's interstate." She rubbed her temples. "Juan and Carla went back to the hospital to talk to the grandmother. She told them about the stuffed monkey Georgia always slept with. It was the last gift from her parents before they died. Something that means a lot more than the pony."

"So they expect you to get some vibes from that. So what? The kid's not going to know where she is and you already have his face. What's this going to get them aside from more heartache for you?"

"I have to try, Renny. Maybe I'll see more of the truck or the front of the house. Or maybe I'll just be able to know she's still alive. If she's alive, she can be rescued. That has to be worth more than a little heartache."

"Don't try to placate me. It won't be a little heartache." She pulled Summer close for a hard hug. "Don't think I'm letting you out of my sight. I don't give a shit what those cops say."

Summer leaned into the hug and found some strength. "Like static cling."

"You're supposed to say glue."

"I've never been accused of being common." Her laugh was only a little shaky when Renny pulled a face.

The ride to the station was made in silence. Summer spent the time focusing on the good things in her life. Whatever she got off of Georgia's toy she would remember the great day she'd spent with her parents, the joy in Chelsea's eyes and the strength of Renny's support. After the headache and the horror faded, she'd have that to fall back on, to prop her up. And she'd have Renny right by her side, ready to help her slay dragons.

"I think you should stay at my place tonight," Renny said as she turned into the station parking lot. "Look at all these cop cars. Shouldn't they be out turning over bushes?"

"I hope they're not here for me." She swallowed hard as a knot threatened to settle in her throat. "They can't expect me to talk to all of them."

"No fucking way that's happening." Renny exhaled. "We're probably overreacting. They're probably here for a briefing about the remains." She slowed and pulled into a spot at the back of the lot. "Coincidence."

"That's as bad. What'll they say after they see me coming in, talking to Vince? They promised they wouldn't give out my name. No way they can keep it quiet with this many law enforcement officials around."

"Where's your phone?" Renny held out her hand. "I'm calling him. He's coming out here to us or we're taking this meeting off-site." She searched until she found the last incoming call, then hit Reply. "No, this is Renny. What's going on? We're not coming in there with a packed house. You promised her anonymity...We can do that." She ended the call and handed Summer the phone. "The feds are here. They called the briefing without consulting the locals or the state. We need to go around back. Someone will let us in."

Juan met them at the door, sorrow etched on his face. "Thanks for coming." He led them to a small office outside of the holding cells.

Summer considered it lucky they were empty, though they still made her nervous. Reminding herself they weren't for her didn't help. "Where's Dani?" she asked, her gaze fixed on the ragged stuffed animal sitting on the conference table.

"She decided keeping an eye on the briefing was more important," Juan said and gestured for them to sit. "Making sure we don't get any unexpected visitors while you're here." He closed the door before joining them at the table. "As you can see she loved this monkey very much."

"Yeah." Summer traced the bald spots with her eyes. Her bedmate of choice had been a unicorn her dad won at a carnival. Taking a deep breath, she took it into her hands and—

she was sitting on the floor inside the funny-smelling room, hoping he wouldn't come today, hoping something bad would happen to him while he was gone. When she'd heard him drive away hours ago in that truck that made a lot of noise, she'd tried to open the door but it was locked. Always locked. The windows were nailed shut and had black stuff on them so she couldn't see how to get away even if the door wasn't locked.

She heard the truck long before she heard his footsteps coming down the hallway. She shrank into a corner when she heard the lock turn, then held her breath when the door squeaked open. She wanted to look away, cover her eyes when the man walked in, but she couldn't. He was smiling. She hated that smile more than she hated the mad look. The smile meant he was going to hurt her again. Her heart hammered in her chest as she looked around, but like always there was no place to go. No place to hide from him and his long arms that grabbed her and shook her every time.

"How's my little sweetheart today?" He dangled a candy bar. "Got you a chocolate bar. Like the one you stole from that store you like to walk by on your way home from school. Guess what? They got your picture in the window." He chuckled. "Got one of me, too. 'Course I don't look like that anymore." He rubbed his smooth chin. "Those cops think they're so damn smart. I'm smarter. Come over here and get this, little girlie."

She shook her head. "I'm...I'm not hungry." She cringed and held up her hands to shield her face when he started toward her. "Please. Please don't hurt me," she begged.

"Where's the gratitude? You little bitches are all the same. Look at me," he demanded. "You'll look at me if you know what's good for you."

She dropped her hands and was blinking away tears when she noticed the open door. He never left the door open. Never. She wet her dry lips. This was her chance. She couldn't blow it. "Maybe I am hungry a little bit." She stood, held out her hand and didn't flinch when he stroked her arm and called her his best girl. "Thank you very much." She took the candy bar and slowly unwrapped it while she tried to plan. She had to make sure he didn't notice the door. Taking a big bite, she made noises like she was enjoying it. When he smiled and sat on the bed, she raced for the door, pulled it shut, heard the lock click into place. Let him see what it was like. But she hadn't gone more than five steps before she heard his footsteps behind her. A sob lodged in her throat. She increased her pace. The key! She forgot about the other key. The one on the chain around his neck.

Her chest felt tight as she rounded a corner. There. The front door. She fumbled with the knob. It was locked. No key. There wasn't a key. She pulled on the knob, sobbing. Pain exploded in the back of her head, then darkness...

"Summer. Summer, come back."

The rough jostle of her shoulder jerked her back. Blinking her eyes, she became aware of the throbbing in her head.

"Hurts," she said in a little girl voice, then grabbed her head and squeezed. "Hurts."

"She needs drugs," Renny told Juan. "This gift of hers isn't free. At the very least it comes with a bad headache. A Coke, no, ginger ale would go good with that."

"I'll be right back."

"Wait," Summer called out before Juan left the room, then wished she hadn't when her headache got a headache. She breathed slowly in and out until it was a dull roar. "Pen and paper. He's changed his looks. And he's been back to the store near where he snatched her. Bought her a Hershey's chocolate bar. Not nuts. It's her favorite. Oh, yeah. He drives a truck that backfires a lot. Now you can get the drugs." She closed her eyes and laid her head on the table. "Are you going to say 'I told you so'?"

Renny rubbed her back. "That would be no. You gotta do what you gotta do. I might wish it otherwise, but then you wouldn't be you."

"She might be dead," she said quietly. "Probably is. She tried to escape and he...he caught her, Renny." She blew out a sharp breath as tears pooled in her eyes. "What if what I have to give isn't good enough? What if he's already killed her?"

"You can't take that on, Summer. You've given the cops more than they've ever had. Because of you they know about this guy, about what he's been doing. It's only a matter of time before they find him and shut him down."

"But that won't help Georgia." She wiped at her cheeks, searched for her center. She couldn't afford to lose focus. She may have been too late for Georgia, but maybe, just maybe, she wouldn't be too late for the next girl.

Juan entered the room with Vince right behind him. "Ginger ale and what passes around here for aspirin."

"Pad and pencil," Vince said, placing the items in front of Summer. "The briefing's over, so I'd say in a few minutes we can get you out free and clear. I can't say enough how thankful I and the department are that you're willing to work with us after the rocky start. I've seen for myself how much this takes out of you."

"I wish it was more. Wish I could do more."

"You've done more than your share," Vince said. "Don't ever doubt it. Now it's up to us to do our part."

That helped. Summer exhaled, picked up the pencil and drew a monster. His face structure was the same. The absence of a beard and mustache added to the removal of gray in his hair made a big difference in his appearance. Summer wasn't sure she would have recognized him if he passed her on the sidewalk. And he was counting on that anonymity to slip by, to keep doing what he did. He was in for a big surprise.

When she thought she was done, she looked it over and made a few tweaks.

"That's the same guy?" Juan asked.

"Master of disguise," Renny said. "Maybe that's why he's never been caught."

"Why are you frowning, Summer?" Vince asked. "What's wrong?"

"He looks familiar." She chewed on her lip while studying the sketch. There was something about this guy, the eyes. She shook her head. "I can't...I can't figure out where I know him from. He just..."

"I'll make a copy, get it out." Vince picked up the pad. "I need you to think deep. Try to tie his image with something. Might help you to remember where you saw him." He strode off, looking like a man on a mission.

Juan pulled out a chair. "Do you know if you've seen him in the last few years?"

"Has to be. I'm fairly sure I didn't know him in New York. Doesn't help much, does it?"

He patted her hand. "Actually that's good. Tells us he's probably very familiar with this area. That his hideaway is somewhere around here. As soon as Vince gets back with the sketch you should be good to go. We've taken up enough of your time." He pulled a card out of his shirt pocket. "Give us a call if you think of anything, no matter how small it might seem."

It was Carla who brought a copy of the sketch. She had a cool nod for Summer, then a warm smile for Renny. "You have a ride? I'm off the clock till tomorrow. We could catch a drink."

"I have my car," Renny replied, her voice as cool as Carla's nod. "And I don't think Summer's up for a drink. I imagine you realize it's been a tough evening for her."

Carla frowned. "I was thinking you and me. Of course, Summer's welcome to tag along if she chooses."

"Earth to Carla," Juan said, clearly amused. "Buy a clue."

"What?" Carla's gaze sharpened as she looked from Renny to Summer. She shrugged. "Some other time."

"Obtuse," Renny said as they walked to her car. "Can you believe her? Some other time? What was that supposed to mean? She's lucky I was more concerned about getting you out of there than slapping her down. Stupid bitch."

"You know what she meant. When you're not saddled with me," Summer said, more amused than angry at Carla's dismissal of their relationship. "Does that mean you're going to be dumping me soon?"

Renny grabbed her hand and linked their fingers. "Not until you've made good on your promises. I think it was dinner, diamonds and something more than a mine? Until then I stick."

Summer's smile echoed the warmth she felt inside. "Looks like dinner in Atlanta. I've already taken you to the best restaurant Seneca has to offer."

"I was thinking Paris. Dinner, the Eiffel Tower, hot sex in the Red Light District." She wriggled her eyebrows. "Best of all, guaranteed not to run into a certain someone. That's not to say I find throwing up in the street unattractive."

"Ha." Summer tried to look indignant. "An abbera—" She came to a standstill as realization dawned. "Shit! Oh my God. Oh my God."

"What? What's wrong?" Renny demanded. "Not another vision thing."

"How could I not see it? How could I be so blind?" She beat against her head. "It was right there."

"Right where?" Renny gave Summer a little shake. "What's going on?"

"Rich's father. He's the one."

"What? Summer, are you sure?"

"He looks more like he did then. The first vision. The time he found Rich and his mom in the closet." She closed her eyes for a second. Just one second to steady herself. "His eyes aren't red, they're golden. This is going to kill Rich. He just can't catch a break."

"He's alive," Renny said, stroking Summer's back. "Sounds like a break to me. Let's get this over with."

They hurried around to the front of the building, arriving as Vince and Juan were leaving.

Vince's eyes narrowed as his gaze focused on Summer's face. "You remembered something."

"I don't know the last name. First name is Stan. He went to prison for killing his wife about twenty years ago. Rich Slator is his son. I mentioned him before, but he's not in this. He's just another victim of his father."

"Son of a bitch," Vince said, running a hand over his hair. "I remember that. Stan Ralston. My rookie year. Got called to the house and saw what he did to her. Son of a bitch managed to escape while being escorted to court for sentencing down in Tifton. Never did find him. And we looked plenty. Damn." He took what looked to be a steadying breath. "Looks like we owe you again."

"Stopping him is payment enough."

"Count on it." He walked away barking orders into his two-way radio.

"Anytime you need, anything. Call me," Juan said before rushing after Vince.

"I don't think he'll be so lucky this time," Summer said, watching them enter the building. "He's not expecting them. Doesn't expect them to make the connection."

"They didn't make the connection, you did. Remember that. We should go before the rest of them come back."

"Yeah, I guess Vince will be the one leading the briefing this time." That made her feel better. Maybe apprehending Stan would bring closure to Vince and to Rich. For herself she wasn't sure if Stan's capture would help balance the scales for being unable to save Georgia. That death was going to weigh on her mind a long time.

CHAPTER TWENTY-FOUR

Summer awoke, sweaty, her throat dry as the desert and her heart pounding. Taking care not to wake Renny, she got out of bed. She'd thought knowing the identity of the abductor was going to drive the nightmares away. She'd been wrong. Very wrong.

In the kitchen, she filled a glass with cold water, drank it without pause, then held the cool glass against her heated forehead. She couldn't say how many times the scene of Georgia's attempted escape had played through her dreams. Splice in the final closet scene with Rich and you had a recipe for seriously disturbed sleep.

The click of Chazz's nails against the tile floor almost made her smile. "Did I wake you?" She gave him a deep body scratch that had his tail going crazy. When he licked her face as if saying thank you, she felt the lingering mist from the nightmare dissipate and her brain click into first gear.

A glance at the microwave showed it was just after four. She wondered how the search for Stan was going. Having a name to go with the face didn't make finding him any easier. Not when he'd managed to stay off the radar for so long.

And how had he managed that? From what she'd read, a lot of girls went missing each year, but surely someone should have noticed the twenty-five with the same attributes—blonde, blue eyes, seven- to eight-years-old. Of course one of them had been from Florida and cooperation between states was more than likely nonexistent, given how little communication there was between the different organizations within the states. He probably knew that. Probably counted on it in picking his victims. Probably smirked about it as he trolled around the southeast for victims, then transported the girls back to Seneca and disposed of them when they outlived their usefulness.

Summer's breath caught in her throat and she ran a hand over the tightness in her chest. She couldn't help thinking that poor Georgia, by trying to escape, had outlived her usefulness. Had unknowingly brought on what the monster saw as the ultimate punishment. She wondered if once Georgia realized what was happening she'd experienced a second of relief that she wouldn't be violated anymore.

She was up to twenty times twenty before the tightness eased enough to allow her to take a decent breath, to push thoughts of violation and death to the back of her mind. She'd done her best. Done all she could do. It wasn't her fault Georgia hadn't made it outside, giving Summer an opportunity to see the house and surroundings in hopes of being able to place the location. A location where others had been kept, then discarded with, she imagined, little more thought than he gave to his trash.

What made a person like that? It had to be more than mother issues. Were some people truly born evil? She had a hard time believing that one. If that were true, they'd have some defect in their genes and pass it along to the next generation. She rubbed the goose bumps on her arms.

"What are you doing awake?" Renny entered the kitchen, rubbing her eyes.

"Too much on my mind, I guess."

"Worrying about whether they caught him, huh?" She laid her head on Summer's shoulder. "I'm sorry it's keeping you up."

"Me too. I have to be at work in a little over four hours."

"Take a day. You deserve it."

"I'd worry more with nothing to do. With work I can escape for a few hours at a time. And getting a dig in at Marcia has become something to look forward to."

Renny leaned back, gave her the look. "Oh, there's an important reason to go to work."

"I know sarcasm when I hear it."

"Good. So tell me what really has you up before the crack of dawn."

Summer hesitated, gave a quick grimace. "Nightmares. Kept switching from Georgia to Rich and back again. I'd hoped…" She sighed. "Never mind."

"No. I want to hear. Please?"

"I had this idea it was done. That I'd sleep the sleep of the righteous and wake up without, you know, 'it.'"

"And by 'it' you mean the psychic stuff?"

"Yeah." She looked away from Renny's probing glance, afraid of what Renny might see. "I couldn't do it before the accident. When I was younger I might have been able to pick thoughts out of the air, but it was little things. Fun things to blackmail my siblings with. As I got older that ability faded away to almost nothing. I thought I missed it. Wrong, wrong and more wrong. I don't want this ability to experience other people's misery. To live through the kind of stuff nightmares are made of. Why me? God, why me?"

"It's your heart." Renny tapped Summer's chest. "Not saying I know a lot about psychic phenomenon. Let's face it, nobody does really. Since getting to know you, I have done a little research about how blows to the head can lead to so-called psychic abilities. In some cases it seems more about using the brain to its full potential."

"And in my case?"

"It's that and that big heart of yours reaching out to someone who's suffering." Renny shrugged her shoulders. "Lame, I know, but I'm sticking by my unprofessional theory."

"So I have to find a way to decrease the size of my heart and I'll be cured?"

"Exactly. Expect my bill in the mail."

"Ha ha."

"Why is it you've never jumped into my head?"

"Hmm. No suppressed deep, dark horrors? I don't know. Maybe you have a thick block in place to keep them in and me out. That would come in handy in show biz."

"Never let them see you sweat. One of Eve's favorite sayings. She taught me early. Doesn't work so well when you're trashed."

It wouldn't, Summer thought. Another good reason for her to continue to abstain from alcohol. She couldn't control the process sober. Drunk she'd probably get hit from all sides, sliding into one head after another. She shuddered.

"What?" Renny demanded, rubbing Summer's arms.

"Just considering what might happen if I got trashed. It's downright scary."

"Ever done it? Get trashed, I mean."

"Once. High school graduation party. I came to in my front yard with my mother standing over me. Took me hours to stop puking and almost three days to feel like I wanted to go on living. Never felt so bad. That is until my mother grounded me for a month. Felt like a damn baby, but hey, lesson learned."

"So little chance of it happening now, right?" Renny asked, eyebrows arched. "I'd say that's a useless worry ready to be ditched. Right?"

Summer shrugged, refusing to give in to the smile that wanted to break out. She could be absurd if she wanted to. Hadn't she earned it? "Awake at four o'clock," she finally said. "Well, okay, it's closer to four thirty now, but you get the drift."

"Not good enough, Baxby" came the quick retort. "You have more important things to worry about. It's all about priorities. You're wasting your worrying resource. When you use that up, it's gone. Then when something big pops up, bam! You'll be a sitting duck, trying to worry and failing. I see it all the time."

Her gaze zeroed in on the twitching of Renny's lips. "Why are you up?"

"Who knows?" Her smile was sly. "But then I'm not the one who has to get up and go to work in four hours."

"Bitch," she said, giving in to the smile this time. "Is this some kind of reverse psychology?"

"Only if it's working. Is it?"

"Seems to be. But then you do have that effect on me. Pushing me back to blue by standing up for me when I'm puking my guts out, promising to kill off asshole cops or staying awake with me when I'm sure you're sleepy as hell. You've got mad skills."

"Whoa. That's…I was going to say 'sweet,' but the word's too tame for what you expressed." She cupped Summer's face and gave her a tender kiss. "I feel empowered."

"It's my truth, Renny." She gave back the kiss, adding a little more. "Not that I mind the extra points I must be racking up. It must be taking away from the universe I owe you."

"Just lost 'em."

"What? No!"

"Oh, yes. Boasting of points makes them worthless."

"So not fair. After the hard week I had I should get—" She broke off and slapped her forehead. "I'm so stupid! Oh my God. I think I know where he might be."

"What?"

"Remember Rich talking about his hard week? The tax bill for property he didn't know he owned? What if his father put the property in Rich's name?" Summer raced to the bedroom and her cell phone. "Come on, answer," she said after three rings. "It's Summer. You need to find out the address of property owned by Rich Slator…Because he mentioned getting a bill for property he didn't know he owned…No, I don't have his number…Don't have his address either. Ask the feds. They know everything about everybody…Yeah, yeah. Just hurry, for Georgia's sake." She ended the call and zipped up to ten times ten before the urge to throw the phone across the room faded.

"In his defense he was probably up most of the night," Renny said from the doorway.

"Shouldn't be allowed to sleep," she grumbled. "Not until that monster's in a cage." *Not until we know if Georgia's alive or dead*, she thought, but she didn't give voice to the thought as she paced. Saying it would mean she believed there was a chance Georgia was still alive and that was a belief she didn't want to let in. Couldn't allow the hope to take hold in case it didn't come true.

"Is that part of the reason you're up?" Renny asked, coming closer. "You don't think you deserve to sleep?"

"If I sleep I'll dream and I'm tired of dreaming. As wired up as I am now, I wouldn't sleep anyway. I should go so you can go back to sleep."

"No. It's dark. At least stay till it's light."

"Renny, my bike has three lights. Bright, bright lights. People might take me for a UFO, but if anyone is out there they'll see me. Did I mention the reflective striping on my bags and my jacket? My mom bought my gear and she wasn't taking any chances. I'm always careful."

"Call me as soon as you get home."

"How can you go back to sleep if you're waiting for me to call? Come on, Renny, I've ridden in the dark plenty of times." She took Renny's hand and brought it to her lips. "Thanks for being concerned. Any chance I can see you tonight?"

"Don't try to change the subject. I'll sleep *after* your call."

Summer grabbed her jeans, preparing to put them on. "You win. About dinner?"

"I'll let you know when you call."

The early morning air was moist and unexpectedly warm, creating a dense fog. Even with her headlight Summer had trouble seeing more than a few feet in front of her. The streets were empty and eerily quiet as she made the trek west to downtown. She was glad to get her muscles working. Glad to feel her heart pumping from something other than fear and horror.

As she sped through the dark and the quiet, a feeling of being invincible filled her. For the first time in a long, long time, she believed she could do anything, be anyone she wanted to be. That was so different from a few days before. She wanted, no, needed to remember this feeling, laser it to her memory banks to take out and hold close when doubts set in. She knew herself better now and knew that doubt would set in.

Summer rode onto the sidewalk in front of her building. Swinging a leg over the crossbar, she spotted a familiar figure in the front doorway.

"You out for an early morning ride?"

"Something like that." Judging by Jay's eyes and the bulging corner convenience store bag, she figured he was on a munchies run. "You out for an early morning shopping trip?"

His smile was mellow as he held the door open for Summer to enter. "Something like that." After a couple of tries he managed to swipe his card for access to the elevator lobby. "You hungry from your ride? Got some good eats." He held up his bags.

"I'm good." She pushed the Up button. "You're not working today?"

He shook his head. "Worked this weekend so I could get off. Jake's b-day today." He lowered his voice. "We scored some good shit if you wanna, like, you know, partake."

She covered her laugh with a cough and pushed her bike into the elevator. "I got, like, work later. Tell Jake happy birthday for me."

"Sure. If you, like, change your mind we'll be hanging all day. Most likely score some pizza for later."

"Tempting. Work or pizza. Work wins out."

"No prob." He leaned back and closed his eyes, moving his head as if he were listening to music.

When they reached their floor, Summer turned left while Jay turned right. She was at her door before she remembered to check in with Renny. After reassuring her that everything was good, she changed into workout clothes and hit the treadmill for a long, hard, mind-emptying run.

She was telling herself not to think about the search when her doorbell rang. As she crossed the living room her phone rang, followed by her cell phone. Her first thought was that they'd found Stan. "One second," she called and checked for caller ID. "Hey, Mom. Was I supposed to call?"

"Have you seen the morning news?"

From the urgency in her mother's voice Summer guessed it wasn't good news. "No."

"Turn it on right now. I'm surprised reporters aren't at your door. How could they do this to you?"

"Me? Why would they want me?" The doorbell pealed again. "Listen, there's someone at the door. I'll call you back."

"Make sure it's not a reporter before you open the door. And for God's sake, turn on the TV."

Summer grabbed the remote, turned on the TV, then went to open the door. The smell of cannabis surrounded Jay like cheap perfume as he leaned against the doorjamb.

"Hey, remember when that girl went missing and you didn't, like, watch the news so I had, like, to tell you about it so you'd, like, be safe?" he reeled off, then took a breath. "Well, you need to, like, turn on the news today 'cause you've been, like, totally unmasked."

"Not the news again. I won't ask you to clarify. It's obvious you've been partying already."

"Yeah." He nodded his head, smiling. "But this is some serious shit. That dude said you told the police he had something to do with that girl that went, like, missing. Are you, like, some kind of undercover detective?"

Any other time Summer would have found the admiration in his voice amusing. She left him standing in the doorway and returned to the TV. Sure enough her photo flashed full screen accompanied by a voice reciting information about the accident, the coma, the miraculous recovery and the long time in rehab.

"No, no, no!" was all she could say.

Then her photo was minimized and moved to the top right corner of the screen, making room for a taped interview with Rich. He was seated in what was obviously his living room, flashing that practiced smile of his, as he tried to convince the pretty female reporter he was being persecuted because the police were incompetent. That the cops were basing everything on a supposed psychic, one he had proof was, in reality, a drunk.

Summer clenched her jaw when the photo of her throwing up was flashed on the screen. To think she had been sorry for this asshole, she thought as she rubbed against the tightness in her chest. She had to go up to twenty times twenty before she could take a deep breath. Before she could listen to the remainder of the interview. Then she could only shake her head in disbelief while Rich went on and on about how he was being set up. About how he was being billed for property he didn't own. Property Summer had purchased in his name to set him up. Even through her growing horror, Summer wondered if Rich were watching the replay. If he was realizing he looked like a raving lunatic answering the reporter's question on why he was being set up by claiming Summer had a thing for him he didn't return. "He's fucking crazy."

She barely noticed when Jay closed the door and settled on her sofa. How could she when they wisely cut away to a female reporter stationed in front of the police station? When that reporter, her expression somber, reported that Summer Baxby's psychic involvement in the case had been verified by a confidential source within the police department?

"See, see," Jay said excitedly, pointing to the TV. "They, like, revealed your secret identity." His eyes grew wide. "Dude, now the killer, like, knows that you know. Oh, man. You need to chill out at our place till this smooths out? Got munchies, remember?"

Summer looked at him and despite the dire situation almost laughed. Maybe she should take a few hits of whatever he was smoking. Everything would be simpler. She wouldn't be worried that her life was being turned upside down. That it was now fodder for a sensationalized story by every reporter in north Georgia. She turned off the TV. "Thanks, but no. I have a place to go when I need to." Which she would, when she figured out what the hell she was supposed to do next.

"Cool. I'm gonna, like, head back. You need a place to duck, we got you covered."

No sooner than she'd shut the door behind Jay than both her cell phone and the landline started up again. She managed to convince her mother there was no need to ride to her rescue, then did the same with Keile, followed by Kevin and Liz. Later she interrupted Juan's apology, telling him more politely than the situation called for to lose her number, turned off her cell phone and let it fly. The resulting "thunk" as it hit the carpet and skidded under the bed wasn't very satisfying.

As she paced the living room floor, her only consolation was that Renny was sleeping through the commotion. That she didn't have to be added to the list of people Summer had to worry about being worried about her. But that wasn't enough to stop the churning in her head. Everything was screwed up. *No,* she thought, *Rich had screwed everything up.* For her, the police and for himself. It wouldn't be long before an enterprising reporter dug up the connection between Rich Slator and Rich Ralston and then, from there, to Stan Ralston. From there they could get an old photo of Stan and compare it to the person of interest in the Georgia Zackery kidnapping case. Rich was going to get more attention than even he wanted.

Doesn't really matter, she decided. If Stan kept up with the news, and chances were good that he did, he was probably gone. That hurt to think about, since it meant Georgia was gone as well. Gone before she'd had a chance to live.

She didn't wipe at the tears as she remembered how Georgia's eyes had lit up around the puppy. How happy she'd looked at the thought of her grandmother being convinced to keep the puppy. How for that moment she'd been uplifted with hope.

Before she consciously thought about it, she had the pad open and was drawing Georgia with her eyes lit up, a smile on her face. She filled page after page as her imagination took hold. When the mind hop took place, she wasn't prepared—

"Remember, you make a sound and I'll kill you. Got me?"

Georgia gave a half nod, afraid of what the man would do if she moved too much. He'd been acting real crazy since he woke her up early and dragged her out of the house. Now she was tied up in the back of his van. They were going somewhere far away, he said. But first he had to take care of some old business. Her belly had hurt at the smile on his face when he'd said that.

She waited a minute after the door slammed to try to get her hands free from the rope. But it was tied too tight and the man came back too soon. She listened to him whistle as they started moving again. If he was in a good mood, maybe she'd get to eat today. Then she'd be stronger to fight him.

"People are stupid. You remember that, little girl. Tell them what they want to hear and you can get anything you want. That stupid son of mine never did learn that." He chuckled. "Got a nice surprise for him. A family reunion. You behave I might let you get on the swings. For old times' sake…"

Summer came back with a throbbing head to match the pounding on her door. For a moment she imagined it was Stan come to get her for her part in his discovery. Then she recognized Renny's voice and hurried to the door. "We have to go to the park," she said, holding her head. "He's got Georgia and he's meeting Rich at the park. The swings. He said he might let her swing for old times' sake. No," she said when Renny reached for her cell. "They'll scare him off. We can call when we get there. Get a description of the van, the tag number."

Renny nodded and pulled her close for a hard hug. "You should have called me." She exhaled and released Summer. "That's all I'm going to say for now."

They took the elevator to the underground parking area. "Good thing you gave me the code. I saw a news truck pull up. Wonder why it took them so long to get here?"

"The condo's not listed under my name. It's under my mother's maiden name. Have they made the connection between Rich and Stan?"

"No. They're too busy digging into your past. They sent a crew to your parents' place."

"Shit! I didn't think of that."

"Don't worry. They weren't home or didn't answer the door." Renny sped through a yellow light, doing twenty miles over the speed limit. "You know, if the police are smart, they're watching Rich. They'll probably beat us there."

"Then let's hope they have enough sense to keep out of sight. One look at them and he's gone."

Renny slowed as they reached the parking lot. "White van."

Summer's breathing quickened. "She's tied up in the back. What do we do now?"

"Make the call, then you and I'll go for a walk. Too bad I didn't bring Chazz. He'd be perfect cover."

She reached for her pocket before remembering she'd pitched it after talking to Juan. "No phone."

"Hang on." Renny pulled into a spot, then removed her phone from her jeans pocket. "Good thing I put his number in my phone. Vince, it's Renny Jamison. You're going to want to get to Central Park. We believe Stan is here and he has Georgia with him. Old white van with license plate number GAF13958. Georgia's tied up in the back." She ended the call and turned to Summer. "Ready for a walk?"

"We can pretend to be out for a run," Summer said. "We're dressed for it."

"Gotta stretch first, right? Do we know if he has a gun?"

"Gun? What the hell are you thinking, Renny?"

"That he's not getting away with another child. That it's two against one." She dug around in her glove compartment. "And that we have this."

Summer's eyes widened. "What in hell is that?"

"Taser. Strong enough to make him shit his pants according to the package it came in." Her smile was feral. "Come on. I promise not to move in on him unless it looks like he might bolt."

"That Taser won't stop his van," Summer muttered.

"I have no intention of using it on the van." Renny opened her trunk.

"Don't tell me you have another one back there?"

"Utility knife. You said she was tied up. And it can be used for other things, if necessary." She thrust it at Summer.

They walked to the entrance of the park and made a show of going through stretches while keeping an eye on the van. To Summer it seemed like it had been hours since they'd phoned for backup. Just when she was afraid Stan might get impatient and leave, another car pulled into the lot. "Rich," she said as he exited his Toyota Camry and looked around nervously.

"We need for dear old dad to get out of the van," Renny said, stretching her arm. "And where are the goddamn police?"

"Hopefully on their way." Summer tried for casual as she took another peek at the van. "Time to run. He's looked this way at least twice."

"We'll run until we're out of sight, then cut back through the woods, using the trees for cover."

Behind the cover of trees they watched Stan exit the van and walk toward his son.

Rich's steps faltered before he jerked to a stop. "No!" he screamed and held up his arms as if to protect his face.

"Run, idiot!" Renny hissed. "If only he'd run we'd have a shot at the van."

As if he'd heard her, Rich turned and raced for his car.

When Stan hurried after Rich, Summer was up and running before her conscious mind registered it. She reached the back of the van steps ahead of Renny and pulled on the back door. "Locked!" she said, breathing hard. "Stay here. I'll check up front." She reached the front of the van and wanted to scream when the keys weren't in the ignition. Fighting back panic, she searched under the seat and again came up empty.

"Uh, Summer. You need to hurry up."

"They're not here. What do we do now?" she asked when Renny joined her.

"Hope Rich keeps his dad occupied until the police get here."

"What?" Summer watched in horror as Stan dragged Rich out of his vehicle, then pinned him against it while squeezing his neck. "We've got to help him. You zap him after I distract him."

"How are you planning to do that?"

"I don't know." She shot across the parking lot, glad that the noise Rich was making masked her footsteps. "Still trying to beat the hell out of your son, Stan?" she said loudly.

Obviously startled, Stan turned his head. Summer could tell the second he recognized her. His eyes narrowed and his lip pulled back into a snarl. "You!"

She made herself smile as if she didn't want to wet her pants, as if she weren't facing her nightmare. "Yeah, me. End of the road for you, Stan. Brought down by a woman. That has to hurt your tiny ego."

Rich took advantage of Stan's loosened grip to bring up a knee and give his father a solid shot to the balls. When Stan pushed back from him and bent over at the waist, adrenaline propelled Summer forward. She plowed into him, sending him to the ground facedown with her on his back. She had a moment to wonder how rugby players did it without padding before Stan recovered enough to struggle.

"Now, Renny!" she shouted even as she took a fist to the temple that had her seeing stars. Before she could recover, Stan's body twitched from the shock of the Taser, bucking her off his back.

"You okay?" Renny asked.

"Yeah." Summer scrambled back to Stan and searched his jacket pocket for keys. "Yes! Go set her free. Set Georgia free." She threw the keys to Renny. "Rich, give me your belt. We need to tie him up."

"I'll take care of him," Renny said with relish. "This baby has plenty of charge left." To prove it she shocked him again and smiled through his grunts. "You're not going anywhere, are you, Stan?" She held out the keys to Summer. "You should be the one to set her free. You've been with her from the beginning."

Summer didn't need to be told twice. As she raced back to the van, she heard the sirens. Then the key was in the latch and she was pulling the door open. "Georgia? My name's Summer." She held out her arms. "You can come out now. The man can't hurt you anymore."

A response was a long time coming. "I'm tied up."

"I have just the thing for that." Summer talked about nothing, keeping her voice bright and cheerful as she climbed into the back of the van. Seeing the bruises on Georgia's face and arms, she wanted to take Renny's Taser to Stan's balls. Instead she talked about how brave Georgia was as she cut away rope.

Once Georgia was free, she fell into Summer's arms and burst into sobs.

"You're going to be okay," Summer murmured, putting her arms around a shivering Georgia. The mind connection was instantaneous. As Georgia sobbed, memories of what had been done to her flashed through her mind and, because of their connection, through Summer's mind as well. It was almost too much for Summer to bear. She didn't bother to wipe away the tears streaming from her eyes.

Gradually the sobs died, her's and Georgia's, and Summer became aware of the conversation going on outside of the van. From the sound of things, she had Renny to thank for having the time to comfort Georgia. "We need to get you checked out, sweetie. Make sure everything is okay."

When Georgia whimpered and tightened her grip, Summer thought her heart would break.

"I'll stay with you while the doctor makes sure you're okay." *Make sure you stay that way*, she vowed.

"Promise?"

"Promise."

EPILOGUE

Summer put down the charcoal pencil and sighed. It was done. Wiping her fingertips on a soft rag, she looked around the bedroom Renny had had remodeled into a studio, from portrait to portrait. Fifteen girls. Well, the fifteen he'd admitted to, she corrected. The fifteen whose bones had been found in his burial ground. The fifteen who mostly turned out to be from poor families and under poor supervision. Easy pickings, he'd said. Doubly victimized, Summer thought.

"But not sixteen," she reminded herself, deliberately looking at the photo of a smiling Georgia and her black Lab companion, who was inexplicably named Spot. Georgia didn't always smile, but when she did it reminded Summer of the sun rising to greet the morning. Of late, those smiles were coming more frequently and seemingly with more ease.

Georgia was also losing that haunted look and putting on weight. She still had nightmares from which she woke up screaming, thinking the mean man had locked her up. Spot was always the first one to bring her out of the nightmare. Sometimes she was able to fall back asleep. Other times Summer transferred her to their bed, where Georgia could be bookended by her and Renny. Where she could feel safe and loved.

She was their little miracle. A survivor, who was working hard to leave the past behind her. A survivor, who'd held Summer to her promise to stay with her through the physical exams and the endless questions by the police, something Georgia's grandmother hadn't been able to do due to her continued bad health. Somehow staying had morphed to daily visits. And then, with the passing of Georgia's grandmother, into legal guardianship, which had turned into an anchor holding the three of them together. Not underwater, though, but above it, floating side by side through hell and high water until they realized they belonged together. Until they were a family.

The clicking of nails on the hardwood floor heralded the arrival of Chazz. Renny wouldn't be far behind, wanting to remind Summer it was time to stop. Time to get ready for something happy. She swiveled around to greet Chazz and watch Renny enter, sweaty from her late morning workout. The tingle deep in her gut had only gotten stronger over the last three years. "All done," she said before Renny could ask. "All fifteen."

Renny crossed the room to look at the latest drawing. The one of the young autistic girl from Florida. The first body found. "How do you feel?"

"I don't know." She leaned into Renny, needing the comfort, the connection. "Good, I guess. They can't be forgotten now. They're more than a name."

"Thanks to you. And thanks to you there were only fifteen. You should be getting the accolades, not that damn task force," Renny said heatedly, referring to the made-for-TV movie about the abductions that was due out in the fall.

"Don't need it when I have you going to bat for me." She brought the back of Renny's hand to her lips. "And the cops couldn't very well give me an award and at the same time deny I provided them assistance. We've talked about this before, love. Let it go. I don't want the notoriety. Not for that." She wanted the notoriety for her art, for the show occurring in two months—the first since the accident.

"I guess. But there should be a way."

"Karma. I got a huge deposit in my account. But if somebody wanted to, say, write a book about it that would be okay." She gave Renny a sly smile. "A book where the main character has psychic powers and the ass-kicking capabilities to take down the perpetrators herself."

"Fiction then?" Renny asked, brows arched.

"Exactly. I'd need a cool moniker. Warrior Psychic. Artist by day and protector by night."

Renny laughed. "What am I going to do with you?"

"Love me?"

"There is that." She pulled Summer close for a kiss. "We'll talk more about this book later. Now it's time to get ready for the party. If I remember correctly, your mother threatened to stomp our muses to pulp if we were late to another thing."

"Strictly posturing. She loves you and your books too much to lay a finger on your muse unless it's for stroking." Summer gave the portraits one final look. She was done. Not with the head hopping or with tortured souls, but she was done with these girls. Had done good by these girls. "You know, I got it pretty good. I got you, I got Georgia, I got my family. But most of all I got back to blue."

Bella Books, Inc.

Women. Books. Even Better Together.

P.O. Box 10543
Tallahassee, FL 32302

Phone: 800-729-4992
www.bellabooks.com